Jasmine Somers Makes Amends

Amy Rainbow lives in a cottage beyond the Malvern Hills. As a slam winning performance poet, Amy has supported Ian McMillan, Attila the Stockbroker and John Cooper Clarke. She has won prizes for her flash fiction, and her prose and poetry have been published in various anthologies. Her first poetry collection, *Poems of the Unrequited*, tells tall tales of love, loss and drunken unicycling. A fully qualified philosopher, Amy's hobbies include hula hooping, juggling, stargazing and drinking rum. She was born on Friday the thirteenth.

www.amyrainbow.co.uk

Jasmine Somers Makes Amends

by

Amy Rainbow

Jasmine Somers Makes Amends
Amy Rainbow

Published in 2013 by Purple Pixie Press
Malvern, Worcestershire, United Kingdom.

Designed, printed and bound by Aspect Design
89 Newtown Road, Malvern, Worcs. WR14 1PD
United Kingdom
Tel: 01684 561567
E-mail: allan@aspect-design.net
Website: www.aspect-design.net

A copy of this book has been deposited with the British Library Board

ISBN 978-0-9926900-0-7

To LL for her bravery and inspiration
and to those of you with the courage to make your amends.

I wrote this book instead.

Acknowledgements

With thanks to Caryn and Claire for their sisterly support,
to The Common Readers,
to Sarah, Li, Kev, Catherine and Di,
and to anyone who has ever had the grace
to forgive me.

amend: verb

to put right

to change for the better

to remove or correct faults

to become better by reforming oneself

amends: plural noun (in phrase: **make amends**)

to compensate or make up for wrongdoings

one

It was a sunny spring morning when she rang. Sixteen years without a peep and then...

'Jasmine, hi. It's Sophie.'

'Er... Sophie?'

'Sophie Styles. From uni. It's me!'

Sophie Styles – the drinking man's crumpet. How could I forget? 'Wow! Sophie! How *are* you?'

'Well, you know. I'm working things through. You?'

'Not bad. Look, Sophie, I'm actually in the bath at the moment.'

'Oh, right. Well, it doesn't matter then. It can wait. But, Jasmine, I do need to speak to you soon.'

Need? Why on earth would she need to speak to me after almost two decades? Oh God, she was dying, wasn't she? That was it – she was phoning to say goodbye.

'Sophie, what is it? Are you all right?'

'I'm fine,' she replied, and I could hear from her perky blonde tone that she wasn't dying at all. Not even ill. I bet she was one of those people who never caught a cold and put it down to a positive attitude.

'I'm glad you're OK, Sophie. Maybe we can catch up properly soon. You know, another time?' I'd only shaved one armpit, for goodness sake.

'Right. You get in touch when you're ready then,' she said.

Ready? What an odd thing to say. As I remembered it there wasn't a great deal of intellectual preparation necessary for a one-to-one with Sophie Styles.

'What's this about, Sophie?'

Silence. Now, that really was *not* the woman I remembered. Maybe she *was* about to die. Perhaps she was putting a brave face on the whole thing. Not that I could see her face, obviously. I could imagine it though – all cheeky grin and twinkling eyes, none of the subtle wrinkles or sagging skin that the rest of us pretended to laugh off. She'd look gorgeous on her deathbed, have men weeping over her beautiful little corpse.

'Sophie?'

I heard her draw in a deep breath. Whatever she'd contracted must be spreading inexorably throughout her body. It would have started in her lungs. I waited for her to speak, but instead she let out a long sigh. Could she be on the ventilator already?

'Soph? Talk to me. I think I know why you've rung. I'm so sorry.'

It turned out that what I took for laboured breathing was a combination of relaxation technique and chain-smoking. One of the handy hints she'd picked up at her Alcoholics Anonymous meetings, she explained. I guessed she meant the yogic breathing; cigarette smoking seemed an unlikely health tip, even from a bunch of alcoholics. Ex-alcoholics. Recovering alcoholics. Whatever.

Life, it appeared, had not turned out so perfectly for old Soph. A few years back she'd lost a job that meant a lot to her, or was it a boyfriend? Anyway, the upshot was that she took to the bottle, and the bottle, it seems, quite took to her. She ended up losing the boyfriend, or the job, whichever one she hadn't lost in the first place, and to comfort herself – yep, you guessed it – she drank. Now, you might think that an allegedly intelligent person would, at around this point, have a think; take stock, as it were.

'Hey,' they might say to themselves, *'this drinking thing isn't such a good idea. It's ruining my life and it's expensive and sometimes it makes me vomit. Perhaps I should stop.'*

To be fair to Sophie, it did sound as if she was trying. And I was gaining a fascinating insight into her murky underworld, although I honestly couldn't see what relevance any of this had to *me*. Besides, my Peach Melba face-mask was beginning to itch.

'OK, Sophie. Let's start again shall we?' I used the patient voice I normally saved for the children at school.

'Start what again?'

'Could you tell me why exactly you wanted to talk to me? It sounded important.'

'Ah, yes, that.' She paused.

I attempted to turn the hot tap on with my toes, but my foot slipped and knocked a half-full jar of lemon zest bath crystals over the floorboards. Well, it wasn't half-full any more. I waited, pondering the possibility that prolonged contact with Dead Sea mud could have adverse effects on delicate skin.

Another loud exhalation of toxic fumes. Perhaps she *was* going for that lung-disease after all.

'I'll get straight to the point then, shall I?'

'Please do,' I said. I'd noticed that Sophie's thoughts had a tendency to wander.

'This is part of my Twelve Step Recovery Programme.'

'I see,' I replied, hoping she'd elucidate.

'It hasn't been easy, but I'm on the Ninth Step now.'

'Great. Sounds like you're doing well then.'

'One day at a time,' she laughed.

So I laughed, baffled as to where the joke could have been. 'Remind me, which one is the Ninth Step?'

'Sorry, yes, it's the Make Amends Step.'

'Ah, right, the Make Amends Step. And what precisely does that entail again?'

'You know, just… making amends for the past – looking back at stuff you did wrong and putting it right.'

'What, *all* of it? Even the little things like cheating in exams or stealing someone's boyfriend?'

'Yes, *all* of it,' she replied, with more gravitas than I was expecting. Perhaps she'd found religion, as so many people do when they've given up hope of finding anything else. Then I remembered that episode with Graham at the end of our first year. Maybe I shouldn't have mentioned boyfriend-stealing.

'Oh, Sophie, I really am sorry. About you and Graham, and me and Graham. I'd had far too much of that punch and—'

'Who? Oh, Graham. No, we'd pretty much agreed to call it a day by then. Rather intense, I found him. Bit weird, to be honest. Anyway, no, it's nothing *you've* done. It's me. What *I* did to *you*. I wanted to apologise and I'm hoping you'll let me make amends. Does that sound OK? Because if not, then that's fine. I'll respect your decision and leave things as they are.'

What *she'd* done to *me?* Was she serious? True, at times I'd found her aggravating and ingratiating, and I'd always suspected that she wasn't *quite* as stupid as she made out – some ploy to flatter the men around her, I guessed – but she'd always struck me as ridiculously, well, *nice*. Yet here she was, on the brink of confession, primed to own up to committing a sin so horrifically underhand that she'd been consumed by guilt ever since. Whatever could it be?

My breathing had quickened, blood pounded in my ears.

'Sophie, ring me back in five minutes.' I hosed myself down and scraped off the mud mask. This was going to take some concentration.

Sitting under my duvet, wrapped in damp towels, I glared at the silent phone. My teeth were chattering, my imagination running wild. What on earth could she have done? Dan. It had to be something to do with Dan.

I could see them now in my mind's eye, my Adonis of a boyfriend and his bit of fluff, banging away in the common room while I was dissecting the finer points of Aristotelian metaphysics in the college library. How *could* he? A seventeen year relationship built on infidelity and deceit. Why had I been so gullible? How would I ever learn to trust anyone again? But then I remembered how Dan had always shared my bewilderment at Sophie's popularity. Soppy Soph, he used to call her. And he's always preferred brunettes. Dan and Sophie? What a ridiculous idea. So if it wasn't that, what *had* she done?

I envisaged a giggling young Sophie tampering with my first year Philosophical Aesthetics exam paper, the disastrous result of which had brought my end of year average down to an embarrassing 2.2. I imagined her breaking into my room and finding what I kept in that bottom drawer. I watched her whispering lies about me to my closest friends and – worse – my enemies.

What *was* it she'd done to me? Why had she phoned? Why couldn't she have left me alone? Whatever had happened, however awful, surely I was better off not suspecting a thing? But now I was about to find out the truth and I didn't want to hear it. I didn't want to know. I didn't want to know!

The phone rang, interrupting my pictorial panic. I grabbed the receiver. 'Sophie? What happened? What did you do? I need to know!'

'All right, Jasmine. Calm down. Well, do you remember that night we all walked out to Trent Bridge after Rock City?'

'Um...'

'There was a full moon and you'd convinced everyone that it would look amazing reflected in the river. Guess we'd all been drinking and smoking quite a bit. Took us hours to get there. Do you remember?'

'Not really.'

'You must do. You were with that odd little medic. Joe? Johnny?'

'James! Of course.' A third year Stone Roses fan with floppy hair and the cutest button nose.

'It had clouded over by the time we reached the Trent, hadn't it? No moon; just wind and drizzle. I was freezing.'

'Yeah, why didn't you have a coat?' I asked. 'Bit silly at that time of year.'

'Oh, I'd lent it to Rachel to wear home. Hers had been nicked from under our table and she had a cold. I couldn't let her walk home just in her dress. Anyway, you did me a huge favour.'

'Did I? What, on the way to that greasy spoon café we found in the market?'

'No, after they chucked us out. God, it was pouring. Remember we waited for the taxis in a bus shelter on the main road?'

I did. Two taxis, eight spaces, ten people.

'Look, Sophie, I'm sorry about that, but I *had* to get back. I was presenting my tutorial on Akrasia the next morning.'

'Akrasia?'

'Moral incontinence. Can't stand it. And James clearly had to come with me. It wouldn't have been safe for me to walk that last bit across campus on my own.'

'Jasmine, it's fine. You were really kind.'

'Was I?'

I remembered clambering onto the warm back seat of the taxi, shaking off my hood and pushing my hands into the fleecy pockets of my thick coat. Sophie and Helen stood on the pavement waving goodbye, their bedraggled fringes dangling like rats' tails over tired eyes.

'Hang on,' I shouted into the rain from our cosy cab. 'It's going to take hours for you two to walk all that way. Look at your top, Soph, it's soaked through already. Here, take these.' I reached out of the window, offering her the spare pair of gloves I'd found in my pocket.

'Thanks, Jasmine. That's really considerate,' she replied, slipping them on.

It was the least I could do.

My tutorial was an unmitigated success, despite the hangover, and by its conclusion my tutor, as well as my four fellow ethicists, could not contest my assertion that they were all morally incontinent. I had convinced them of the cruelty, general evil, and blatant speciesism inherent in the meat and dairy industries, and yet they had failed to pledge their allegiance to the vegan – or even the vegetarian – cause. Each one of them was choosing to continue doing what they knew to be wrong. Hypocrisy, I declared, abounds.

I'd gone to the union bar afterwards to celebrate my indisputable powers of reasoning. Friday lunchtime flowed into Friday night, and the weekend was soon upon us. I hadn't given Sophie Styles's soggy jumper or my old gloves a second thought. Until the phone call, that is.

'It can't have been a pleasant walk home. The others should have let you and Helen go in a taxi; two of the men could have at least offered.'

'Oh, it was no big deal,' Sophie laughed. 'Luck of the draw, I guess. Listen, about your gloves – I meant to give them straight back but I felt so ill the next morning. Stayed in bed all that weekend, actually. Taught me to carry emergency funds on me at all times though!'

'So you're phoning about my gloves?'

'Yes. I'm sorry, Jasmine. I didn't mean to keep them. I wore them loads in case I saw you, so I could return them and say thank you properly. I never even did that. I feel awful.'

'Look, there's no need—'

'No, let me finish. It's important. By the time I saw you again I'd got used to wearing them and you'd bought some more anyway and I… I kept them. I wasn't in a good place at the time, I can see that now. I was too self-absorbed and inconsiderate to realise how my actions might affect others. I was selfish and ungrateful, and when you'd been so thoughtful as well. I never forgot what I did and I've always felt bad about it. And now I want to make amends.'

'You want to make amends?' I spluttered, once I'd stopped laughing. 'My tatty pair of gloves has been gnawing away at your conscience all these years? Is that the worst thing you've ever done?' Saint Sophie, I ought to start calling her.

It wasn't the worst thing she'd ever done though, not by a long way. Some of her misdemeanours involved calculation, dishonesty and downright deceit. A few were… well, to be honest I was shocked that a woman with Sophie's private school education and Pony Club background could have sunk so low. But what a fantastic concept.

'Sophie, just run this amends thing past me again, will you?'

And I was hooked. The whole idea fascinated me. Making amends for past transgressions, putting ancient wrongs to right. You simply made a list of bad deeds done, phoned a person up, expressed some sort of regret, then moved on in life with a renewed sense of righteousness, tempered with humility. I liked it. I liked it a lot. Absolution for atheists. Catholicism without Christ.

'You're not seriously going to do this are you?' Ruben asked, pouring the last of the Bordeaux into my glass. He'd listened attentively as I'd recounted tales of carefree college days and the whole phone call from Sophie.

I downed my warming wine and clunked the glass onto his rustic coffee table. 'Yes, Ruben, I really am going to do it.'

'But you can't have much to make amends for, surely? Unless you count every incident in the glove-borrowing league, which would make the whole thing take years to finish.' He turned away to squeeze more logs into the wood burner.

This did need some reflection. Off-hand I could think of a dozen minor misdemeanours, a few medium scale trespasses and one or two offences which I could never... Well, some things were best left undisturbed. Clarity was needed, and the empty wine bottle glinting in the hearth was reminding me that this was possibly not the time for fine-tuning my plan. I watched the dancing flames through the stove's cracked window.

'I've no idea how long it will take. But I want to give it a go. You know how I hate moral weakness. This is my chance to go back and put everything right.'

'Everything like what?'

I understood why Ruben was puzzled. I'd hardly led the life of a dissolute sinner. But the timing was perfect. I was, relatively speaking, still in the first stages of my new life, and what better way to make a genuine fresh start than to absolve past indiscretions and begin again?

'Come here,' said Ruben. 'And stop frowning like that.' He pulled me closer and kissed me with wine-stained lips. 'Come to bed.'

'I can't,' I replied. 'I need to start my list. Where's that notepad gone?'

Ruben kissed me again and undid the bow on my top. I'd never understood the allure of the older man, but when I'd met Ruben, I suddenly got it. He could do things to me with one glance, with one touch, that other, younger men had failed to achieve after hours or even weeks of effort.

'Come to bed,' Ruben repeated, taking my hand in his.

How could I resist that broad lopsided smile, those soulful, feline eyes? My moral expedition could wait. My planning could wait. This, on the other hand, could not.

It'll be fine, I told myself, as Ruben led me towards his bedroom. I'll start tomorrow. Make a list, say sorry, move on. How difficult could it be?

two

I love the slivers of weightlessness at the very start and end of the day – those moments between consciousness and sleep. I try to hold on to that feeling of floating free in an infinite universe, where I could be anyone, anywhere, anytime. But each night and every morning, this freedom falls away as I slip into oblivion or wake to a real and irrefutable world. There is no Heaven, but this is my taste of Nirvana, my glimpse of Moksha. I can see why lifetimes are spent in pursuit of their attainment.

It was the smell of freshly baked bread and the sound of Ruben's soft voice which seeped into my awareness that Sunday morning, drawing me from my world of slumber. I loved it when he sang in Spanish. Songs from Andalusia, songs from his childhood. I rolled over to look at the hand-carved clock which hung above the doorway. Almost ten. I'd get up soon.

'Morning, sleepy!' called Ruben, as he passed the bedroom door with a vase of daffodils. He'd often done half a day's work by the time he roused me. 'Want some breakfast?'

'Mmm, please.'

Ruben soon reappeared with a fully laden tray, which he slid onto my bedside table. 'Would madam prefer to dine with the curtains open or closed?' he smiled. 'I would recommend the first option, if I may, as the garden is looking particularly fine this morning.'

He was right. A hazy sun shone through the willows onto the

dancing surface of the stream. The narcissi and tête-à-têtes which stood in huddles around the lawn's edge swayed in the breeze. Kerria and clematis were already flowering, although the late crocuses and snowdrops had not yet faded.

'Let's walk down to the village later,' I said, as Ruben handed me my coffee and sprawled out next to me on the bed. 'We could pop to The Plough for lunch.'

'Not today, young lady. You're going nowhere.' He wriggled under the covers, put his arms around me and laid his head gently on my chest.

'Ru, you're terrible,' I laughed. 'We can't spend the whole day in bed again. And mind my drink, will you?'

He sat up, took my cup and returned it to the tray. 'Terrible? Me? A whole day in bed indeed. That's not what I had in mind at all. Come and see.'

He grabbed my hands, pulled me to my feet and led me to his study. I wasn't normally allowed inside; this was where he did his translation, and he insisted on separating work from play. His desk had been cleared, so that instead of the usual pile of dictionaries and muddle of documents, it bore a single notepad, one biro and the flowers he'd picked earlier. Ruben was looking at me expectantly.

'What's this?' I asked. Had he dragged me away from breakfast just to show me he'd tidied up? It was a rare occurrence, but nonetheless...

'It's for you. So that you can stay here to write your list. I didn't want you to go straight home.'

My list? Oh my God. My list. Did I seriously intend to seek forgiveness for all my trespasses? And was this the place to begin, in the company of the very man who regularly led me into temptation? Admittedly, I didn't take much leading, but that was beside the point. No, the whole thing was ridiculous. It wasn't as if I'd committed myself to going through with anything. And it was such a beautiful day.

'I can find you another pen if you want,' frowned Ruben. 'I thought you'd like purple though.'

'No. Sorry. It's wonderful. Thanks. It's just... Well, I'm not convinced that there's much point. I mean, who's going to benefit from me raking up the past?'

'Rubbish. I know what this means to you, Jasmine. You spoke so passionately about it last night.'

'Yes, but...'

'Look, I know I was dubious, but I think you should go for it. Anyway, I *know* you. If you say you're going to do a thing, you do it, no matter how hard. I love that about you. So I want to help.' He wasn't going to let this one go.

'OK, maybe I *will* do it. But not today. Look how lovely it is out there.' I gestured towards the window and the open fields beyond. 'We should be out walking, collecting mushrooms, frolicking by the stream.' If edible fungi couldn't sway him, then the promise of al fresco fun surely would.

'Frolicking?' Ruben shook his head and tutted. 'I am not so easily seduced, you know. Now, I seem to remember that you have work to do.'

'All right, I give in. I'll start the blasted list. I'd like to finish my breakfast first though, if such a luxury is permitted.'

'Take your time,' Ruben replied. 'I'll run you a bath.'

I put my arms around him and pulled him close. 'Why didn't I meet you twenty years ago?' I mumbled, savouring the warmth of his lips on my neck.

I knew the answer though. Twenty years ago I'd been a green-haired idealist, intent on overthrowing capitalism and eradicating the world's injustices through a subtle combination of direct action and the frequenting of hardcore punk gigs. While Ruben was playing happy families and negotiating business deals in Granada, I was writing letters to leaders of oppressive regimes, and chaining myself to the entrance doors of murderous fast food outlets. No, we'd met at the right time, Ruben and I, and we were both enjoying every moment we had together, making the most of what we knew could never last.

'Breakfast! Go!' he ordered, pushing me playfully towards the bedroom. 'You have a busy day.'

I decided to create a loosely chronological catalogue of my wrongdoings. If Tasha was to be believed, there would be plenty of material from our formative years for me to work on. But then, sisters were bound to recall their younger siblings' innocent mistakes in a bad light. I began to ponder. What *would* Tash tell me to put on my list?

I remembered the hole we'd made in one of dad's fencing panels in our back garden in Briar Street. That had been Tasha's idea though. I had merely pointed out the two wobbly slats of wood and showed her how you could ease them aside to reveal a narrow window onto the Hicklings' vegetable patch.

According to Tasha, we'd stumbled across a breach in universal matter. As the chosen two, we were duty-bound to work the laths loose and be the first to step into the mystical realm which lay beyond. Ever-trusting of my big sister, I spent whole evenings by myself, diligently edging the timbers to and fro, as quietly as possible, so as not to arouse the suspicion of any non-believing adults. Tasha, meanwhile, remained indoors, preparing for our pioneering voyage. When I was eventually able to swing the enchanted slats back and forth like a pair of parallel pendulums, we stepped through our portal and found ourselves in the middle of a row of potatoes no more magical than our own. Tasha, undeterred, took this temporary setback as a sign that, for now, we should spend more time simply playing with our neighbours.

For a while, one of our favourite games was off-ground tag. This was usually based at our house, as the Hickling girls had less furniture to clamber onto. Our enjoyment of this sport was ruined forever one Thursday after teatime – a result of the messy incident which Tasha subsequently forbade me from mentioning. When my turn had come to chase the others, I quite legitimately pursued them along the hallway and into the downstairs loo, where, in her panic, Tasha leapt for the safety of the toilet seat. Now, I still maintain that Tasha was the last person to use that toilet, but she was adamant that *I* was the idiot who'd left the seat up and was therefore to blame for her soggy embarrassment and spoiled slipper. I hardly ever used that toilet anyway since the thing with the spiders at Halloween, so why she held me responsible I never understood.

No, it was no good trying to work out what *other* people considered me accountable for. I was certainly not prepared to take the blame for things I hadn't done. I needed to consider what *I* felt bad about.

Where to start though? The smallest thing? The earliest thing? This was going to be harder than I'd expected. There was so much to think about. Maybe it was time for a coffee break. Yes, I'd be more lucid after some caffeine and a bit of sugar. Hadn't Ruben said something about vegan doughnuts, or was that a dream? I replaced the lid of my unused pen and dropped it onto the pile of blank paper. How many pages was Ruben expecting me to cover? From the study window I could see him on the drive, tinkering away, head half hidden in the engine of an ancient Lotus 7.

I pushed the window open and leant out. 'Hey, Ru!'

'What's up?' he called, without shifting his attention from the incommodious engine.

'Nothing. Time for a coffee break, that's all. Coming in?'

'Coffee's not for another half hour,' he shouted, still not looking up at me. 'You keep at it.'

Ruben and his timetables. He'd lightened up a lot since we'd met though, and suggesting that I stayed on longer than usual to write my list… Well, that meant progress.

I shut the window. The last thing I wanted to hear while I was stuck indoors was the cheery chirping of a bunch of exultant birds. Slumping down into the chair, I grabbed the lilac biro and began to scribble. Stuff regimented record keeping. This was supposed to be fun. Or was it? I wasn't really sure. In any case, a good old-fashioned brainstorm was what was called for. It was simply a matter of getting it all down; I could sift through and edit later.

By the time Ruben appeared, smeared in grease and engine-oil, and proffering a mug of the finest in fairtrade Peruvian, I had covered almost two sides of A4.

'Wow!' he exclaimed, squinting to make out my enthusiastic scrawl. 'Have you finished?'

'Yep. Easy peasy,' I replied. 'All done. Can I come out now?'

'Well, I guess if you've done *everything*. I always said you were a fast worker.'

'I shall ignore that comment. And yes, I *have* done everything. It's all there – right up to the end of primary school.' I waved the paper under his nose.

'Primary school? You mean when you were nine or ten? I thought you meant *everything*.'

'Eleven. Primary school finishes when you're ten or eleven. I've included that whole summer holiday too.' It was a Sunday, for God's sake, a day of rest. That would do for now, surely?

Ruben was not impressed. 'You can do high school after the coffee break, then adulthood this afternoon.'

'Secondary school. We didn't have high schools in my day.'

'High school, secondary school – it's the same thing, isn't it?'

'Not at all. High schools are mixed ability. Mine was a grammar school. Didn't your dad teach you *anything* about England when you were little?' If I could keep the conversation going, there was a chance I'd be excused from the remainder of my task.

'Grammar school? You mean your parents *paid* for your education?' Ruben exclaimed in mock horror. 'You told me they were socialists!'

'They were. My education was free. We just had different schools for different abilities.'

'What, better education for clever kids? Doesn't sound very fair and equal to me.'

'That's not what I said. Anyway, we took an exam when we were near the end of primary school—'

'Ah, yes. Primary school. Where your little list ends.'

So he hadn't forgotten. It probably didn't help that I'd rolled my sheets of paper into a scroll, which I was now pointing directly at his chest.

'Ruben, you're a slave driver. As a lover, you are almost perfect, but if you were my boss...'

'OK, truce,' he laughed, raising his arms in a gesture of surrender, hampered considerably by the steaming mug of coffee in each hand. 'Now take your drink and come outside. I thought we could try those doughnuts.'

I took my mug, and Ruben turned to head for the stairs. After a few paces he stopped and looked back at me over his shoulder, a grave, theatrical frown across his face.

'And what do you mean, I'm *almost* perfect?'

We sat quietly for a while on the crooked bench which overlooked the stream. The sun was higher in the sky now, its light no longer filtered by the trees. The warmth on my face and the tinkling of the water took me back to those early morning walks during my months in Perpignan. Strolling alongside the canal, hand in hand. Café noir at our favourite bistro near the citadel. Sweet Arnaud. Had he ever opened that bookshop he used to daydream about? How long had it taken him to get over my departure? No time to even tell him I was leaving. And there was no way I could have contacted him afterwards. I mean, how could I possibly have explained? What justification could I have given for what I did? But that was all years ago. A different lifetime. He'd have been fine, I knew it. Poor Arnaud. Some things were best forgotten.

A flash of turquoise and orange woke me from my reverie, as a kingfisher darted upstream and disappeared behind a grassy outcrop on the opposite bank.

'It's amazing,' said Ruben, licking the sugar from his lips.

Was he referring to the brightly-hued bird or the doughnuts we'd just polished off? I nodded, conveying my appreciation of the marvels either of nature or dairy-free confectionery, whichever was appropriate.

'I Googled *Twelve Step Recovery Programme* earlier, while you were asleep,' he continued. 'I got sixteen million results!'

We weren't discussing ornithology *or* cakes then.

'Sixteen million?'

'Yep. The whole Twelve Step thing was started by Alcoholics Anonymous eighty odd years ago. It's been so successful that the same methods are now used by Narcotics Anonymous, Debtors Anonymous, Sexual Compulsives Anonymous, Workaholics Anonymous… I could go on.'

'Please don't,' I said. 'I get the picture.'

'Did you know there's a group called Clutterers Anonymous?'

'No.'

'Ridiculous, isn't it? I mean, they'd have us *all* on some sort of recovery programme, the Americans, if they think we need therapy to force us to spring-clean more often.'

'I imagine the problem's more serious than that,' I replied, although cluttering did sound pretty trifling. 'I wonder if we could get you a referral from Dr Wilson. Car Collectors Anonymous. There may be hope for you yet.'

'You can mock, but you're the one following The Programme. Oh, that reminds me…' From his back pocket he produced a folded piece of paper that he must have printed off that morning. He smoothed it out on the table in front of us and pointed to a paragraph headed *Step Eight*. 'See? Today you should be examining past errors with the aid of an experienced supporter. That will have to be me.'

'Stop talking like an Alcoholics Anonymous handbook,' I said, scraping the dregs of doughnut sugar from the plate with my finger. 'And I'm not following anybody's programme, I'm just making amends. Anyhow, look at the stuff before that: s*tart by recognising the lack of control over your addiction…* blah, blah… *feelings of uselessness and self-pity will disappear… acknowledge a power greater than yourself which can give you strength…* I mean, none of this waffle is relevant to me, is it?'

'Unless you count me as the power greater than yourself,' said Ruben. 'Women far wiser than you have accepted this truth, Jasmine, and found great peace and fulfilment.'

'Oh, shut up, Ru. You don't half talk rubbish sometimes.'

'Why, thank you. Anyway, when you've done the amends bit you're meant to start afresh, live by a new code of behaviour and help others who want to clean up their act.'

'I have no intention of changing a thing,' I said, 'and absolutely no desire to become some kind of missionary.'

'Too much of a non-conformist for any kind of missionary position, eh?'

That did it. I gave Ruben a shove in the ribs with my elbow. 'I'm not talking to you any more,' I said, turning away for added effect.

Ruben groaned, and I looked back to see him clutching his ribs, face contorted, eyes screwed shut.

'Christ, Ru, I was only messing around. Are you OK?'

He was rocking slowly back and forth. What if I'd broken a rib? I brushed his dark fringe aside.

'Are you OK?' I repeated.

'I am, but you won't be!' he laughed, grabbing me and pulling me from my seat.

'Ruben Antonio, you're a scoundrel.'

'And you love it,' he replied, as we fell in a heap onto the daisy-strewn lawn.

'Do you know what?' he asked.

'What?'

'We've never made love in the garden.'

'I thought you wanted me to get back to work.'

'There's always this afternoon,' he said, kissing me to prevent further fake protest.

To rejoice in current sins or regret past ones – the choice was not a tricky one. Vague concerns regarding neighbours popping in on their way home from the Easter service quickly evaporated, and soon there was nothing in my consciousness but the heat of Ruben's touch and the softness of his skin on mine.

three

Once, when Dan and I were going through one of our difficult patches, I'd asked my mum how she'd put up with Dad for so long. I was expecting her to come out with the usual nonsense about love and trust and good communication.

'It all boils down to whether you'd rather be right or happy,' she'd replied.

I'd mulled this over for some time. The problem was that both Dan and I would far rather be right, every time. The pair of us preferred to go to sleep on a quarrel, miserable but intellectually unvanquished. As for compromise, to me that simply meant *nobody* getting what they wanted. I could see what Mum meant though. With Ruben, it worked out fine; I'd rather be right, he'd rather be happy. So in anything that mattered, I'd get my way, which made *me* happy, and he'd avoid the big confrontation, which made *him* happy.

And so it was, that after our impromptu outdoor amorousness, Ruben conceded defeat and took me for that pub lunch. It was my suggestion of taking the Lotus rather than walking that clinched the deal. A quick spin to assess the tuning, he agreed, would indeed be prudent.

I'm not a car person, but speeding along country lanes with the wind in my hair, I almost felt like a movie star. Except that in the movies you're never aware of the kamikaze flies which head straight for your mouth, nose and eyes. The other problem with the Lotus was that unlike any other convertible, whose soft top can be controlled at the flick of a switch, its lid had to be manually removed and left at home. If the weather changed half way through your day out, you were pretty much stuffed. The faintest white wisps drifting lazily across an azure sky, however, posed no threat to us today.

We steered clear of weighty conversation over lunch – nut roast and all the trimmings for Ruben, stuffed peppers on a bed of rice for me – so I had a chance to prepare my case.

Rolling his post-meal cigarette, Ruben, as I'd predicted, took up from where he'd left off earlier. 'I just think you'd be better off doing things by the book,' he said. 'Literally, I mean.'

'What, the Alcoholics Anonymous handbook?'

'Yes. It makes sense to finish Step Eight before embarking on Step Nine. It's more logical.'

'Logical?'

'Of course. Write the whole list first. It will mean you're properly prepared. Mentally. And I'm sure you'll find creating a record of your offences therapeutic in itself.'

I very deliberately wafted his cigarette smoke away from my face. 'But I'm not *doing* all the steps. And what do you mean, therapeutic? I hardly think I'm in need of therapy, thank you very much.'

'That's not what I meant and you know it.'

'You do realise you're starting to sound like the psychoanalysis-obsessed Americans you were mocking only this morning?'

'Jaz, I'm just saying—'

'Look, if I do go through with this thing I will most certainly be doing it *my* way. And my way involves tackling one chunk of life at a time.'

'The first of which, handily enough, takes you up to the end of primary school?'

'Precisely.'

Ruben flicked his ash onto the floor.

'I appreciate your support, Ru, but I'm not an addict and I'm not a sufferer of some sort of freakish behavioural disorder.'

'I don't remember suggesting that you were.'

'So there's really no need for psychological scrutiny from concerned bystanders.'

Ruben stubbed out his cigarette and shrugged.

I admit that I may have been a little harsh, but this was going to be demanding enough, without other people sticking their oar in and telling me how it should be done. Besides, my early years were fairly straightforward compared to, well, the bits that I wasn't too keen on looking at just yet.

'One day at a time,' Sophie had said.

I could see what she meant.

I left Ruben's not long after we'd returned from our extended lunch break. The journey home usually took me a good hour even with no traffic, and I needed the whole evening to tie up some loose ends. There was a week of the Easter holidays left, and I was planning to utilize the next few days to make good headway with my mission. Aware that I was never able to fully focus on the task in hand if other duties remained unfinished, I aimed to clear the decks so that I'd be ready to go first thing in the morning. Thunderous Holst and heaps of laundry, washing up and unanswered emails left no opportunity for apprehension.

Only when I turned off the bedside lamp and shut my eyes did I become fully aware of the churning in the pit of my stomach. I hadn't even eaten. How could I have forgotten to eat? I was turning into my nan. A good night's sleep was what I needed. All I had to do was to stop thinking and relax. Where *had* I left that book on meditation? I could do with sorting out the bookshelves tomorrow, come to think of it. There was probably loads of stuff I could take to the Amnesty bookshop. Might as well have a rummage through that junk in the shed while I was at it.

No, no, no. The charity shops could manage without my cast-offs for one more week. Procrastination may well be the thief of time, but if I kept my wits about me I could avoid becoming its victim. I was going to have to be strict with myself. I needed to concentrate on my amends. Targets. I should set targets. I could do this. Couldn't I? I rolled onto my back and pulled the duvet up to my chin. I needed a strategy. But where to begin? As my breathing slowed, the echo of a familiar voice cut across my fragmented thoughts.

'You start at the beginning, Jasmine.'

Mrs Wilkinson? It was, it was Mrs Wilkinson. I was being offered counsel by the ghost of my old headmistress. Just what I needed.

'You start at the beginning,' the voice repeated, *'and you keep going until the very end.'*

How many times had she given me exactly the same advice? Wasn't one of the benefits of any afterlife supposed to be enhanced knowledge and wisdom? Apparently not.

'Is there anything you want to tell me?' That same stern voice.

I was standing in the school corridor, staring at the wooden rectangular blocks which jig-sawed together to make a floor. When I grew up, I'd like to make floors like that.

'Nothing at all, Jasmine?'

I shook my head. The dining hall doors swung open behind

me, and the mingled aromas of rhubarb crumble and disinfectant wafted over us. I wanted to go home.

'All right. Back to your classroom. But if you ever think of anything you ought to tell me, you come and find me, won't you?'

'Yes, Mrs Wilkinson,' I mumbled, and the scene faded to darkness.

I was up early the following morning, and with the help of Friends Reunited and a pile of telephone directories, by eleven o'clock I'd tracked her down. Mrs Wilkinson had not yet reached her final resting place, but her penultimate one, according to her former neighbour, was a rest home called Valley View.

It was hydrotherapy hour when I rang, so I entrusted a camp-sounding care worker with my garbled message. I wiped my damp palms on my jeans before replacing the phone books and Yellow Pages on the bottom shelf. This was no big deal. She'd have no idea who I was, after so long. I wandered into the kitchen, turned the kettle on, and started to put the dry crockery away.

Earl Grey and a digestive biscuit – the combination certainly *sounded* healthy, even if it was an unnecessary calorie intake. I might put my feet up for the rest of the morning, maybe finish that book. Initial contact had been made, albeit indirectly, and taking on more than one misdeed concurrently would only split my concentration. That pasta salad should still be fine for lunch, then I'd tackle the shed.

The trill of the landline made me jump.

'Hello?' I said.

'Mrs Somers?'

My surname was one of the few things I hadn't given up when I married Dan. 'Ms,' I corrected.

'I beg your pardon?'

'It's Ms Somers.'

'Right-e-o. I'm calling from Valley View.'

'Oh, hello. Yes, sorry, yes. I spoke to you earlier.' I stood up straight and smoothed down my T-shirt.

'Mrs Wilkinson will be ready for you at three.'

'Oh, no, I don't need to *see* her,' I said. 'We can sort it out over the phone. There must have been a misunderstanding.'

'I doubt it, love. Mrs Wilkinson says she'll see you at three.'

'Right. Thank you. Three o'clock then.'

How had *that* happened? I checked my watch: quarter to twelve. Plenty of time. The drive shouldn't take much more than half an hour. Like me, Mrs Wilkinson had ended up not far from where she'd started out. All I had to do was eat and get changed. I couldn't hope to make a good impression, but a decent outfit might encourage leniency.

The wrought iron gates of Valley View swung open on my approach, and I followed the tarmac driveway through an avenue of limes. I pulled up in the far corner of the visitors' car park, which, apart from me and my yellow Beetle, was deserted. No wonder she'd been so keen for me to go and see her. I had twenty minutes to kill, so I searched my handbag and glove compartment for inspiration. Nothing.

The house was obscured from view, but I imagined a smaller scale version of the old lunatic asylum I'd passed on my way here. It had been converted into smart apartments now, but had still operated as some type of mental hospital when I was young. None of us had a clue what actually went on there, but rumours of ice baths and electric shock treatments were enough to keep the worst of our undesired behaviours in check.

The most dreaded phrase throughout my childhood? *'They'll send you to Farley Hall!'* From adults it came as a threat of where we'd end up if we were too inquisitive or wayward or rude. From other children, it was a warning that we were not quite one of the crowd. Anyone who didn't fit in might end up being carted off to the madhouse.

That was all I'd been trying to do that day – fit in with the crowd. Of course I'd known it was wrong, but Karen had assured me that because nobody would be upset, it didn't really count.

'I bet you anything,' she'd told me, 'no one will even notice.'

Mrs Wilkinson had noticed though, caught the three of them red-handed. Karen and Gillian had got off with a week of lunchtime detentions, but Sam had been made to give her librarian's badge back too. There'd been no reason for anyone to suspect my involvement, and despite their other failings, at least my classmates hadn't grassed on me.

But that was decades ago. What on earth was I doing, sitting outside some retirement home, fretting about such a petty issue? My old headmistress was sure to be busy crocheting blankets and darning socks and whatever else pensioners occupied themselves with these days. A quick phone call was a far better idea. Less intrusive. Far more appropriate. I put my seatbelt back on and was reaching for the ignition key when a round, beaming face pressed itself against my window.

'Is that Mrs Somers in there? Blimey, you can't see a thing through this glass, can you? Is that safe?'

I unclipped my seatbelt and slipped the car key into my jacket pocket. There was no going back now. I waited for the face to move away from the window before easing my door open.

'Mrs Somers?'

'Ms.'

'Oh, Lord, me and my memory! You're here for Mrs W then?'

'I am, yes.' Given today's number of visitors, it was safe to assume that we had the same Mrs W in mind.

'Good job you're punctual. She's a stickler for detail, that one.'

'I know.'

'Are you a relative then, love? Only, we didn't think she had any.'

'No. An ex-pupil.'

'Oooh, crikey. Glad she wasn't *my* teacher. I mean, she's a big softie underneath, but she puts the fear of God into some of the junior staff. Anyway, can't stand here nattering all day. Come on, this way.'

I followed my guide across the car park and along a blue brick path which led past an ivy-covered stable block and towards the main building. The house itself was a mock Tudor monstrosity, the aesthetic appeal of which was further diminished by a variety of flat-roofed extensions and metal fire-escapes. One swipe of a security card allowed us entry into what looked and smelt like the lobby of a cheap hotel.

'Plonk yourself down over there and I'll pop and see if she's ready for you.'

I examined the worn grey sofa which I'd been ushered towards and decided to stand and wait. Flecks of yellowing paint clung to the ceiling and half a dozen assorted wheelchairs formed a row against one wall like discarded shopping trolleys. Were these what they used for taking the senile ones for their electro-convulsive therapy? Or was that illegal now? How I hoped I'd snuff it before I was forced to live in a place like this. I wondered whether Mrs Wilkinson was bed-ridden. What if somebody asked me to feed her? I was no good at things like that. In any case, there were people here who were employed to carry out such tasks. Too badly qualified to do anything better, I supposed.

'Mrs Somers?' The moonlike face was peering round a battered MDF door.

'Ms.'

'Beg pardon?'

'It doesn't matter.'

'Right, well, she's ready to see you, our Mrs W. Up in the library, she is. Come on.'

A wave of nausea hit me. The library? Why the library? She couldn't possibly know, could she? I wished I'd gone to the toilet while I was waiting.

We scurried through a maze of bare corridors, and up a steep staircase to the first floor.

'Must keep you fit, working here,' I said, in an attempt at casual banter.

'Ooh, you're a cheeky one. You'll be asking to see my muscles next!'

I forced a smile, but his suggestion intensified my feeling of sickness. We came to a halt next to some glass-panelled double doors, one of which bore a brass plaque embossed with the words, *Harold Wilkinson Memorial Library and Meeting Room*.

'Is that Wilkinson as in *my* Mrs Wilkinson?' I asked.

'Harry was her husband, if that's what you mean. Must be ten or eleven years since he passed away, poor sod. Alzheimer's, embolism, strokes – you name it.'

We stood silently, gazing at the plaque. What state was I going to find Mrs Wilkinson in? Would she be crumpled and drooling? Would she know who I was? Would she know who *she* was?

'You'd better go in, love.' He sounded kind now. Maybe he did have qualifications. Maybe it didn't matter.

'What's your name?' I asked.

'Mark,' he replied. 'Mark Stevens. I haven't upset you have I? Oh, me and my big mouth!'

'No, Mark, you haven't upset me. Thank you. Thank you very much. I'll go in then, shall I?'

'Not without knocking, if you know what's good for you,' he winked, and bustled off back the way we'd come.

So this was it: time to begin in earnest. I stood squarely in front of the doors and took a deep breath. I felt inside my bag for my bottle of spring water. Damn, I must have left it in the car. I lifted my right hand to knock, but left it hovering in front of me for a moment, before lowering it to my side. I swallowed hard. A few more deep breaths. Come on, Jasmine, this is meant to be one of the easy ones. As I raised my hand again, the doors swung open and a regal figure dressed entirely in crimson held out her bony arms in greeting.

'Little Jasmine! Oh, you haven't changed one bit!' she cried. 'Apart from the pigtails and freckles. Do come in. How lovely to see you.'

We sat down in a pair of armchairs next to a large leaded window.

'Look at that,' said Mrs Wilkinson, peering out beyond neglected rose beds and a faded lawn. 'That's the only reason I chose this place for Harry. It's hardly The Ritz, is it? But the views. Most of that's Herefordshire.' She made a sweeping gesture towards the undulating meadows and farmland which gave Valley View its name. 'And that's Wales over there. You can just about make out Hay Bluff.'

'Lovely,' I mumbled.

She turned to face me. 'You're not here to talk about the landscape though, are you, Jasmine?'

'No,' I replied, studying the patterns on the floral carpet between us. I wouldn't have been surprised to see parquet flooring in here. Maybe it had been covered up.

'Is there something you want to tell me, dear?'

I shook my head and braved eye contact. 'I came to see how you were, that's all.'

The wrinkles across Mrs Wilkinson's pale forehead deepened. 'How thoughtful. Well, I'm not so bad, considering.'

'Considering?'

'I had a tough time of it after the amalgamation,' she said. 'Then my husband's health pushed me into early retirement. I looked after him for as long as I could, but after the second stroke...'

I clasped my hands in my lap and gave what I hoped looked like an empathic nod. This was one of my teachers; I shouldn't be hearing about her personal life. That wasn't how it worked.

'Listen to me going on,' she smiled. 'What about you, dear? I've heard you're working over at Henwick Grove. You always were a bright girl. I'm sure you make an excellent teacher.'

'Henwick Grove? How did you know that?'

'Oh, young Kerry Porter works in the kitchens here. Calls herself Kerry Marsh now. Married one of the Marsh twins. The sporty one. She keeps me up to date with all my ex-pupils.'

'I don't remember her,' I said.

'Well, she knows who *you* are. You must have made quite an impression. She was a few years below you. Looked up to you, no doubt.'

'Looked up to me?'

'Well, you were a formidable troupe, even after your sister

left. And how is the great Natasha Morley-Somers? I read a review of her latest book in *The Guardian* a while back. C.S. Lewis in stilettos, they called her. What an image!'

'I'm sure she'd be happy with the comparison,' I said. 'And she does enjoy a bit of glamour.'

'But you were the one with real brains, weren't you, Jasmine? I knew you'd do well. I never saw you as a teacher though. Always questioning the rules, as I recall. I'm very proud, you know.'

'Actually, I'm not a teacher,' I said, re-examining the carpet.

'Oh. But Kerry said—'

'I *am* at Henwick Grove, but I'm a classroom assistant. I didn't finish my teacher training.' It was nothing to be ashamed of. I was *good* at my job.

'I see,' she nodded, raising an eyebrow. 'Well, that's an important rôle, of course. I'm sure the children adore you.'

'It wasn't too hard for me or anything,' I continued. 'The teacher training, I mean. Just bad timing.'

'I must say I'm surprised you didn't finish it. You were always such a determined girl. Not one to give up without a fight. Or with one, come to think of it. But I suppose we all change as we grow older, that's only natural.'

'I *haven't* changed. I'm not a quitter. I just couldn't... There wasn't... You wouldn't understand.'

'I'm sorry, Jasmine. Take no notice of an old woman. You don't need to justify yourself to me. I'm sure you had your reasons.'

'I did, yes.'

'But you know, if you do want to talk about it...'

'No. Thank you. That's not why I'm here.'

'No, you're here to see how I am. Isn't that what you said?'

She cocked her head to one side, a burgundy starling awaiting my reply.

How was it that mums and teachers always knew when you had something to hide?

'There *was* something else,' I muttered.

'These things are better out than in, believe me. Go on.'

'You probably won't remember…' I stalled, biting my bottom lip.

'I do remember, Jasmine. I remember it very well.'

'But I haven't… I didn't… How could you…?'

'Tell me how it happened, Jasmine. I'll pour us both some tea.'

It was a wet Friday afternoon during the autumn term of my final year at Brockhill Junior. Sam and I, as the school's non-fiction librarians, had been asked to take a friend each to help us tidy the bookshelves after the infants' weekly visit. Sam picked her best friend Gillian, and I picked Karen Phillips. I knew that more than one of my friends would be disappointed not to be chosen, but Karen carried a lot of clout, and it wouldn't do me any harm to be seen getting pally with her.

Sam and I took our responsibilities seriously, and between the four of us we managed to sort and stack the books, sweep the floor and rearrange the beanbag corner, with plenty of time left before the end of school. Gillian decided that we ought to rejoin the rest of 4B in the art room but Karen convinced Sam that we'd be better off staying put, and that we deserved a rest after all the clearing up we'd done. I wasn't too fussed either way and certainly didn't mind missing another twenty minutes of decorating harvest festival baskets with pine cones and dead leaves. And I could see that we all had to do the same thing. It was no good two of us going back; we'd either finished the job or we hadn't. So we stayed.

The produce we'd brought in for that morning's special assembly was piled up on two trestle tables in the Myths and Legends corner. There were cans of condensed milk and tins of corned beef, jars of dried things that looked like shrivelled peas, packets of tea bags, pots of homemade jam, apples, potatoes and a load of other stuff that I couldn't see anyone being grateful for, even if they were poor and hungry and old. Mum had sent in spam and tinned peaches, which she said would go down a treat with the toothless OAPs.

'When my teeth fall out,' I'd told her as we'd walked to school that morning, 'I'm going to eat custard and ice cream, not tinned meat and fruit.'

There was nothing remotely decent in the heap of food. No chips or fish fingers, no Monster Munch or fizz bombs. But something had caught Karen's eye.

'Ginger biscuits!' she shrieked. 'They're the best.'

'Are they like ginger beer?' I asked. 'Because that's revolting.'

'Of course not,' Karen sniggered. 'They're biscuits, aren't they? They taste like biscuits.'

'Well, I don't know, do I? I've never tried them.'

'You've never even had ginger biscuits? *Everyone's* had ginger biscuits, haven't they?' She turned to face Sam and Gillian, who nodded fiercely, eyes wide, mouths firmly shut.

'Shall we have some now then?' suggested Karen, I supposed to all of us, although she had turned back to look at me.

'Nah,' I said. 'Not hungry.'

'You can take some for later then.'

'Is it time to go back yet?' I ventured. I scanned the magnolia walls for a clock which wasn't there.

'Are you chicken or something?'

Why was she picking on *me*? And when I'd chosen her as my helper as well. I looked to Sam and Gillian for support. Sam was scraping dirt from under her fingernails, Gillian's eyes were roving over the food mountain next to us.

I faced Karen squarely. 'No way am I chicken,' I said. 'But it's not ours, is it? We can't just take it. That's stealing.'

'You see? Chicken!' Karen turned to the others and began flapping her elbows in and out like wings, making a horrible clucking noise in the back of her throat.

My two friends quickly joined in, until the three of them were clutching at their sides laughing.

My face grew hot and I could feel my chin starting to quiver. I was *not* going to cry.

'Nobody will even notice,' Karen continued, giving up the chicken impressions. 'I bet you anything.'

'Of course they will,' I replied. 'We can't just take a great big packet of biscuits each.'

'Durr. They're not proper packets, stupid. Look.' She leant across some boxes of Angel Delight and fished out a matchbox-sized plastic parcel. 'There's only two in there. Probably nicked from a café or something anyway.'

'What about the old people? They might not have enough money to buy their own biscuits.'

'Nor have I,' she said. 'And I know for a fact that you don't get pocket money either.'

'Yeah, well, I don't really feel like biscuits today.'

'Do what you want,' Karen shrugged, 'but I still think you're chicken. Anyway, the old people won't know the biscuits were here, so they won't miss them, will they?' She waggled the packet in front of my face and put her left hand on her hip. She looked like one of the Pink Ladies from *Grease* except with no chewing gum.

'Oh, give those to me and stop making such a big deal about the whole thing,' I said, grabbing the biscuits from Karen's hand and shoving them into my cardigan pocket. 'Now, let's get back to class before the bell goes.'

I'd throw the stupid things in the bin at the corner shop on my way home. Next time I'd ask someone quiet like Vicky or Matthew to be my helper.

As I opened the door, I realised that the others weren't following me. They were burrowing around amongst the heap of groceries, and giggling.

'Come on,' I urged. 'We ought to get going.'

'All right, don't get your knickers in a twist,' said Karen. 'There's another bag of peanuts in here somewhere, I'm sure.'

There probably was; I'd seen Luke with a whole armful of them in the service earlier. How much did they think they could smuggle out though?

'I'm going back to class,' I said. 'I'll see you there.'

I stepped out into the corridor to see Mrs Wilkinson striding towards me. I froze.

'All done?' she asked.

I stared up into her penetrating eyes.

'All spic and span?' she tried again.

'Oh, the books. Yes. Spic and span.'

'Have the others already gone?'

'No, they're still… finishing off.'

She raised an eyebrow. '*Are* they now?'

As she headed for the library door, I scarpered back to the safety of my classroom, where the rest of 4B were sitting at their desks with their arms folded. All eyes turned towards me as I did my best to sneak in unnoticed.

'The wanderer returns!' bellowed Mr Bennett. 'How nice of you to join us.'

Somebody in the back row snorted. I glared at my teacher. He was only pulling my leg, but I'd had enough of being laughed at today.

'Right, very quietly, put your chairs up please… I think I said quietly, 4B... That's better. William, there's no need for chatter, thank you. Are you with us, Joe? That's it, in your own time! Dear me… OK, let's see who's standing nicely when the—'

Mr Bennett's last words were drowned out by the clanging school bell and the cheers of twenty six of my happy classmates, looking forward to the weekend ahead. I pushed my way through the milling crowd, grabbed my coat and bag from my peg in the cloakroom and legged it all the way home.

Dumping my school things on the back doorstep, I ran down past the shed and the greenhouse, and picked up Mum's trowel from where she always left it, on top of the water butt. I tiptoed between potato plants and eased myself into the space behind the compost bins. It stank, but I didn't care. I dug and dug until the hole was deep enough for *any* plant, then snatched the plastic-coated ginger biscuits from my pocket and dropped them in.

When I'd refilled the hole, I covered the soil with stones and leaves so that when the police came to search the house and garden, I'd have left no clues which could lead to my arrest. I wondered if they'd started going through the bins on my route home yet. I thought of the tramp my dad had told us about, whose picture was in *The Evening Gazette*. He wouldn't stop stealing things and nobody knew if he did it on purpose so that he could sleep in the police station, or if he couldn't help it. The tramp told the judge that it wasn't his fault and that he didn't mean to take things, so the judge decided he must be some sort of maniac, and sent him to Farley Hall. I wanted to know if the tramp had ever stolen ginger biscuits and whether he liked them any better than ginger beer.

I remained indoors for the rest of the weekend, cleaning my bedroom and finishing my project on Ancient Greece. I'd seen *Miss Marple* with my mum once when I was off sick with the mumps, so I knew that how I behaved now could be used as evidence. I tucked my Help the Aged badge inside my pop-socks and forced them down behind the radiator using Tasha's ruler. They were bound to confiscate that badge, and I'd worked hard to get it, collecting jumble for the bring and buy sale and taking in silver milk bottle tops for the *Blue Peter* Appeal.

When nobody came to question me at home, I realised that they must be waiting for me to return to the scene of the crime. The Monday morning tummy ache I reported to my mum was for once not imaginary. Mum shrugged and told me about the boy who cried wolf and the meeting she was going to at ten o'clock to discuss the zebra crossing by the new sports centre.

She waved goodbye at the phone box on the corner as usual. If I waited on the pavement outside the playground until the bell went, there was less chance I'd be spotted by Mrs Wilkinson and her team of detectives. At breaks and lunchtimes I planned to race up to the end of the playing field as soon as we were let out, and sit behind the biggest conker tree. Karen, Sam and Gillian wouldn't be on my table until maths that afternoon, so I'd have all morning to think of a way of swapping places with one of the slower girls at the front of the classroom.

Mr Bennett let me sit out of gym, saying I looked peaky, then after playtime we joined 4H in the studio to watch television. I usually enjoyed *Look and Read*, but this morning I was finding it hard to concentrate. Anyway, I'd seen this one before and preferred the one with the *Magic E* song in it. My favourite bit was usually where they showed the story about the peregrine falcon. But today it was the final episode, where the egg-thieves are caught and sent to prison – even Mr Trim who had seemed like a goody to begin with. I was sure that Mrs Wilkinson had asked the BBC to put the programme on especially. I couldn't stop thinking about the tramp in *The Evening Gazette*, and whether the judge would decide that I was a maniac too.

By lunchtime, news of the harvest produce theft had somehow leaked out, and the whole school had an opinion on the criminals and the punishment they deserved. The whole school except me, that is. I knew from my experience of *Miss Marple* that if the others spilled the beans on me they'd get off more lightly. They were bound to tell. And as the first to sneak out with stolen goods I supposed I was officially the ringleader.

Karen, Sam and Gillian weren't in the hall for dinner, so at least I could sit down without having to make sure I faced away from them like I'd had to in science first thing. The bad news was that it probably meant they were in the head's office right now, telling the police all about me and my sticky fingers.

I mixed the lumpy gravy into my mashed potato and squashed it down flat. Jason was always grateful for extra sausages, and after I'd slopped both of mine on top of his, my plate looked empty enough to keep the dinner ladies off my back. I sidled over to the serving hatch and swapped my plate of pulp for a ladleful of crumble covered in a pale yellow poster-paint-like liquid. Luckily, getting rid of pudding was never a problem with Jason McKenzie on your table.

As soon as I was allowed, I took my bowl and beaker over to the trolley. Miss Miller dropped my spoon into the red washing up bowl and slopped my last drops of custard into the blue one. Even with an empty tummy, the mushy mix of leftovers made me retch, and I ran out of the dining hall as fast as I could.

'Straight to your classroom today,' Miss Miller shouted after me. 'It's wet play.'

No hiding behind the conker tree for me then.

With the doors swinging shut behind me, I stopped next to the sports trophy cabinet to catch my breath. If I went into the toilets I could probably stay there for most of dinnertime without anyone noticing I was missing. Two steps forward and there she was, Brockhill Junior's very own private investigator, come to make a citizen's arrest.

'In a hurry, Jasmine?' asked Mrs Wilkinson, her bulldog body blocking my path.

I shrugged. I had the right to remain silent.

'Is there anything you want to tell me?

I bit my lip. I was not about to crack under pressure.

'Nothing at all, Jasmine?'

I shook my head. If the others hadn't already told on me, I certainly wasn't about to drop myself in it.

A loud knocking sound broke off my account.

'Come!' boomed Mrs Wilkinson.

I blinked, and turned to see Mark breezing in through the library doors. He was proffering a large oval plate. His impeccable timing made me wonder how long he'd been waiting just outside the room. Mrs Wilkinson nodded towards the coffee table. Mark placed the plate precisely at its centre.

'Ginger biscuits,' he said, glancing between the two of us, 'as requested.' He hovered next to my chair for a moment.

I waited. Did Mark know what I'd done as well? Had my

punishment already been decided? Was kleptomania still penalized with incarceration? I wanted to go home.

'That will be all thank you, Mark,' said Mrs Wilkinson.

'Right-e-o, Mrs W. Buzz down if you need anything, won't you?'

I listened to Mark's footsteps die away before I spoke. 'How did you know? The others swore they didn't tell you.'

'Oh, Jasmine,' she leant over to pick up a biscuit, shaking her head but smiling. 'I can tell a guilty child when I see one. And you barely exchanged a word with Samantha or Gillian after that day. I know Karen wasn't ever a real friend, but you three had been thick as thieves before then. Do pardon the pun.' She took a big bite out of her biscuit. 'Mmmm,' she nodded, pushing the plate towards me.

'No. Thanks. I've never been able to stomach the things.'

Mrs Wilkinson finished her ginger biscuit and reached over for a second one. At least a dozen remained, lying in silent accusation in front of me. I settled back into the armchair and crossed my legs to shield the vile discs from my sight.

'I'm sorry,' I said. 'You trusted me and I let you down.' I reached into the top pocket of my jacket and pulled out my long green librarian's badge. 'I came to give this back.'

'Oh, you silly girl. You earned that badge. It's yours. What good is it to me?'

'But Sam had hers taken away. And I let you down too.'

'There were other issues involved in Samantha's case, but that needn't concern you. And you were one of the most dedicated librarians Brockhill ever had, so stop all this nonsense about letting me down.'

'But I stole and I lied and I concealed evidence and—'

'You took two biscuits, Jasmine. Hardly a hangable offence.

And you didn't lie to me about it; I never gave you the opportunity.'

'But weren't you *cross* with me? Weren't you disgusted?'

'A little disappointed, yes. But we've all done things we're not proud of, you know, most of them a lot worse than this. Besides, you punished yourself enough, don't you think?'

'What do you mean?'

'Those extra hours you put into the lunchtime book club, helping out with the infants' reading scheme, organising that charity concert – all fuelled by your guilty conscience, I'd say.'

I'd never thought of it like that. I looked at the badge glinting on my outstretched palm. Perhaps I did deserve to keep it. 'But I should have owned up. You gave me a chance, didn't you, by the dinner hall the next day? You see, I *did* let you down.'

'I knew you, Jasmine. I know all my pupils. I said that if you ever wanted to tell me anything you were to come and find me.'

'But I didn't, did I?'

'You did, Jasmine, don't you see? You're here now. I knew you'd come one day.'

I put the badge onto the arm of my chair and rubbed my temples with both hands. Was I really that predictable?

'So why now?' she asked.

'I... I wanted to make amends.'

'Aha, it got you too, did it – the dreaded drink?'

'No. It's not like that. It's just... something else.'

She leant back to look at me properly. I could tell she was weighing me up. Coke addict, smack head, gambler – which had I become? I wouldn't see her again; what did it matter if she got me all wrong? Besides, I'd had enough of talking. This was more gruelling than I'd expected. At least if she'd heard of The Programme I wouldn't have to explain.

'So, how do you plan to make your amends?'

'Well, I thought I could just say sorry. Which I have.'

'And do you feel better for it?'

I thought for a second. 'No. Not at all.'

'Then perhaps more is needed.'

'You think I should say sorry again? And I could find the other three and apologise for not owning up. I could find the people who were meant to get the biscuits and take them some more.'

She laughed. 'I don't think you'd have much luck finding any of those old folks still alive.'

The memory had become so vivid, I'd forgotten how long ago the whole episode had taken place. I felt my cheeks burning.

'I'm sorry, Jasmine, I don't mean to make fun. I'm not sure that raking things up for the other girls would be helpful though. Remember they will all have their own take on things. And they'll have dealt with it in their own way.'

'So what else can I do?'

She was my headteacher; I wanted her to tell me the answer. And she did.

'How about becoming a regular visitor here?'

'You mean as a penance?'

She smiled. 'Not a penance as such, more a mutually beneficial arrangement. Come and keep us oldies company, bring us all a bit of cheer from the outside world. It could be fun.'

I doubted that very much, but if I was able to give something back, my pilferer's guilt might be assuaged.

Our agreement finalised, I didn't linger for long. We stuck to lighter topics and swapped information on the whereabouts of a few more of my former classmates before I made a move to leave. I felt slightly dazed and disorientated, and unsure of how embarrassed I ought to be about what had just taken place. I probably needed a nap, or at least a lie-down on the sofa.

'How does next Sunday suit you?' Mrs Wilkinson asked as she escorted me to the door.

'Sunday? Oh.' When she'd mentioned regular visits I'd been thinking along the lines of every six weeks, once a month at a push.

'Saturday would be fine if that suits you better, but Sunday afternoons are always so dead.'

I pulled the door open. My eyes were drawn to the words on the brass plaque: *Harold Wilkinson Memorial Library and Meeting Room*. The old woman's last word hung between us as she waited for my reply. What else did I have planned for Sunday? A spot of weeding and a *Midsomer Murders* DVD?

'Sunday's perfect,' I said. 'I'll look forward to it.'

The raised eyebrow. She could see straight through me.

I cleared my throat. 'Well, I'll see you next week then, about three?'

'Splendid. I'll let the others know. They *will* be pleased.'

As we said our goodbyes a thought hit me. 'Shall I bring some biscuits?' I asked.

'What a lovely idea.'

Smiling, I turned and strode towards the staircase. This amends thing was going well. I might even start to enjoy it.

On rounding the corner, a clear voice floated after me. 'Oh, but Jasmine,' called Mrs Wilkinson, 'perhaps something other than ginger biscuits.'

four

Clearing out the shed and garage kept me occupied for the next couple of days. I decided to leave the bookshelves for now; sorting books had somehow lost its appeal. By Wednesday evening I'd filled four black bin liners with rubbish, five cardboard boxes with bits and bobs for the charity shop, and a musty hold-all with the tools and gadgets that Dan still hadn't got round to collecting.

On Thursday morning I loaded the boxes into the car to drop them off on my way to the Co-op. The lack of empty parking spaces in front of Oxfam forced me to drive further along the row of shops, until I spotted a gap between two delivery lorries. Years of jostling for space in the staff car park had honed my manoeuvring skills, and I squeezed in with no trouble. Barely had I hoisted the first box out of the boot when I was accosted by an elderly gentleman with the air of a frail Albert Einstein.

'Do you want a hand, my dear?'

'I think I can manage, thanks,' I said, balancing the box on my left hip and reaching up with my right arm to shut the boot.

As I stooped to pick up my handbag from the kerb, a silver candlestick toppled from the box and clunked onto the pavement between us.

'Here, let me help you,' he said, and swept up the bag and candlestick with an agile bow. 'Oh! Lovely, lovely. Does he have a partner?'

For a moment I thought he must be referring to himself. A ranting Gollum escaped from Middle Earth: '*Does the graceful old man have a partner? Oh no, my precious, he is all alone...*' I was being mugged by a demented hobbit. Great.

'Look,' I ventured, 'how about you keep the candlestick but give me back my handbag?'

Gollum didn't seem to have heard me, but was squinting into the box which I was now clutching to my chest.

'Ooooh! He *does* have a partner. Let me see her. What a beauty!'

I attempted to step backwards as he extended a scraggy hand towards me, but with my back against the Beetle I had nowhere left to go. I would have screamed or given him a sharp kick in the shins if I hadn't been certain that the shock would have killed him. So instead I looked on, motionless, as he eased the matching candlestick from my hoard and lifted it high into the air.

'A perfect pair,' he marvelled, without taking an eye off his find. 'Quite a scoop. Most people favour Oxfam to us. More trendy, I dare say. Shall we?'

He gestured sideways with his pointy head, causing silky white strands of hair to fall over one eye. I looked past him to a shop front I'd never noticed before. Headless mannequins in cocktail dresses and ponchos posed nonchalantly between cuddly toys and china tea sets. Large blue letters painted above the window display read *Help the Aged*. Of course.

Gollum skipped through the open doorway with Granny's apparently priceless silver, my Barbie-pink handbag dangling over his shoulder. What could I do but follow?

The reek of Parma violets and mothballs which hit me on entering, vindicated my staunch aversion to charity-shopping. The thought of using somebody else's hairbrush or wearing dead people's clothes made me feel sick.

Gollum placed Granny's candlesticks one each side of the till and stood back in admiration. 'Come and look at these beauties, Betty,' he called towards the back room. 'Best find of the month, I'd say!'

'Shove 'em in t' storeroom,' came the reply. 'I'm sortin' knickers.'

The old man shuffled his feet and coughed. 'You must excuse Elizabeth. At times she can be somewhat... How shall I put it? Uncouth? She has a heart of gold though. Pure gold.'

I forced a smile. I had no interest in Betty's manners. All I wanted was to reclaim my bag, dump my stuff and transport myself to the safe familiarity of the Co-op wine aisle. 'Should I leave this box here?' I asked, lowering it onto the glass counter.

'Yes, yes,' said Gollum. 'I'll help you in with the rest.'

Help The Aged or Oxfam – it was all the same to me. I shrugged and headed back out to the car.

Peering into the boot, I picked the lightest-looking box for my sprightly companion to carry. No family heirlooms in that one, only an ornamental copper kettle, a set of paintbrushes and a handful of DVDs. Gollum had already spotted something though.

'Ah, *Riverdance*!' he cried. 'Such magical choreography.'

'A bit of a fan, are you?' I asked. There was no accounting for taste.

'A bit of a fan?' he spluttered. 'Dancing was my life! My first love, my last love, my only love. Alas, she deserted me many moons ago and broke this foolish heart of mine. Oh, she's a mean mistress.' Resting a hand across his narrow ribcage he gazed wistfully into the distance, where a bin lorry had just become wedged between two metal bollards. 'I can still do a perfect tango, you know, and a mean rhumba. In here, at least.' He tapped his right temple with a gnarled finger and sighed. 'Body refuses to cooperate, that's all. My dancing days are over, I'm afraid. I can still watch though. Watch and dream...'

It was a shame about the dancing, but growing old was a fact of life. At least he didn't have to endure the shabby décor of Valley View, day in, day out. I rattled the box I'd been holding out for him. The Co-op wine shelves were calling. His speckled green eyes darted back to me, earnest and moist. He'd been serious about the broken heart.

It took us a while to shift the remaining boxes. Out of pity I'd asked him a couple of pertinent questions, and surprised myself at my interest in his replies.

As a shy young clerk he'd taken lessons in all the basic dance steps from a friend of his mother's so that he wouldn't make a fool of himself at village get-togethers. This, of course, was where all the pretty girls were to be found. The pretty girl who mattered most was Margaret Cooke, the spectacular eldest daughter of Dr Cooke, local GP. Week after week, Miss Cooke's admirers would gather round, clamouring for the merest morsel of her attention, swooning at each astute remark. The men she deigned to dance with were the luckiest in the whole world.

'Good things come to those who wait,' young Gollum's mother would always tell him.

So he waited for Margaret Cooke to tire of other suitors. He waited while a dashing physicist swept her off her feet. He waited behind the yew tree in the graveyard of St Mary's Church until the beaming couple emerged, man and wife. And then he moved away.

'We didn't share one dance,' he sighed. 'Not a single one.'

'So dancing wasn't your *only* love.'

The old man's eyes lit up again. 'My only *true* love,' he said.

'True and requited. Together for over half a century.'

'And you never married?'

'I never found anyone who could compare.'

Whether he was referring to the charms of Margaret Cooke or the lure of the dance I didn't discover, as our conversation was interrupted by a fierce yell which came from the back of the shop.

'Ruddy perverts!' bellowed Betty-the-Uncouth. 'Knickers I can cope with. But this filth… What *is* our country coming to?'

Time for me to take my leave. The old man thanked me again for my donation and apologised for his sentimentality. It was rare to find people who really listened nowadays, he lamented. I assured him that it had been a pleasure to meet him and to hear his story.

'Goodbye then,' he said, as I headed for the door.

A simple goodbye didn't seem sufficient somehow, after such an outpouring, but what else was there to do? I could hardly hug him. I glanced back from the doorway and couldn't help chuckling.

'What is it?' he asked. 'Something I said?'

I pointed at his shoulder. 'You've still got my handbag.'

'Oh. So I have. It's not really my colour, is it? Although it's comfy enough. Perhaps I should get myself one of those newfangled manbags.' He walked towards me, hooked the bag over my arm, then raised my hand to his lips for a gentlemanly kiss. 'Farewell once again,' he said with a small bow. 'May your life be rich and joyful.'

'Goodbye,' I said, 'and thank you.' I wasn't sure what I was thanking him for, but I meant it all the same.

I resolved to phone Penny when I got home. It would be good to arrange a night out before term started. Things were always too hectic at work for a proper natter. I might even see if Tash would be up for a houseguest for a night or two. She usually took time off for the kids' holidays and I could do with a change of scene. Catching up with her and Phil and the boys would be great too, of course.

My supermarket shop was a quick one; there was no point buying much fresh stuff if I was going to be away for the next couple of nights.

I reached home just as the postman was pulling up onto the kerb opposite. If I timed it right, I could make a dash for the house before he collared me for one of his state-of-the-world rants.

'Morning!' he shouted, sprinting across the road. 'Only the one for you today.'

'If it's another bill, you can keep it. Or better still, return it to sender. Tell them I've emigrated.'

He held out a light blue envelope. 'Doesn't look like a bill to me. I reckon that's proper ink pen. You know, I hardly ever deliver real letters any more.'

'I think you did mention it.'

'The odd birthday card, maybe. But it's only a matter of time before those become obsolete, if you ask me. Do you know what my daughter sent me for my birthday this year? A flipping text! What good's that to me, eh? I can't stick a text on my mantelpiece, can I?'

'That's awful,' I frowned, recalling all the last minute birthday greetings I'd sent by text or email. 'But it's nice to know someone's thinking of you, isn't it? And there's always the environmental aspect to consider. Saving paper, I mean.'

'Environment? Pah! Too lazy to get off her behind and walk

down to the Post Office for a card and stamp, more like. For her own dad as well! You work your fingers to the bone for your kids, and are they grateful? Are they hell. You're a sensible girl not having any kiddies, you know. Worse than leeches, they are. Love mine to bits, mind.'

Sensible? So is that what I'd done back then? Made a sensible choice?

'Are you OK, love? You look a bit... odd.'

'No. Yes. I'm fine. But I need to get this lot in the freezer before it's ruined.'

He glanced down at my reusable and totally see-through string shopping bag. 'In the freezer? What, French bread and salad?'

'I've, er... I've got a bit more in the car.'

He looked over at my locked car on the drive, then back at me. 'Right. If you say so. Anyhow, I'd best get on my way. Junk mail to deliver!'

Inside, I plonked the ingredients of today's lunch and my cheap bottle of wine onto the kitchen table. Why was everyone so interested in whether I should have kids or not? Dan had always told me that people were just showing an interest. Don't let it bother you, he'd shrug. He honestly didn't know what all the fuss was about. But then there were a lot of things that Dan didn't know.

I carried the unopened envelope back into the sitting room, examining the neat gothic script and trying to make out the post mark. The only handwritten letters I usually received were from my parents. There was the odd scribbled poem from Kevin Anderson – star of my special needs literacy group – but those didn't count. In any case, this certainly wasn't from Kevin; he leant towards wax crayons and reused envelopes sealed with gaffer tape. It couldn't be from my parents either, not unless they'd surreptitiously sold up their dream home in Malaga and resigned themselves to English property prices and our abysmal weather. I had to admit, my postman had a point for once: there *was* something exciting about getting a proper letter.

I opened the envelope, eased out the thick, pale blue sheets of writing paper and unfolded them. The same gothic script covered the pages, giving the whole letter the grandeur of an ancient and precious scroll. At the top of the first sheet was yesterday's date and the sender's address: Valley View. Could Mrs Wilkinson have changed her mind about my regular visits? Had she decided that I'd suffered enough and now deserved to be let off the hook? I rearranged the cushions behind me, pulled my feet up onto the sofa and began to read.

My dear Jasmine,

You cannot imagine how delighted I was to see you again on Monday, after all these years. In coming to visit me, you demonstrated the courage and honesty which I recognised in you from your first days at Brockhill. You may well have forgotten all about little Thomas Knowles and the tadpoles, but I assure you that I have not. Apologies. I digress.

I have a suggestion to make ~ an offer, let's say ~ and I wanted to put it in writing to ensure that you are able to give the matter ample consideration. The thought did occur to me when we were talking two days ago, but I was concerned that it would be too much for you to take in. I know all too well how much energy these confrontations with one's past can sap.

I shall not recount my own tale in full; I'm sure that its outline, at the very least, will be a familiar one. For whoever we are, whichever drug we choose, our stories are the same. We all have our own demons which allow us ~ perhaps push us ~ into addiction and the selfishness which accompanies such an illness.

During my difficult years it was alcohol that I used as my prop. It gave me the strength to face the world; it numbed my agony as I watched my husband in his; it eased my dread of facing another anguishing day with him or a lifetime without him.

When, for him, the end finally came, I prayed that it would come for me too. All I wanted was for the pain to stop. God heard my prayer, Jasmine, and he led me to Alcoholics Anonymous. It is with my hand on my heart that I tell you how those meetings, those fellow sufferers, and, of course, The Programme, saved my life.

You say that it is not alcohol with you. I do not ask you to reveal your secrets to me. Your journey will still be hard. There will be days when you are on the point of despair, ready to go back to familiar ways. I know that you have the strength to persevere and to restore yourself fully to health and a mindful life. I pray that you know this too.

My concern, Jasmine, is not for your motivation or your willpower but rather your direction. You seemed a little confused as to the best course of action regarding making your amends. Do I infer correctly that you are no longer with a support group and that you are acting without a sponsor? An admirable ambition, but in this case I fear that independence is unwise. As you are well aware, The Twelve Steps are a serious undertaking, and I cannot stress enough how vital it is to have the guidance of one who has trodden the path before you. If you feel that there can be no reconciliation between your sponsor and yourself, then I should be honoured to offer my support. When you are further on in The Programme, you will realise the importance of helping other sufferers, both to them and to yourself and your own recovery.

Please think about all that I have said. We can discuss the issue further on Sunday. I truly believe that it would be a joy and an honour to be your sponsor, Jasmine, and to introduce you to the wonders of Benestrophe.

Yours in utmost sincerity,
O.M. Wilkinson

P.S. The general preference here seems to be for bourbons or custard creams.

I reread the letter but still it made no sense. The first part was simple enough. Clearly I should have corrected her misapprehension concerning my addiction, or lack of one. But after that I got a little lost. Why did she think that everyone on

The Twelve Step Recovery Programme was looking for sponsors? Did some addicts get *paid* to give up their booze or pills? No, surely the general public would know about something like that. The tabloids would be certain to find some lanky teenaged girl who'd not only had a baby at sixteen to get herself a plush council flat, but who'd also forced herself into alcoholism for the extra tenner a week. There would be an outcry. The sponsorship system would instantly be scrapped.

Senile dementia – it was the only explanation. I must have seen Mrs Wilkinson on a good day. Then she'd written the letter on a bad one. What *had* I let myself in for? Another challenging visit to Valley View, for one thing. My old headmistress was going to ply me with words of wisdom, then attempt to bribe me out of my make-believe addiction. Plus she seemed intent on fixing me up with the exotic-sounding Benestrophe. He, at least, might be real. A foreign care-worker perhaps – Greek or Italian. Maybe I should ring and speak to a member of staff before I set off on Sunday, see what state she was in. With any luck she'd have forgotten all about our arrangement. I refolded the sheets of paper, stuffed them back into the envelope and propped the letter up against a vase on the mantelpiece.

If I was going to sort out this break at Tasha's I needed to get a move on. She'd most likely be out and about with the boys at this time of day, so I tried her mobile. She picked up straight away but didn't speak. From the muffled shouting it sounded as if she might be at the swimming baths.

'Tasha, are you there?'

'Hey, sis. Hang on. Just let me... That's better. Hello, Jaz? Can you hear me?'

'Where on earth are you, Tash?'

'Farm park. Hettie Hen's World of Adventure. We're with

Amanda and her girls. Remind me to keep the au pair on in the holidays next time, will you?'

'Tash, I was thinking of driving down to see you all. Just for a couple of nights. Maybe Friday and Saturday? Tash?'

'Ow. No, Felicity, that hurts. Sorry? Friday? As in tomorrow? No can do, sis. We're off to Alton Towers. The boys have been begging me to take them for months.'

'Just Saturday then?'

'Felicity, stop. I don't care if your mum lets you do it to her, Finn doesn't like it. Saturday? Yes, that should be... Oh, no, rugby tournament in Oxford. How about Sunday? I could practise my cashew nut roast.'

'No, Sunday's no good. I've got to visit somebody else.' Possibly. I didn't feel up to explaining my renewed contact with our old headmistress.

'OK, well I might have a weekend off in June if that's any good. Come away from the ducks, Stephanie, there's a good girl.'

'All go in the world of fantasy fiction then?'

'Lectures mostly, it's such a... Stephanie, put it down. Stephanie! Don't you dare... Oh, Christ. Sorry, sis, Stephanie's just thrown a duck-egg at Charlie. Amanda was only meant to be buying ice creams. Lord knows where she's disappeared to. It's all right, Charlie, it'll come off. I'll speak to you soon, Jaz, yeah? Charlie, we can wash your hair as soon as we get home. Come on, don't cry.'

'Right then—' I began, but was cut off by a drawn out squeal.

'No, Felicity! Not on the piglet—'

The line went dead. I took in a long, deep breath through my nose and let it out in a slow, silent whistle. It was one of the de-stressing exercises we'd been given to teach the kids at school. I loved my family, but from a distance it was easy to forget how exhausting they could be. A night out with Penny would do. I'd stay at Ruben's on Saturday evening and then on Sunday... Well, I'd have to wait and see.

My evening with Penny didn't provide the opportunity to discuss everything I'd hoped to: i.e. myself. She was unable to leave the house as her black Labrador was about to have pups and needed her support.

'What about me?' I wanted to shout. *'I'm your best friend, aren't I? I need support too, you know!'*

'That's fine,' I'd said, 'I'll bring round some plonk and a DVD.'

I knew how soppy Penny was. She'd be jumping up every five minutes to check on Mitzi, and would find it impossible to hold a coherent conversation, never mind a constructive one.

We passed a pleasant enough couple of hours getting tipsy and watching Thelma and Louise's doomed but bizarrely uplifting attempt to reach the Mexican border. Geena Davis's motel room antics with Brad Pitt caused the tiniest flutter in my wine-filled stomach as I imagined my first encounter with the mysterious Benestrophe. Greek rather than Italian, I decided, with chiselled features and smoky eyes. All the charms and exoticism of Ruben, but with the lithe body and unstinting enthusiasm of a man at the peak of his sexual vigour.

'I think Mitzi's waters have broken,' announced Penny from the living room doorway.

'I didn't think dogs had waters,' I said.

'Of course they do. It's what the puppies float in. In the uterus.'

'Aren't they born in their little sacs?' I asked. 'Like lambs?'

'How would they get out?'

How was *I* supposed to know? It was *her* stupid dog. My eyes flitted back to the screen. Thelma and Louise were sitting in the diner and had just realised that Brad Pitt had run off with all their money. Even in supposedly feminist movies they managed to sneak it in, didn't they? Go ahead, sisters, be free! Enjoy your emancipation! But take too much pleasure from life and you'll be punished.

'Maybe the bitch eats them,' said Penny, only slightly slurring her words.

'Who, Thelma?' She'd lost me. 'Or Louise?'

'What? No, the dog. Maybe she eats the sacs. She must do. Like cows licking the gunk off their calves' faces. Gross.'

'So that can't be her waters then,' I pointed out.

'Well, there's a big puddle on the floor, so if it's not... Oh, Mitzi, you *bad* girl. Outside! Go on, out!'

I turned the sound up to compensate for the door-slamming and mop-and-bucket-clanking coming from the kitchen.

'Don't worry about waiting for me,' Penny called. 'I know how it ends.'

'Oh, OK,' I replied, turning the sound down again so that she wouldn't realise how much she'd already missed.

So, she knew how it ended. I wished *I* knew how things would end.

'Need a top-up?' Penny was standing behind the sofa, peeling off her pink rubber gloves. 'Better keep these handy,' she said. 'I'll be glad of them if one of the pups gets stuck and I have to—'

'Listen, I'm going to make a move.'

'You can sleep here if you like. There's plenty of room now that... Well, I could make you a bed up in the back room.'

The back room. Jane's office. Until last Christmas. Until Jane had stumbled in drunk one night after an office party and announced to her partner of ten years that she'd met the man of her dreams and was expecting his child.

I watched Penny as she picked thick black dog hairs off the arm of the sofa.

'Thanks, Pen, but I'd better be getting back. Loads to do in the morning. You know how it is.'

She didn't know how it was – I hadn't told her – but she nodded anyway.

'Do you want to take your DVD?' she asked.

'Don't worry. You can bring it into school next week.'

'Urgh, school. Don't remind me.'

'Never mind,' I consoled. 'Only five weeks till half term.'

'Thank goodness for that.' She passed me the coat I'd left hanging over the banister.

I put it on and wished her good luck with the dog. 'And if anything goes wrong or you're at all anxious,' I said, 'it doesn't matter what time it is or what you're worried about. Anything at all, seriously, don't hesitate to ring the vet.'

'Thanks,' she said. 'Are you sure you don't want me to call you a cab? It's almost twelve.'

I declined her offer. I fancied a walk, and it was a safe area of town. Although it paid to be cautious. As I set out for home I took my house keys from my pocket and clenched the pointiest one between my thumb and first finger, ready to pierce the eyeballs of potential muggers. With my other hand I eased a hairpin from my topknot and bit the rubber blobs off the ends of the metal. Now I was primed to skewer my assailants in the jugular. Blinded and bleeding, I would leave them disinclined to mess with me again.

The most notable event during the walk home, however, apart

from seeing a squashed badger near the Sainsbury's roundabout, was receiving a text from Ruben. There was nobody in sight, so I dared to slip my carefully-crafted weapons into my pocket for a moment so that I could look at my phone.

'Hope we're still on for Saturday. Looking forward to reading your new lists. That's not all I'm looking forward to… ;-) xx'

Good old Ruben. I might only see him once a week but at least he gave me his full attention when we were together. No badly behaved kids or incontinent pets to distract him. I hadn't told him anything about my visit to Valley View, so it would be good to see him. I could tell him about Mrs Wilkinson's letter and her weird sponsorship idea. I knew he'd agree that the old woman had lost the plot and that there was no sense in me continuing to visit. I'd be wasting her time as well as mine. I might even tell him about the harvest festival biscuits. Honesty, I resolved, could well be the best policy. I'd keep quiet about Benestrophe for now though. No point stirring up negative emotions.

I paused for a moment under a lamppost to compose my reply.

'Looking forward to seeing you too. Loads to tell you. If you're VERY nice you might get that massage…xoxox'

Yes, I was looking forward to the weekend. I knew I could rely on Ruben. He was bound to agree with me. I had faith in him to talk good sense. He always did.

five

'What do you *mean*, I shouldn't call her a fruitcake? She's a loon, a complete loon!'

Ruben blew a cone of smoke rings and flicked his cigarette end into the hearth. 'It's just not nice to use words like that, Jaz. I'm surprised at you, to be honest.'

I didn't like this – *I* was the disapproving one: his smoking, his diet, all those vintage cars and their ridiculous fuel consumption. This wasn't fair.

'Well, you didn't meet her, did you? Dressed in red like some queen mother. You haven't read her letter either. I'm telling you, she's nuts.'

Ruben winced. He stared into the cold fireplace. When he finally turned to face me, his eyes suggested a sadness I'd never seen before.

'What on earth's the matter?' I asked.

He looked at me for a moment, then slowly shook his head. 'It's nothing,' he said, 'Nothing's the matter. I was going to ask you what she'd written, that's all, this teacher of yours.'

'You're sure you're OK?'

'I'm fine. Now tell me about the old woman. Why are you so convinced she's mad?'

'Well, she thinks I'm a junkie, for a start, and she wants to pay me.'

'To take drugs?'

'No, to not take drugs.'

'She said that?'

'Yes, she says she wants to be my sponsor.'

Ruben smirked.

'What? I hardly think it's *that* amusing.'

'It's not *her* I'm laughing at – it's you!'

'I'm only telling you what she said. What's so funny?'

'She's not talking about giving you money,' he said, still laughing. He was beginning to irritate me.

'And how on earth would *you* know? Ruben!'

'Because I read up on it, didn't I? While you were still tucked up in bed last Sunday.'

'Read up on what?'

'The Twelve Steps. One of the fundamental guidelines is that you should have a sponsor – a mentor to help you through the whole thing.'

'Yes but sponsor doesn't mean that, Ruben, it means... Oh. A mentor. I see.'

Ruben was watching me, a ridiculously self-satisfied look on his face. I guess it wasn't often that I made a mistake.

'OK, so she isn't trying to bribe me. Maybe she's not *totally* batty. But you didn't see her, she was...'

'Dressed in red? Hm, a sure sign of insanity.'

'Oh, shut up.'

He shut up, but smugness oozed from every pore.

'And stop looking at me like that.'

'Like what?'

'You know like what.'

He batted his eyelids and made a great show of averting his gaze to the beamed ceiling. 'Better?'

'Not really. And say something, will you?'

'I thought you wanted me to shut up.'

'Well, I don't any more. I want you to tell me what to do.'

'Mm, I like the sound of that.' He looked at me, reached one hand out towards me and slowly ran his fingers over my cheek and down my neck, until his hand rested on my shoulder.

I pulled away. We'd have time for that later. I needed to get my thoughts straight first. 'I mean, I want you to tell me what to do about the mentoring thing.'

Ruben sighed and took out his tobacco, dropping it onto the table next to his Rizlas. 'I knew what you meant, but what is there to say? You'll need all the help you can get, from what I can tell. And you've made it pretty clear you don't want *me* involved.'

'I never said that, Ru.' At least I didn't think I had.

'Look, I know you hate accepting help from people, but she might be able to teach you a thing or two. Who knows?'

'I do *not* hate accepting help,' I said. 'It's just that I never need it.'

Ruben stared at me, eyebrows raised, as if he'd somehow proved a point.

'What?' I asked.

He started to roll another cigarette. 'Accept her offer. At least she'll know all the rules.'

'What rules?'

'That's my point: I don't know. The rules of The Programme. Like not harming others. Or yourself.'

'Why would I want to harm myself? You mean suicide?'

'Of course not. No, there's something about not making amends if it could harm other people.'

'But how would it?'

'Don't ask me. Ask your teacher. Maybe like if you apologised to your sister for sleeping with her husband, when she didn't *know* you'd been sleeping with her husband, so then they got a divorce.'

'But I'd never do something like that. Christ, Ru, is that what you think of me?'

'Don't be ridiculous. It was an example, that's all. Of when you might be better off keeping quiet.'

'And carrying on with Phil behind Tasha's back?'

'Well, obviously you'd have to finish it.'

'Why?'

'Because you're meant to be becoming a better person.'

'You're saying I'm not good enough?'

'No, Jasmine, I'm telling you what Step Nine is about.'

OK, so maybe he wasn't trying to wind me up; he wasn't Dan. But me and Phil? Honestly! Ruben had seen photos of my family as well. Could he really see me cavorting with Tasha's gangly, bald-headed professor of a husband? Did he credit me with *no* taste? But if Mrs Wilkinson really wasn't mad after all, maybe she would be a useful guide.

'Fine. I'll let her be my sponsor. As long as she's not too domineering.'

Ruben muttered something about domineering women, but I decided it was best to ignore him.

'Anyway, Ru, how's your week been? What have you been up to?'

'Me? Well now, I thought you'd never ask…'

Our evening played out like all our Saturday evenings: we talked, we ate, we drank, we made love. Afterwards, as we lay entangled, I wondered how long we could stave off the rot's onset if we rationed our liaisons to once a week. Would I still be madly in love with Dan if I hadn't had to look at his face over the breakfast table every single morning, if I hadn't witnessed his fortnightly clipping of toe-nails and nasal hair?

With Ruben it would be different. It *was* different. We had an understanding and we had our own lives. We were *not* going to fall in love.

'Are you still awake?' I whispered.

Ruben let out a sleepy 'Mmm', and pulled me closer.

'Ruben, do you think we'll ever hate each other?'

Silence.

'Ru, I said—'

'I heard you.'

'Well?'

'Oh, Jasmine, why are you—'

'Will we ever hate each other? Yes or no?'

Without speaking, he kissed my questioning lips, my fingertips, my shoulders, my neck... He didn't need words to make me understand. We were together *now*, and that was all that mattered. We were together, and that was enough. I let go of my thoughts and sank into his warmth.

After breakfast, I'd tempted Ruben back to bed, and it was gone eleven by the time I'd showered and dressed. The sky was thick with clouds, although it looked decent enough for a walk along the stream or up Fosse Hill. But Ruben had a document which needed finishing before lunchtime, so with his promise of a walk when I next came over, I left him with his dictionaries and ring-binders, and set out for home.

I always enjoyed this drive, marvelling at the transformations in the Gloucestershire landscape week by week, and observing the differences in the villages and towns I passed through, as Cotswold countryside gave way to the more familiar

Worcestershire farmland.

I had no intention of arriving early at Valley View this time, which meant I should be able to squeeze in an episode of *Midsomer Murders* before leaving home. Some nice gentle killing was always a pleasant accompaniment to cold leftovers eaten from my lap-tray. It was comforting to know that, whatever the number of fatalities, and however complicated the crime, within two hours Inspector Barnaby and his latest side-kick would have things wrapped up, with time for a quick pint at the local before supper. The villagers of Midsomer Worthy and Badger's Drift would be left in peace to their bell-ringing and flower-arranging. And I would be left with the prospect of being biscuit-bearer at a musty old folks' home.

She was in the library again when I arrived. Today she was swathed in lime green, with what looked like an olive chrysanthemum pinned into her shiny hair. I'd preferred the crimson.

'Jasmine, Jasmine!' she beamed. 'How good of you to come back.'

'Well, I said I would. You didn't doubt me?'

'No, no. Of course I didn't. And I trust you received my letter?'

'Yes. I did.'

'I do hope you weren't offended. As I said, it really would be an honour…'

'I'd love you to be my mentor. Thank you. There are a few things I need to explain first though.'

I told her about Sophie's phone call and the gloves. I talked about Dan and the divorce, about Ruben, and how far I'd come in the last eighteen months.

She listened intently. 'So you never *were* an addict? Hmm.'

Surely my lack of a habit hadn't disappointed her?

'Not to worry,' she continued. 'As long as you've thought this through. It's not something to be taken lightly, you know. You can't treat The Programme as a game.'

'I wouldn't. I'm not. I want to do it properly.'

'Ah, but picking and choosing the bits that suit you, well, I'm not sure about that.'

'But I don't *need* to do the whole thing. The Twelve Steps would take ages. And the first seven aren't relevant to me anyway.'

'Oh, I see. So tell me, what *are* those first seven steps, Jasmine?'

'Well, I couldn't tell you *exactly*, but it's more the amends part that I like the sound of.'

'You like the sound of it?'

'I mean it sounds as if it would be useful. Like it would make me… you know… grow. As a person. It helped you, didn't it?'

'It did. I can't tell you how much. Such different circumstances though.' She turned towards the window and the views which had brought her here.

What if she withdrew her offer now that I'd revealed myself as a fraud? Yesterday I'd been determined to see things through on my own. But this threat of desertion… She was my only crutch. No, she couldn't leave me.

'Who knows where I might end up without any guidance?' I said.

Mrs Wilkinson shook her head and smiled. 'All right, we'll see what we can do, shall we?'

I'm not sure how long we sat there, planning my route, plotting my journey. She seemed satisfied with the tattered brainstorm I'd taken along to show her, but disagreed with my idea of tackling the past, chunk by chunk. An honest assessment of my entire history was deemed vital in the psychological preparation for Step Nine. So Ruben had been right. Again. Absolute truthfulness was another requirement, both with myself and with her, as my mentor. And although actual harm was to be avoided, I must not allow mere pride to prevent me from owning up to potentially humiliating episodes.

Concerned at the open-endedness of our strategy, I had the bright idea of setting a time limit. I was willing to set aside a fixed number of hours per offence, or, if Mrs Wilkinson preferred, a couple of months to cover the whole business. If she'd had a piece of chalk and a board rubber in her hand, I swear she'd have slammed them down on the table in front of me.

'A couple of months, Jasmine? A couple of months? It can take years, you know. It can take a lifetime. Step Nine never truly ends, because we are human. We remain fallible, so there are always amends to be made. Don't suffer the misapprehension that you can do this little project and then carry on as if nothing has changed. Because things *will* change, you mark my words. *You'll* change, for a start.'

'I realise that,' I said. Although I didn't.

'So if you only have a couple of months to spare—'

'No, I can take longer. It was a stupid suggestion. Forget I mentioned it.'

Her clenched fists poked out from lacy lime sleeves. I allowed time for her and her locked jaw to calm down while I affected a rereading of my list. After a few minutes, I realised that it was down to me to reignite the conversation.

'Right,' I hazarded, 'I'll complete Step Eight before I next see you then, shall I? All of it. Properly.'

'If you are able to find the time,' she replied.

I really had put her out. 'And then you can help me decide my next move. I'm not sure I could do any of this without you. You always were a great teacher.'

'Enough! Flattery, my dear Jasmine, will get you everywhere. Now come on, we've a room full of starving oldies downstairs, hankering after your bourbons.'

Meeting the other residents wasn't as painful an experience as I'd been expecting. Most of them seemed fairly normal. It wasn't until we were arranging next week's visit that I remembered what I'd anticipated would be the highlight of my day.

'Oh,' I said, 'you were going to introduce me to Benestrophe.'

Mrs Wilkinson's face lit up. 'You *are* keen, aren't you? I think that's enough for one day though.'

'You want me to wait another seven days?' What if he wasn't on duty next weekend? It might be a *fortnight* till we met. Maybe more. 'I could always hang around for a while longer,' I said.

She was not about to be swayed. 'I'm glad you're so interested, but I'm sure it can wait until Sunday.'

'I'm honestly in no rush to get off.'

'*You* may not be in a hurry, but I certainly am. You enjoy the odd game of poker, Jasmine?'

'I prefer gin rummy, myself. Or snap.' This lot looked more like bridge fans and whist drive enthusiasts than hardened poker players, but you never could tell.

A wizened hustler bared his gums at us as he and his Zimmer frame shuffled past. 'Coming down to the den, my flower?' he asked.

'I'll be with you in a moment, Berny,' said Mrs Wilkinson. 'I'd better warn you though, I'm feeling lucky today! Jasmine, I'm sorry to rush you...'

'No, no. That's fine. I've got heaps to do anyway.' What with *The Archers* omnibus to listen to and another Midsomer murder to solve.

'Super. Well, same time next week then. You'll find your own way out, I trust? And be sure to put maximum thought into that list of yours. I'll be awarding points for effort.'

'Right. Of course. I'll do my best.'

She pushed herself up out of her chair. 'Jasmine, you do make me chuckle.'

'Do I?'

'I shan't be awarding any points. It was a joke.'

'Oh. I see.'

'You'll be fine. All you have to do is start at the beginning—'

'And keep going until the *very* end. I know.'

'Ha! You remembered. Marvellous!'

'You'd better go and find Berny,' I said. 'He'll be sneaking a look at your hand otherwise.'

'I wouldn't put it past the old weasel. Until Sunday then. And there's something I'd like you to do for me.'

I'd do it. Anything that would help me set things straight, put right my past. Extra biscuits? Hypnotherapy? Public confession? I was prepared to do whatever it took. 'What is it?' I asked. 'Tell me. What do you want me to do?'

'My dear girl,' she replied, 'it's very simple. I would like you to stop looking so worried.'

six

The first week back at work after a break was always hectic. Teachers were keen to make a start on the new term's topics and the children wanted to tell us and each other every detail of how they'd spent their Easter holiday.

On Wednesday evening I'd had to go and meet Penny's ridiculously tiny puppies, which were now a whole five and a half days old. Concerned that Penny might gift wrap one of the bundles of fluff and give it to me as an early birthday present, I swore that if it came to it I'd help her find homes for Ziggy, Pixie, Rusty, Rudi and Ozzy.

So it was Thursday before I had the chance and inclination to begin my list-making homework. I'd managed to escape from the staffroom by four o'clock, and apart from nipping to the garage for petrol, I had no other pressing jobs. At home, I sorted my things out for the following day's work, made a packed lunch, then prepared myself a stir fry. I took my time over dinner, catching up on last week's newspapers and finishing the crossword, before washing and drying up, and putting everything back in its place in the kitchen.

I checked my watch; it was still early. I'd have a good few hours to put into this list-writing. If it proved to be too much of a bind, I could always leave some for tomorrow. I poured myself a large glass of Californian rosé and glanced out of the window. The grass could do with being mown, but it would have to wait.

A cop-out it may have been, but I planned to ease myself into the exercise by typing up my previous list. That shouldn't take too long and would get me into a suitable mood for delving into my memory's darker recesses. I balanced my laptop on the arm of the sofa, spread my crumpled sheets of paper from Ruben's over the cushions next to me and keyed in a title.

Music! What *was* I thinking, sitting down at my computer without putting any music on first? I walked over to the CD rack, and searched for something soothing yet stimulating. I wanted pretty melodies but no distracting lyrics. Julian Bream – he'd do. A nice bit of classical guitar. I turned the volume down a few notches, then returned to the sofa. A gulp or two of wine and I was away.

Julian was nimbly plucking his way through Torroba's *Fandanguillo* by the time I'd deciphered my scrawl and transferred it onto the screen in front of me. The two pages condensed to almost nothing, once it was all laid out neatly and the doodles had been ignored. I decided to enlarge the font to give the document a more substantial appearance. That was one of my handy hints for our special needs kids: if you don't have much to write, make your letters bigger and leave lots of space between your words. I didn't know if teachers marked the stuff any differently, but at least the children felt they'd achieved something by filling a whole page. Right now, sitting back to admire my work, I could relate to that. I clicked on 'print', poured myself some more rosé and ran upstairs to retrieve the page from my printer.

It had been strange enough seeing my deeds written out by hand, but having them right here in print was even odder. An official log of all my dubious behaviour – not even Saint Peter bothered with this kind of paperwork. Or maybe he did. Maybe he created individualised records on his heavenly laptop as he hovered by those pearly gates. I took another sip of wine and attempted to look over my list with the critical eye of Saint Pete.

Step Eight
Stage One (Birth to End of Primary School)
By Jasmine Somers

Off-ground tag / toilet seat incident (not actually my fault)
Stan the Hamster
Making Louise cry
Harvest Festival – ginger biscuits
Bogus tummy aches (do they count? – Mum not fooled)
Tasha's diary
Baking conkers (cracked anyway – overcooked?)
Fly in Eccles cake
Breaking fence (coerced)
Telling Claire about tooth fairy
Pulling knob off wireless
Cutting worms in half
Mum's teapot
Spying on Tasha and Jason
Using Dad's toothbrush on Fluffy
Prank phone calls
Tasha's dress
Billy Prosser (he deserved it)
Mint ice cream > Fluffy to vet
Jason McKenzie (**everyone** called him Podge)
Egg and spoon race
Kerplunk marbles down drain
Dad's tobacco

It didn't amount to much. It didn't even fill that one page. Good old Saint Pete wouldn't have had much to pull me up on if I'd snuffed it before I'd reached my teens and roller-skated on up to meet him at Heaven's door. The juicy stuff came later. I rummaged on the shelves above the printer and pulled out an empty pink document wallet. Brushing off the dust, I slid my single sheet of paper inside.

Julian Bream strummed the last few bars of his *Burgalesa* as I came down the stairs, then he left me in silence. I swapped Bream for Beethoven, pressed the repeat button and settled back into my contemplation corner on the sofa.

So, eleven years down, twenty six to go. It made sense to split those years into two batches. Secondary school and uni would take me up to the age of twenty one. I could tack on my gap and PGCE years to even up the life stages a bit.

Except that I couldn't separate my life cleanly into stages. What I did back then didn't finish then, did it? It wasn't a one-off, like the biscuits; it couldn't be hermetically sealed into a specific point in history, allocated a neat dot on the timeline of my existence, because it was still with me – an ugly ink splodge, seeping outwards, colouring relationships and staining lives.

I got up, marched into the kitchen and grabbed the rosé. I took it back into the living room and sat down. Right, time to bite the bullet. No separating out the years, no faffing about with chronology. Better out than in, Mrs Wilkinson had said. Well, it was coming out; it was all going to come out, and I had no idea what that might mean. Just another drop of wine first. Where *had* I put that glass? If it wasn't on the table, then it must be on the window ledge… or maybe on the shelf… Oh, sod it. I scooped up the bottle, and with one hand, between swigs, set to work on word-processing my past.

Step Eight
Stage Two (Secondary School until Now)
By Jasmine Somers

4th Year Maths exam
Fruit picking
Bee Keeping Club
Irving's NLP books
Fake Valentines > Suzanna Hunt
Hockey lessons / showers (pervy teachers)
Newspaper round
Tasha – itching powder
Beckie Reynolds
Bubble gum dispenser
Tasha's diary (again!!)
Scratching Bob Marley
Essay 'sharing'
Graham (whoops!)
Trip to Bath etc.
Museum entrance fee
Flying saucers
Claire's dad's vodka / water
Tent pole
TV licence

Blah, blah, blah…

It's all so bloody petty. It's all so irrelevant and I can't even remember anything else because all I can think about is what I did to Arnaud and to Dan and I can't even type it and I don't even want to think it and some things you can't ever make amends for and there's nothing I can do and I shouldn't have started this and just this tiny bit has taken me ages but now I've got to finish so I'll do it but it's not going to do any good so...

Arnaud – I'm sorry, I'm sorry, I'm sorry
Dan

I clicked on 'print' and heard the whirring of the printer upstairs. I turned off the computer and the sickening grandiosity of the *Moonlight Sonata.* Heading for the kitchen to pour my dregs of Californian sunshine down the sink, I kicked over my empty glass. So that's where I'd left it. I took my pink folder upstairs and shoved the freshly printed sheet inside without looking at it.

A cursory tooth-clean would have to do; there were two mirrors too many in this bathroom, and I couldn't face my own bleary-eyed, deceitful reflection. I undressed quickly and dropped my clothes into the washing basket. Closing the door of my room, I crawled into bed, pulled the covers over my head and wept.

If it hadn't been the first week back, the following morning I'd have been tempted to phone in sick. It wouldn't have been dishonest; I *was* sick. As far as I remembered, I hadn't actually *been* sick, but as I tried to force down some marmite on toast, I certainly wasn't far off. And my head... I'd simply have to hope for a quiet day, and make sure I avoided loud noises or sudden movements. A quiet day and an early night – that sounded good. Then tomorrow I'd see Ruben. Maybe I could cook us something special, or there was that new Italian place in town he'd been wanting to try. Urgh, food. Why was I thinking about food? Sleep was all I wanted right now. Or at least a rest. Only one more day to go. Ruben had promised me a lie-in and a lovely walk. I would refuse to think about anything serious until Sunday afternoon's appointment with my octogenarian life-coach.

The school day passed without incident, and Penny agreed to cover my lunchtime shift in the playground if I took over her personal hygiene class the following Tuesday. A half hour snooze in the sick bay gave me just enough energy to cope with the Friday afternoon free play session.

I was starving by the time I reached home, my half-eaten breakfast still on the kitchen table, my packed lunch untouched in my bag. Neither looked particularly appetising now, so I unearthed a suitably bland soup from the freezer and shoved it into the microwave. While all the goodness was being zapped out of my dinner, I lugged my quilt and pillow downstairs and made myself up a daybed on the sofa. I pulled the coffee table over and covered it with all I might need for the rest of the day: phone, TV guide, remote controls, book, water, cashew nuts and chocolate. Once installed, I did not intend to move until bedtime.

The microwave pinged and I took out my steaming bowl, gave its contents a stir and found a space for it on the table. Might as well get my pyjamas on while it was cooling. On my way to the bedroom, I stepped over the pink folder which must have been lying on the landing floor since last night. Then, turning back, I half-stooped to pick it up, thought better of it, and kicked the thing across the floorboards and under my bed.

The tribulations of the gentlefolk of Midsomer County struck me as too taxing today, so I found my old recordings of *Gardeners' World* and buried myself under the duvet. I really had been neglecting my little patch of garden lately, but seeing other people's perfectly manicured lawns and finely tended plots might inspire me to get out and start hacking. Dan had been in charge of mowing and weeding, fixing fences and shifting soil. I'd always preferred pottering – replanting seedlings, watering vegetables, sweeping up leaves. Now that I was on my own, my enthusiasm tended to wax and wane, and I'd discovered that once I took my eye off the ball for a couple of weeks, the bindweed and brambles were all too eager to seize any unclaimed territory as their own.

As I tucked in to my soup, a ruddy-faced farmer explained how best to care for fruit trees. He was outlining the benefits of organic mulches when my phone started vibrating on the table next to me. Ruben – it had to be. Texting to let me know what he had in store for us tomorrow. Telling me how much he was looking forward to that lie-in. I wondered if he'd be interested in coming to the Spring Garden Show with me in a couple of weeks. Not the sort of thing we usually did together, but he was sure to love it there, and I knew he was planning to replace a few things in his garden. I put my bowl down, picked the phone up and flipped it open. Ruben – I knew it! Mmm, it would be good to see him after the week I'd had. I pressed a key to read his text:

'Can't make this weekend. Something's come up. Hope your week went OK. Catch up soon. xx'

Was that it? '*Something's come up.*' Like what exactly? We *always* met up on a Saturday. Saturday was *our* time. If it was to do with work, he'd say so, surely. '*Something's come up.*' Did he mean 'something' or did he really mean 'someone'? That had to be it. He'd been acting weirdly last weekend. Distant. He'd met some woman and didn't have the guts to tell me. But he couldn't have. He'd never wanted a proper relationship. Neither of us was after commitment. That's why it worked so well between us – we wanted the same things. He couldn't do this to me. We had an agreement, for God's sake. We'd agreed to... What *had* we agreed to? We'd agreed not to get too serious, to meet up while it was making us both happy, and to be honest and call it a day when it wasn't. We'd agreed to let each other lead our own lives and to keep what we had together separate from the daily grind, the mundane. We'd sworn that we'd never limit each other's freedom and never fall into that pathetic trap of becoming whingeing or nagging or, Heaven forbid, possessive. I flipped my phone shut and dropped it onto the table. We'd never said we wouldn't see other people. I'd just sort of presumed.

So, I unexpectedly had a free night tomorrow. That was great – a blessing probably with all I had on my plate at the moment. I could do with catching up on some paperwork, and I'd have the whole of Sunday morning to get on top of the garden. One Saturday evening without seeing Ruben wasn't going to kill me. After all, I managed all right every other night of the week. I managed perfectly well. Look at me.

I gazed around the room. My laptop hung precariously over the edge of a shelf where I must have perched it last night, my wine glass still lay on its side on the rug. There was a pile of post for Dan propped up on the window ledge by the front door, next to a battered Morris Minor manual I'd found in the garage and had intended to take over to Ruben's tomorrow. The paraphernalia I'd so carefully gathered together for my cosy night in was strewn across the table.

'...so with some judicious pruning and a good dose of TLC your apple trees should go on providing you with bountiful harvests for years to come,' leered the beaming farmer from my screen.

'And you can bugger off,' I said, pressing the 'off' switch and plunging him and his green wellies into darkness.

I checked the time: ten past six. Ten past six on a Friday night. Pushing the covers aside, I stood up and took the bottle of water and bar of chocolate from the table. The duvet flowed behind me like a wedding train as I dragged it up the stairs. I'd been planning an early night, so this was fine, absolutely fine. It was such a relief not to be in a claustrophobic relationship, after all those years with Dan. It was great having my freedom, doing exactly what I wanted, when I wanted. No commitments, no ties. This was just how I'd wanted my life to be. Really, it was great.

seven

Sunlight and birdsong streamed through the crack in my curtains when I awoke the next morning. The weekend, at last. I liked Saturdays – leisurely breakfast, the odd magazine, a relaxing drive over to Ruben's... And then I remembered: '*Something's come up.*' Heaviness settled in my chest, a dull ache radiating from the centre of my ribcage. I leant over to the bedside table and switched on the radio. More deaths in Afghanistan and another stabbing in Birmingham. Cheery stuff. I turned the radio off. I was *not* going to lie around moping all day. Food. I needed food. Food and physical activity.

I treated myself to a big breakfast: toast and marmite, a bagel and jam, a couple of oat cakes with peanut butter, and a glass of orange and mango smoothie. I gathered together the latest bundle of unopened bills and cheap insurance offers which lay spread across the kitchen table, and squeezed them into the top drawer. Today felt like an outdoors kind of day.

It was late morning by the time I'd cut back the hedges and hacked the weeds from the top terrace. If I shredded the piles of clippings while I was mowing the lawn, I could dump most of it on the compost heap and save myself a trip to the tip. I fetched the petrol can from the garage and filled the rusty mower's tank. I had let the grass grow longer than usual, and wasn't sure if that meant I should leave the blade high or cut the grass extra short.

I settled for a happy medium, reckoning that I couldn't do too much damage that way. I pulled the starter cord: nothing. I tried again: nothing. I adjusted the throttle setting, took a few deep breaths and gave the cord an almighty tug. The machine shook, let out the faintest hint of a splutter, and then… nothing.

'Fine,' I said, hands on hips. 'We'll play it *your* way.'

I heaved the lawnmower over and examined its underside. No obvious faults, although I wasn't exactly sure what I was looking for. I pushed the thick blade around with my fingers – one full rotation without a problem. I untangled a long black plastic string which was wrapped around the workings. It could have been a thread from my weed control fabric but didn't look strong enough to thwart the mower. Pulling the contraption back upright, I felt a splash of cold liquid on my bare legs. Water? Oh. Petrol. I must have cross-threaded the petrol cap. I unscrewed it and peered into a half empty tank. At least I hadn't wasted the whole lot. Having replaced and double-checked the cap, I gave the starter cable one last yank: nothing. I kicked the mower, swore at it, then turned towards the house, where the postman stood watching me, a white envelope flapping in his hand.

'Spot of bother with the old mower?' Such a perceptive man.

'Not really. It's just temperamental. Is that for me?'

'I'll have a quick look if you like. The wife says I've got the knack. Anything mechanical.' He set his satchel down on my drive and strode towards me and my heap of junk.

I headed up to intercept him. 'Is that for me?' I repeated, pointing at the envelope he was still holding. 'Looks like another proper letter. I thought you didn't handle many of those.'

He passed it to me but walked on, not rising to my conversational bait. I squinted to make out the letter's smudged postmark: Plymouth. Sophie – it had to be.

'Crikey, smells like you've had one hell of a fuel spillage. That's not good.'

'Really?' I shoved the letter into my back pocket. 'There's honestly no need—'

'No, no. I insist. Won't take me a minute. It's often something simple. And it can't be easy… I mean, it must be, you know…'

'Must be what?'

'Well, it must be hard for you now. Being, well, on your own.' His last few words came out in a stage whisper, as if being single was on a social par with suffering from smallpox or seducing the pope.

'I'm sorry, but I don't see the relevance.'

'I'm not being funny. It's just, well, women and machines, they don't really go, do they? Must be hard trying to keep on top of everything. That's all I meant.'

He fiddled with the controls while I stared at him, grasping for a suitable response.

'Did you prime it?' he asked.

'What?'

'Did you push this to prime the engine?' His thumb hovered over a small black rubber button on the fuel tank.

'Possibly. Why?'

He pushed the button three times, pulled the starter cord, and the machine sprang into life. He switched it off and rubbed his hands together. 'Still got the magic touch,' he said with a wink.

'Well, thank you, but—'

'Don't mention it, love. Always willing to help a damsel in distress.'

I opened my mouth to protest.

'No, please,' he said, holding up a hand. 'There's no need to thank me again. Seriously. Like I said, it must be difficult with no man about the place. I'd hate to think of my Catherine stuck on her own at your age. No offence.'

'I hardly think—'

'Listen, love, I'd better get on. Where'd I put my bag? Ah, there it is. That letter of yours looks interesting, by the way. The real McCoy. I don't get to deliver many proper letters these days, you know…'

I watched him pick up his satchel and climb back into the van. Difficult with no man about the place? What a cheek! Still, at least I could mow the lawn now. I wanted to read this letter from Sophie first though. What more could she have left to confess? I climbed the slope to the top corner of the garden and sat down beneath the apple tree.

There was no letter inside the envelope, just a homemade card. In the photo which Sophie had stuck onto the front of the card, a throng of grinning students posed on the steps of Nottingham University's Trent Building. In the foreground was a young Sophie, bottle in one hand, cigarette in the other. Graham stood behind her, looking awkward. I didn't remember him hanging around after they'd split up, but there he was, still loitering. Mikky and Christopher sat on the bottom step, Mikky with his thumbs up, Christopher holding a huge spliff out towards the camera. Simeon's face was half obscured by his shoplifted copy of Sartre's *Nausea*, while Lily and Emma linked arms and waved, like Siamese twins in Doc Martens and stripy tights. Glen was checking his watch; probably had a girl waiting for him somewhere, and Kirk was balancing on his skateboard on the top step. And in the middle of this rabble were me and Dan, oblivious to our friends around us, oblivious to the camera, gazing into each other's eyes, clinging on to each other as if we would never let go.

As I opened the card, an ironed twenty pound note fluttered down onto the grass at my feet. I picked it up and read Sophie's message.

Hi Jasmine,

Hope you're well. I expect you've forgotten all about my phone call by now but I'm sending this as an official thank you and apology about the gloves thing. I didn't know if you still liked pink so I'm sending you money to choose another pair yourself. Or if you don't need gloves just buy something else. Hope you like the photo. What DID we think we looked like?? Say hi to Dan for me when you see him. Still can't believe you guys got divorced.

Take care, Sophie x

She expected I'd forgotten her phone call? If only. It was sweet of her to send the money though; I'd go into town after work one day next week and see what I could find. And as for the card... I'd never seen that photo before. Had we seriously wandered around dressed like that? Sophie and her Diamond White! She'd always been up for a party, was always so carefree. Or at least that's how it had seemed. I looked at me and Dan. How long had we been together then? Six, seven months? All the adventures we had to look forward to. All the excitement and the passion and the fascination of finding out *everything* about this perfect person who you just *knew* you would be with for the rest of your life.

I slipped the card and twenty pound note back into the envelope, took them inside and hid them away in the top drawer with my bills and bank statements. I would eat lunch and then carry on sorting out the garden. What I wouldn't do today was think. I put some rice on to boil, and searched the radio stations for a programme which demanded my full attention. *Death of The West, A Society in Meltdown* on Radio 4 – that sounded ideal.

As soon as I'd finished eating I went back out to confront my lawnmower. It meant missing the last ten minutes of the programme and not discovering whether it would be global warming, nuclear weapon-wielding terrorists or Mexican swine flu that would finish us all off, but hey, what was life without a bit of mystery?

Physical labour felt good. I didn't even mind getting dirty. A flat lawn and level garden would have been easier to manage, but apart from that, this place had been exactly what Dan and I had been after when we'd started planning our move back down here.

I was thinking. I wasn't *supposed* to be thinking. Concentrate on the grass, Jasmine, on the garden. I ought to do this more often. If I got out here regularly enough I'd soon have it looking as good as Ruben's. I thought of Ruben's little house and garden. Had this new woman of his been round there yet? Had they sat and drunk coffee on the bench by the stream? Had they... No! Stop! Focus, Jasmine. Focus on how much better the garden will look when you've finished. And stop thinking about Ruben. And Dan. Stop thinking about bloody men. Concentrate on the mowing. This was great exercise after all. I was doing something useful *and* burning off fat. My calves and upper arm muscles were getting a decent work-out too. It was hard work, but I had to keep going. Once the endorphins kicked in, I'd be well away...

When I eventually stopped to admire my work, however, a

fuzzy ache returned to my chest, having none of the mower's droning vibrations to blot it out. I put the tools away in the shed and garage and went in for a wash.

I needed decent distraction and I needed a plan. Just because I wasn't staying at Ruben's tonight, didn't mean I had to sit in on my own. Not again. I poured myself a glass of apple juice, carried it through to the sitting room and took my address book from the shelf. There must be loads of people I could do with catching up with. I'd barely seen *anyone* at weekends since I'd met Ruben, and I was so tired in the week. Going over to Penny's hardly counted; we'd been friends for so long that she was pretty much family.

I opened the address book on the first page. Alice and Paul: they were more Dan's friends. Al and Celine? They were finding themselves in India. Aga Centre: useful, but not much fun for a night out. Auntie Jean: ditto. Adam Fletcher? Some bloke from Dan's work. Adnan and Razwana: we'd lost touch after Sheffield. Amelia Hetherington: nice enough, but she'd insist on finding out how I *was*. Arthur Williams, Appletons, Antonia and Josh, The Anchor, Annie, Alex, Alfie Taylor, AA… AA? How did the number for Alcoholics Anonymous get in my address book? Dan must have written it in there. But why on earth would he want their number? My life was awash with addicts. Not Dan though surely. He couldn't be. I looked at the entry again: AA – Breakdown Helpline. He'd had a breakdown without me noticing? OK, so we weren't the best couple for communicating, but surely… Oh. AA. Automobile Association. Obviously. I closed the address book and pushed it back into its slot between *Healing Herbs for Women* and *Mammals of the Malvern Hills*. What was I thinking, going through my address book like some desperate loser? I had *plenty* of friends. There must be *someone* free apart from Penny.

I'd just phone around my good mates and see what people were up to.

'So Ruben actually *told* you he's seeing someone else? Wow.' Penny scooped another handful of peanuts from the bowl on the bar and dropped a couple into her mouth.

'Well, he didn't *say* that exactly, but it wasn't hard to work out. I knew there was something up last weekend. I knew it.'

'I'm sorry, Jaz. I don't know what to say. I thought you two were all in love and everything.'

'God, no. Don't be silly. It's not that sort of thing.'

'Oh. OK. So... so you're not upset then?'

'Of course I'm not. It's not like we made any promises. It's just... Well, it would have been nice if he'd been a bit more upfront about things. Honesty, Pen, it's important, isn't it?'

'Yes,' she said, munching on another peanut.

'Men. Why can't they be straightforward like us, eh?'

'You're asking the wrong woman, Jasmine. Not my area of expertise.'

'No, of course. But I mean, if he'd just come out with it... Well, it's more grown-up isn't it? More dignified.'

'You do seem a bit upset, Jaz.'

'I am *not* upset. I thought he had more integrity, that's all. If he'd looked me in the eye and told me he'd met somebody else—'

'What? You think that would be fine? You think that would be easy to hear?'

'Not easy, no, but... Oh, Pen. I am *so* sorry. Christ, I'm an idiot.'

Penny shrugged. 'It's no big deal. It's a long time ago now. Sixteen months and four days. In fact I hardly ever think about her.' She wiped the salt from her hands and downed her Pernod and black. 'Fancy a cocktail?'

We spent the rest of the evening trying out new concoctions and rating other drinkers on looks, style and sex-appeal. At some point in the evening we struck upon the idea of borrowing a convertible from the showroom on the ring road, and heading off on an escapade, *Thelma and Louise* style. The Welsh border didn't hold the same romantic appeal as Mexico though, and besides, we both had work on Monday morning. Instead, we rang for a taxi, its driver taking Penny back to her houseful of dogs and me to my houseful of loose ends.

It was Sunday tomorrow. Time for my next visit to Valley View. I checked the time. Officially it was already Sunday, but I was planning on a long sleep before facing another day. Most nights I liked to dream; I loved to drift and swirl and glide through impossible worlds. I savoured those fragments of time beyond time, delighted in the tastes and promises of limitless liberty and hope. But tonight I didn't want to dream. I didn't want to see the present or the future or the past. I wanted nothingness. I wanted darkness and stillness and peace.

eight

'For goodness sake, Jasmine, perk up will you?' Mrs Wilkinson's yellow sleeves flapped around the brittle bones and loose skin of her arms. 'We're not in the morgue yet, you know.'

'Sorry,' I mumbled, leaning back into the armchair. 'Tiring week.'

'Ah, yes, back to school. I take it that's your homework in there?' Her twig-like fingers reached out towards the folder I was clasping between my knees.

'Well, I didn't really finish it,' I said. 'I've been so busy, what with—'

'Give!'

I handed her the file. I hadn't opened it when I'd fished it out from under the bed that morning, but I knew my list wouldn't look particularly polished. Would numbering the items on it have helped? I watched a spider spin his intricate trap between a brass curtain pole and the dusty bookshelves, while Mrs Wilkinson surveyed my efforts. Her silence did not last long.

'*It's all so bloody petty!*'

'I'm sorry?' My list wasn't perfect, but I hardly thought it was *that* bad.

'*It's all so irrelevant and I can't even remember anything else because all I can think about is what I did to Arnaud and to Dan…*'

'Oh God!'

'Jasmine?'

'I thought I'd deleted that bit. You weren't meant to see... Here, let me take it.'

'You can have it back if you like, but I've read it now. Dan's your husband, yes?'

'My ex-husband.'

'So who is this Arnaud?'

'Arnaud was... He's an old friend.'

'Of your husband's?'

'No, of mine.'

'And your husband and this Arnaud didn't see eye to eye?'

'I don't think they met. Look, I shouldn't have shown you that. It was just, you know, thoughts, ramblings of a drunk. I get over-emotional. Ignore it, please.'

'So you admit that you are a drunk?'

'No, I don't! I'm not. I just was on Thursday.'

'And last night?'

'That was different. I was out with a friend. And how did you know...?'

'I'm well qualified to recognise a hangover, Jasmine. Tell me about this Arnaud. What did you do that was so awful? I do hope you didn't steal his biscuits.'

'Arnaud's at the bottom of the list,' I protested. 'You said we'd start at the beginning.'

'And was that not the beginning of something, Jasmine? Something that is still with you every day?'

'No. Yes. But you're not being fair. I can't do that. Not yet. OK, we won't start at the beginning then. Pick another one. Anything. Choose one and I'll do it. Just not that. Not now.'

She considered me carefully, then her eyes skimmed over the two sheets again. 'If you insist. But these things can't be put off forever. Here, one from each list.' She dragged a pink highlighter across an item on each of the pages and handed them back to me. 'Perhaps those will be more straightforward.'

From my first list she'd chosen *Tasha's diary*. Great. From the second list: *TV licence*. Now, *that* I could deal with.

'If you want to talk through the best way to tackle these two episodes—'

'Nope. Those are fine. I'll do them this week and tick them off, shall I?'

'If you feel that they have been fully dealt with in a week.'

'Oh, yes. I'm pretty confident with those two.'

'Good. Then shall we adjourn to the drawing room?'

She gathered up the yellow velvet of her skirt, and I stood to offer her my hand. I eased her to her feet and we began our winding journey down towards the lounge, where Berny and his poker-playing buddies were no doubt awaiting our presence.

'I do enjoy a good game,' she said, as the lift rattled up slowly to collect us. 'But do you know what I'd really like to have a go at?'

Sudoku? Origami? I shook my head.

'Ballroom,' she said. 'Something gentle. No flamenco or fandangos. I've always loved the dresses.'

The lift clattered to a halt and we stepped in.

'Ground floor, please,' requested Mrs Wilkinson of our non-existent attendant. She chuckled and pressed the round white button herself. 'Can't get the staff these days.'

'Thanks for ringing back, Tash. Everything calmed down a bit now?' I'd tried to speak to my sister as soon as I'd arrived home from Valley View, but without success. Teatime, bathtime, bedtime – her evening routine went on for hours.

'All quiet,' she replied. 'Both boys fast asleep, by the sound of it. Phil too, I bet!'

'At half past eight?'

'Wouldn't put it past him. I sent him up to read their bedtime story and left him to it. Why is it, the more tired my children are, the more manic they get?'

'Perhaps it's just boys. I don't think we were ever like that.'

'Hm, I'm not sure Mum would agree with you there.'

'Maybe not.'

'And if Amanda's little darlings are anything to go by, I'll stick with boys, any day. Three washes it took me to get the smell of duck-egg out of Charlie's hair!'

'Kids, eh?' I tutted.

'Anyway, sis, how's it going? Two phone calls in as many weeks. I *am* honoured. You're OK, aren't you?'

'Yes, I'm fine.'

'Still enamoured with that perfect Spanish lover of yours?'

'Ruben? I didn't say he was perfect, Tash.'

'Er, I think you probably did. "*Oh, those dreamy eyes, that smooth dusky skin...*" You and your foreigners.'

Damn it. I'd forgotten to ask Mrs Wilkinson about Benestrophe again. 'Me and Ruben are fine. And he's only half Spanish. Hardly a foreigner.'

'Looks Spanish, sounds Spanish – that's good enough for me. Mmm, does he whisper sweet Spanish nothings in your ear when you're in bed?'

'Tasha, stop it! I don't ask what you and Phil get up to.'

'Me and Phil? Ha! Well, Finn's two and a bit now so it must be... ooh, getting on for three years since my dear husband and I had sex.'

'Three years? You *are* joking?'

'Me? Joking? Afraid not. Can't remember the last time I did *that* either.'

'Wow, Tash, I had no idea. So, what are you going to do?'

'Do? Nothing. That's the problem – neither of us has the energy to *do* anything. That's the only reason so many couples with kids stay together, I reckon – they're all too bloody knackered to bother getting a divorce.'

'But I always thought you and Phil were really happy.'

'Happy? Yeah, well, I guess we're as happy as most people. I'm not moaning, Jaz. I love the boys to bits. And I love Phil. I'm just, you know, tired.'

'I'm sorry, Tash. I don't really know what to say. Is there anything I can do? Have the kids for a weekend or something?'

'Thanks, that's sweet of you, but I think we're beyond the romantic weekend away phase.'

'I didn't mean… I don't know. It was just a thought. Look, I'll let you get some peace and quiet while you can, shall I? We can talk some other time.'

'Don't be stupid. You haven't told me what you rang for yet. Come on, *I'm* the big sister. *I'm* meant to be listening to *you*, not the other way round.'

'Right, if you're sure. Thanks.'

'So?'

I cleared my throat. 'Um, this may sound a little weird.'

'Oh?'

'It's about when we were little.'

'Yeah, model children, eh, Jaz? I thought we'd just been through all that.'

'Well, I have a sort of confession.'

'Go on.'

'I don't have to tell you this now, or ever, if you don't want me to.'

'Jasmine, you're freaking me out now. What are you on about?'

'It's part of an undertaking. You see I've decided to make amends for everything I've—'

'Sod that, Jasmine. Tell me what you did, will you?'

'OK. Well, you remember those diaries we had in our Christmas stockings one year? The ones with the tartan covers?'

'Yes. You cried because I got the pink one and yours was orange.'

'Did I?'

'Sobbed. And you didn't even use it anyway.'

'Maybe that's because it was orange.'

'Jasmine, is there a point to this?'

'Yes, sorry. Well, I was fiddling around with the locks one day...'

'As you do.'

'And I sort of found out that my key fitted both locks.'

'Uhuh?'

'So I kind of had a quick look through yours when you were out.'

'A quick look.' Tasha paused. 'Just the once?'

'Possibly more than once.'

'Possibly?'

'All right – definitely. Every Monday, when you were at Guides.'

'You read everything?'

'Um, yes. Sorry.'

'And you didn't think it might be a teensy bit wrong to read my diary, my private thoughts?'

'I guess. A little. Not really. It was interesting. I mean, I know it's wrong now, obviously. That's why I'm apologising.'

'And what interesting facts did your snooping uncover?'

'I can't remember much of it, to be honest.'

'Jasmine!'

'OK, OK. It was when you were seeing Vincent so there was stuff in there about him. About you and him. About him being, you know…'

'What?'

'Being your first, um, proper boyfriend.'

'What else?'

'There was loads of stuff about the guitarist from Duran Duran.'

'Mmm. Nick Taylor. Huge crush. Anything else?'

'Just school things, friends, music, and er, something about smoking pot. With Vincent.'

'You were such a nosy little brat. Always spying on me and Vince.'

'Only because I knew what you got up to. And I wasn't nosy, just curious. I didn't even know what pot was. I had to ask Brown Owl.'

'You talked to that old battleaxe at Brownies about drugs? Christ, Jaz, it's a wonder she didn't call Social Services and have us taken into care.'

'Yeah, her and Tawny Owl did keep asking me how things were at home after that actually. I told her I'd read about it in *Jackie* though. On the problem page.'

'You read my *Jackie* magazines as well?'

'Oh. Yes. Sorry. I never told Mum about the dope though. Or about you and Vincent in his brother's Escort.'

'What do you want, sis? A medal?'

'At least I was loyal.'

'A loyal traitor.'

'I was not a traitor. A spy maybe.'

'Much better: a loyal spy.'

'Look, I'm not trying to defend myself. I wanted to say sorry, that's all. Because, well, because I am. Sorry, I mean.'

'And do you think that saying sorry is always enough?'

'No, but I can't think what else to do. And you were hardly Little Miss Perfect, were you? Off getting stoned and having underage sex in the back of some grotty car behind the youth club.'

'Is that part of the apology?'

'Oh, sorry, no. Forget I said that.'

'Do you know something, dearest sister of mine?'

'What?'

'You've always been a tad on the judgemental side, ever since you were big enough to start following me round.'

'That is so not true.'

'It's always so clear cut to you – who's right and who's wrong. And strangely enough, it's never you who's in the wrong, is it?'

'I have moral conviction, yes. But I never judge.'

'Think what you like, Jaz, but it does no harm to take a good look at oneself from time to time. See what others see: someone who's a tiny bit inflexible, obstinate, gullible.'

'What do you mean, gullible?'

'You were sucked in to my first great work of fiction for a start.'

'*Realm of Angels?*'

'I mean my diary, you idiot.'

'What?'

'Made up, all of it. Every single word. Except the bits about Duran Duran. They *were* rather dreamy.'

'Hang on, but Vincent used to come round loads. I don't

believe you.'

'Your prerogative. Of course Vince came round loads; we were best mates. We spent hours discussing Tolkien and Lewis and Barrie. You should have seen his illustrations.'

'But why make stuff up?'

'Because I knew what a prying little cow you were and that my diary would be too much for you to resist.'

'But how did you—'

'I kept a tiny picture of Nick Taylor in there. Figured it would fall out if you managed to open the thing, and you always shoved it back between the wrong pages. Pretty dumb.'

'And what about Vincent's brother's Escort and the drugs and the… you know?'

'Vince didn't even have a brother. Classic only child. But lovely. Dead intelligent and a fantastic artist. Queer as anything though.'

'Vincent was gay? How do you know?'

'Let me see… Well, there was the way he dressed, the way he always hung out with girls at school, the way he loved coming shopping with me, oh and the cute boyfriend, Jeremy.'

'You're winding me up?'

'Not at all. He really was cute: floppy black hair, wistful eyes, gorgeous pout.'

'I don't mean about Jeremy, I mean the whole thing. You spent a year inventing stories about yourself for me to read?'

'Yep.'

'But, Tasha, that's horrible. I was so worried about the drug thing. I can't believe this. It's—'

'Dishonest? Deceitful? I was only writing in my own diary. So who's in the wrong here then, oh non-judgemental one?'

'Yeah, OK, so what I did wasn't great, but… Well, I wasn't expecting this.'

'So what exactly *were* you expecting? "*Hey, so you read my diary, little sis? No worries. Water under the bridge.*" Sorry to disappoint.'

'No, it's just that what's supposed to happen is that I say sorry, and then you—'

'Yeah, well, the best laid plans and all that. Anyway, feeble apology accepted, I guess. But only because the diary was a fake. Jesus, if you'd ever found my real one… I'd have bloody killed you. Was there anything else?'

'Er, no.' There *were* a couple of things, but they weren't on this week's schedule so they could wait.

'Cool. Look, Jaz, I'm going to leave you to mull that one over. I've got a stack of essays to wade through by Tuesday. Good to catch up though.'

'Yes, it's been… enlightening. I'll speak to you soon, Tash. And good luck with… everything.'

'Thanks. We'll be fine, don't worry. See you soon, little snoop.'

I put the phone down and picked up the gold glitter pen I'd confiscated from Meena Zondheim in the science lesson on Thursday. I took list number one from the folder and drew a bold tick next to *Tasha's diary*. Next item? *TV licence*. That should be simple enough. I'd sort it out one afternoon this week after work. It would cost me, but it shouldn't be too difficult. Now, why did that thought seem oddly familiar?

nine

I wasn't feeling sociable at work on Monday. Lessons weren't a problem, but I certainly wasn't up to the staffroom banter in between. During morning break I hid in the stationery cupboard, hunting down red, white and blue crêpe paper to make tricolour flowers for the French Club's *Vogue et Viticulture* display board. At lunchtime I sneaked into Naomi's office to use her phone and sort out the business with the TV licence. I sat down at her desk and dialled the number I'd copied from an old licence fee demand letter the night before. The phone was ringing. I cleared my throat. A click.

'Oh, hello.' I began.

A well-to-do 1950s housewife straight from a Fairy Liquid advert interrupted my carefully planned speech. 'Thank you for calling. All our advisors are busy at present. Please hold.'

Music, ringing, another click.

'Yes, hello—' I said.

The perfectly coiffed lady with the soft hands butted in. 'Thank you for your patience in continuing to hold. An advisor will be with you shortly.'

Music, ringing, click.

'Thank you for calling...'

I put the phone on loud speaker and pulled my legs up onto Naomi's navy swivel-chair. I loved these things. Pushing off from the desk I managed to spin myself round on the spot, just far enough past a hundred and eighty degrees to be able to grab the desk again and perform another revolution. Two more and I felt a twinge of nausea, so began to turn the other way.

'Thank you for calling,' repeated the washing-up woman. 'All our advisors are busy at present. Please hold.'

'Yeah, yeah. I get the picture.' I levered myself away from the desk towards the filing cabinet, alternating spin-directions to curtail my queasiness. I manoeuvred myself back to the desk and glided around it twice, first clockwise, then anti-clockwise.

'Thank you for your patience in continuing to hold...'

'Oh, shut it,' I said. She could at least keep quiet and let me listen to her tacky background tunes. I launched off from the desk, then attempted a three-sixty whilst shunting between the filing cabinet and the fire extinguisher. Whoops, one emptied waste paper basket.

'Thank you for calling. All our advisors are busy at present—'

'I know they're busy!' I shouted. 'We're all bloody busy! This is my lunch hour! I should be eating my lunch! I'm trying to give you money and you'd have me starve to death!'

'Thank you for your patience...'

I skidded back to the desk and yanked the receiver up to my mouth. 'Bugger off!' I yelled at the angelic housewife. 'And no, I will not bloody well hold.' I slammed the phone down and slumped over the desk.

'Everything OK in here?'

I span round to see the deputy head peering through the doorway of his adjoining office. He looked at the bin and its contents strewn across the carpet, then back at me. I uncrossed my legs and dangled them down in front of me.

'Yes, everything's fine. All under control,' I said.

'I thought I heard raised voices and, er, banging.'

'No, no. Well, yes, but I've sorted it out now.'

'Right. Good. I'll, er, leave you to it then.'

'Thanks. I've pretty much sewn things up, I think.'

'Yes, quite. I've, er, got some great books on stress-busting if you ever wanted… you know. Helped me through that nasty graffiti episode.'

'Thank you, Patrick. I'll bear that in mind.'

'Yes, good. You… er… you do that.' He disappeared back into his office and gently closed the door.

I scooped the chocolate bar wrappers and scrunched up balls of paper back into the bin and headed for the caretaker's storeroom. I'd eat my cucumber and pickle sandwiches in peace and pay the TV licence on the way home.

They'd closed down most of the Post Offices in the area to ensure that queuing times in the few that remained were kept well above national average. While I waited, I chewed the plastic tags off the hat, scarf and gloves I'd just bought from Wool 'n' Weave with the money Sophie had sent. I tried on my new accessories and admired my reflection in the tiny mirror on top of the sunglasses display stand. The yarn was soft – far less itchy than wool – although rather warm on such a sunny day. Mauve had definitely been the right choice.

I felt a jab in my ribs and turned to see a walnut-faced granny scowling at me.

'Cashier number four, they said. Hurry up or I'll miss my bus.'

I shuffled over to the counter, shopping bags around my feet.

'Can I help you?' A Scandinavian-looking woman smiled at me from behind her protective layers of perspex and make-up.

'Yes, I'd like to pay for a television licence please.'

'No problem. Do you have your reminder letter with you?'

'Oh, no. I actually have a licence at the moment.'

'Sorry, madam. I thought you were wanting to renew your licence.'

'Oh. Ha. Yes, I can see why you'd think that.'

'So what was it you wanted, madam?'

'I want to pay for a TV licence.'

'But you already have one?'

'Yes. But not for the right year.'

'So your current licence has expired?'

'No, no. My current licence is fine. Although I hardly watch telly, to be honest.'

She wrinkled her nose. 'Madam, I'm not sure how I can help.'

'I need a TV licence for… hang on…' I checked my pockets. 'Won't be a sec.' I smiled at the assistant, who seemed to be admiring my hat. Perhaps they didn't have polyester in Scandinavia. 'Must be in my bag,' I said.

The cashier looked over my shoulder at the growing queue, which prompted Walnut Face to pipe up again.

'If I miss my bus, there's not another one for an hour, you know. And I've got the podiatrist coming at five to look at my corns.'

Mad people in Post Offices: I supposed they were used to it.

Miss Scandinavia was shifting her weight awkwardly from one leg to the other, so I gave her a shrug and a wink to put her at her ease. I pulled the scrap of red crêpe paper from the bottom of my handbag and smoothed it out on the counter. 'Yes, here we are. I need a licence for October 1994 to December 1995.'

She frowned. 'We only sell current licences here, madam.'

'Well, obviously that's what you *normally* do, but I need an old one. It's for fourteen months so I'm prepared to pay for two years if that's simpler. I think they were quite a bit cheaper in those days though.'

'I've only been here since June so I wouldn't know.'

'I expect you could look it up?' I suggested.

She glanced behind her towards a lanky youth who was weighing brown packages, then she turned back to face me. 'Madam, if you have a current licence, I don't think you need to worry.'

'Oh, I'm not worried. I just want to pay my debt. Tell you what, I'll just pay the current fee. I guess I'd owe you interest anyway.'

'So you *do* want a current licence?'

'No. I *have* a current licence.'

She looked at the crêpe paper I was clutching in my gloved hands. It really was hot in here. Her eyes flicked to the cashier on my right, where Walnut Face finished counting her change into a battered leather purse and snapped it shut.

'Malingerer,' the old woman hissed as she hobbled past me and off to her home podiatry appointment.

I faced Miss Scandinavia through the perspex. We seemed to have reached an impasse.

'I suppose I don't need the actual licence,' I said. 'How about I simply give you the money?'

'I'm afraid you can't just give me money like that.'

'I don't mean *you*. I mean the Post Office. I thought they were in financial difficulties? No wonder, if they won't take people's money. Here, have a hundred pounds.' I pushed a wad of notes into the silver tray in the counter.

She took a step back from the perspex. 'I won't keep you a moment, madam. I just need a quick word with my supervisor.'

At last. Someone who could help. If they were old enough

they might even remember how much the licence fee used to be. I retied the new scarf around my neck. How did the sixth formers from St Anthony's do that trendy loose knot thing?

'I gather there seems to be some sort of confusion?'

So *this* was the supervisor? The gangly school-leaver who'd been sorting out parcels? I began to fan my face with the crêpe paper.

'No, no. No confusion. I just wanted to pay for a television licence. You can have a hundred pounds.' I pointed at the money between us, wiped my forehead with my gloved hand and smiled.

'I'm afraid I'm going to have to ask you to leave.' He pushed my twenty pound notes back at me.

'But I want to give you my money!'

'Madam, you're upsetting our other customers.'

'What rubbish!' I exclaimed, and turned to see a young mother pulling her staring toddler past me and towards the door. 'Listen,' I whispered, leaning towards the holes in the perspex, 'I did something bad a long time ago and now I want to put it right.' I slid the money back towards him and nodded.

He didn't move. 'Madam, is there anyone you'd like us to call?'

What *was* his problem? 'Just take the damn money, will you?' I shouted.

A small boy in his buggy began to cry.

'I'm afraid if you won't leave quietly—'

I grabbed the notes and shoved them in my pocket. 'I'm going, OK? Satisfied? Just don't come whingeing to me when your precious Post Office goes bust!'

I pulled my hat down over my ears, gathered up my shopping bags from around my feet, and turned to leave. So much for honesty. As I headed for daylight, a shop full of people averted their gaze.

Dumping the groceries and new items of clothing in my foot well, I locked the car again and continued down the high street. If this didn't work, I'd keep the flipping licence money for myself – blow it on wine and chocolate.

The charity shop's window display had lost a couple of teddy bears but gained a wooden train set and a plastic floral commode since I'd been here a week and a half ago. I paused in the entrance. Help the Aged? I seemed to be doing little else at the moment.

At first I thought the shop had been deserted, but an outburst of grunts and expletives alerted me to the presence of Betty-the-Uncouth in the back room, still sorting knickers no doubt. I took the roll of notes from my pocket, dropped them onto the counter, and turned to leave. Easy. As I inched the door open as quietly as I could, a faded hand-written notice unstuck itself from the glass and drifted to the floor. I picked it up, remoulded the desiccated blu-tac clinging to its corners and pressed the notice back onto the reinforced window pane. *Polite warning!* read the sign. *Shoplifters will be persecuted!*

Thieves. I hadn't thought of thieves. Proof, at least, that I no longer had a criminal mind. I looked back over my shoulder. I ought to put the money out of sight of potential robbers. I let go of the door and it swung shut with a bang. Blast. Running over to the counter, I snatched up the cash and turned the key that had been left in the till. I pressed the likeliest-looking buttons until the drawer pinged open, at which point Gollum waltzed in with a naked mannequin to find me clutching a wad of notes over an open till.

'My dear lady, we meet again.' He bowed his pointy head then brushed a wisp of hair from his eyes. 'What an absolute pleasure, although I fear none of us is presenting ourself in the best light. Constance,' he said, facing his nude but plastic dancing partner, 'return to the storeroom at once. You may come out when bearing suitable attire.' Gollum swept the model from the room then reappeared alone through the bead curtain, dragging a pair of ornately-carved high-backed altar chairs. 'Take a pew,' he chortled.

'So you see, I wanted to dump the money and run,' I finished. 'You *do* believe me?'

'Yes, yes. Of course I believe you. But there's one thing that puzzles me.'

'My motives?'

'Gracious, no! A gentleman never questions a lady's motives. No, what intrigues me is how on earth you got that till open. Darned thing never cooperates when I'm in charge. Not seeking part time employment, I don't suppose?'

'Not at the moment, no.'

'What a shame. There will always be a most warm welcome here for anyone who can operate that blessed till.'

'Thanks,' I smiled. 'Anyway, I'd better be heading off.'

'But your money, my dear?'

'Oh, pop it in the till. Say it's an anonymous donation.'

'I'm afraid that won't work, miss. Betty will have my guts for garters if the books don't balance at the end of my shift.'

'So *you* don't want my money either?'

'Patience, dear lady. That is not what I said. In fact, I know a very deserving cause.'

'Go on.'

'Talking newspapers.'

'Sorry?'

'You've heard of talking books, I take it?'

I'd bought Tasha's boys a *Thomas the Tank Engine* book once, which had buttons to press for various sound-effects – steam train, guard's whistle, stray sheep – but I couldn't see how the idea would transfer to newspapers. I opened my mouth to voice my concern.

'Audio-books, they call them,' continued Gollum. 'I have a few on cassette, but apparently you can buy them on discs these days. Or get them through some kind of computer internet link-up. Goodness knows how that works though.'

'Ah! Right, I'm with you. So the newspapers...?'

'Oh, there are quite a few of us, retired thespians and the like. We read the whole *Evening Gazette* aloud, record it every Friday as soon as it's out, and post it off to subscribers all over the county. Blind or partially sighted, most of them. Helps keep them up to date with local affairs.'

'What a good idea.'

'Between you and me, I think a couple of our customers just like the company – same familiar voices each week. Some old folk get lonely, you know.'

'Fine. A great project for me to support. And rather apt, seeing as the money was meant to be for a TV licence.'

'Yes, well, that's your own business, as I've said. But many thanks.'

I smiled and stood up to leave.

'Wait!' Gollum leapt up. 'I ought to do this properly. If I may?' He bowed, then took my hand. 'On behalf of all at *The Talking Gazette*, I, Frederick Thurlow, would like to thank... I'm so sorry, I don't know your name.'

'Jasmine. Jasmine Somers.'

'I would like to thank Mrs Jasmine Somers for her contribution to our ongoing work. Her generosity has been recognised, and such kindness in offering—'

'Please, it's nothing. I'm sorry but I really must be off.'

'Oh.' He let go of my hand. 'Of course.'

'It's been lovely talking to you again though, Mr Thurlow.'

'Fred. You *must* call me Fred. I insist.'

'Well, Fred. Good luck with the newspaper.'

'One of my week's highlights, our Friday recordings. After *Strictly Ballroom*, of course.'

'Of course,' I said. 'You take care of yourself.'

'Oh, I shall,' he said. 'And thanks again.'

I thought about Fred as I drove home, and wondered how he filled his time between unpaid shifts in the shop and voluntary reading sessions. How sad that a programme about ballroom dancing should be the highlight of somebody's week. Perhaps Mrs Wilkinson had the better deal after all – at least she was fed and watered, and had company at hand when desired.

Once home, I unpacked my shopping and threw together a rice and tofu salad. Carrying my plate and glass into the living room on my lap-tray, I settled down on the sofa for another gripping episode of *Trouble Down Under*.

So, it was only Monday and I'd completed this week's two assignments already. Mrs Wilkinson *would* be pleased. I envisaged a quiet week with no further confessions and no more soul-searching. In fact there would be no need for me to have a serious grown-up conversation with anyone until the weekend.

I chewed on my tofu as Wallaby Bill bravely wrestled with the dingo he'd caught savaging his sheep. Wallaby Bill had struggled to get back on his feet since last summer's bushfires which had claimed the lives of his beloved wife and five children. Losing his left arm in the crash on the way to the funeral had been a bitter blow, but Bill was a fighter, and he'd charmed the nurses as he lay in his hospital bed, drawing up plans to rebuild the farm.

The dingo took a kick to the windpipe and for a moment cowered at Wallaby Bill's feet. Just as the amputee's victory seemed assured, the dingo pounced, knocking Wallaby Bill to the floor, and making me drop a forkful of bean sprouts all over the sofa.

It took a few seconds for me to realise that the buzzing was coming from my mobile. Probably a text from Penny to check I wasn't missing our favourite Aussie soap. I grabbed the phone and flipped it open. It was Ruben.

'Missed you at weekend. Don't want to leave it until Sat. Sorry. We need to talk. I could come to yours. Thursday? xx'

He *never* came to my place. And we *never* met on a Thursday. I didn't like this. If he was going to dump me I'd rather he did it by text. Well, maybe I wouldn't, but I wanted to know *now* what this was all about and why it couldn't wait until Saturday. He was probably seeing *her* on Saturday. Yes, that was it. He couldn't fit me in at weekends any more. The bastard. As if I'd let him come and tell me that in my own home. Tell me how amazing she is, and how happy he is and how he never knew that he could feel this way about a woman. Christ, he had a cheek. No, if this had to happen, I'd go to his. I would plan my speech and leave with my dignity intact, wipe his number from my phone, block his messages and calls. Thank God I'd kept an emotional distance. Otherwise this could have really hurt.

I put down the tray and composed my reply.

'Very busy week but should squeeze in quick visit on Thurs. I'll come to your place. 8pm. I'll bring your stuff.'

Ha, no kisses. Nice touch. Admittedly Ruben didn't have much here for me to return, seeing as he never visited, but there were a few things I'd borrowed over the past year and a bit: books, DVDs, a telescope. I liked the finality of that last statement of mine though – my pre-emptive bid to revoke his upper-hand.

I picked the last of the bean sprouts off the sofa and dropped them onto my plate. I didn't much feel like eating now.

Wallaby Bill was sitting by his camp fire, chewing on what looked like the leg of a roasted dingo, humming *Waltzing Matilda* in the firelight. Good old Bill. No matter what life threw at him, he always came out smiling.

Bill gave his faithful hound Maximilian a pat on the head and a dingo bone to chew on. 'What a day,' he laughed.

I flicked the 'off' button, picked up my glass of wine and swung my feet up onto the sofa. 'Yep,' I agreed. Sometimes Wallaby Bill was spot-on. 'What a sodding day.'

ten

By Thursday teatime I'd rehearsed my farewell speech so many times that I was word perfect. There were various versions, allowing for variations in Ruben's responses, but I knew him well enough to predict his lines pretty accurately. I forced down some beans on toast and coffee, and prepared my lunch and work things for the next day; I knew I wouldn't feel up to doing much when I got home after the showdown later.

I paused by the front door and looked around the living room – at the vase of lilies on the mantelpiece, the stack of unread *Free From Faith* magazines on the corner shelf, the watercolour that Ruben had given me on Valentine's Day. Why did it feel so strange to be leaving? Maybe because the next time I came back, everything would be different. But it wasn't such a big deal. So I was about to become properly single again. So what? The only real change would be to my Saturday nights. That was all. Nothing else would be affected. I mean it wasn't like me and Ruben... It wasn't as if... I pulled the door shut behind me. Best get this over with.

I checked the clock on my dashboard as I approached the cottage: twenty to eight. Maybe I should drive up to the end of the lane and back. I didn't want to arrive too early and look desperate. Oh for goodness sake, this wasn't a first date. He probably wouldn't even notice. I turned onto the drive and pulled up behind a rusty

Jaguar. The Lotus had been partially dismantled, and bonnet, exhaust and both wings leant against the garage wall. I'd miss this place.

I closed my car door and started towards the house. Blast – the box. My feet crunched over the gravel as I walked back to the car. On top of Ruben's CDs and books lay the tatty grey jumper he'd made me borrow for my drive home on that frosty morning last month. I brushed its softness across my face and breathed in the smell of smoke and coffee – the smell of Ruben.

'You're early.'

I threw the sweater back into the box. 'Christ, Ruben, you made me jump!'

'Sorry, I just wondered why you weren't coming in. Come here.'

'Don't, Ru. Here, you may as well take this.' I shoved the box into his arms and slammed the boot shut.

He didn't move. 'Are you all right, Jaz?'

'Of course I am. What's up with the Lotus?'

'Ah, well I'm thinking of replacing some of the panels with carbon fibre composite. Much lighter and stronger than the aluminium. Less prone to corrosion too which would mean… Jasmine?'

'Let's just go in, shall we?'

Inside, Ruben dumped the box in the hallway and led me by the hand to the living room, where the fire was lit and an open bottle and two glasses stood in the hearth. Again he pulled me close, and again I pushed him away.

'Please, Ru. Please stop.'

'Stop what, Jaz? What's up?'

'You know what. Stop acting like everything's all right, like nothing has happened. Let's not make this harder than it needs to be.'

Ruben looked at me for a moment, then nodded. He bent down towards the fireplace and poured us both a drink. As he handed me my glass I saw that same melancholy look in his eyes, the look I'd noticed last time I was with him. At least he felt bad about what he was doing.

'You'd better sit down,' he said.

I knew what was coming. And although I really didn't want to hear any of it, there was a part of me that felt like screaming at him. Why had he ruined everything? *Why, Ruben? Why?* 'Go on then,' I muttered. 'Confession time.'

'It was the way you were describing your old headteacher – nutcase, batty, fruitcake, loon – that's what did it.'

That had made him shag someone else? Of all the excuses! I stared into my blood red wine. 'Ruben, that's pathetic.'

'Maybe. But I want to tell you the truth. I owe you that.'

'We owe each other nothing. No strings, no commitments, no promises. We agreed.'

'Yes, but—'

'Ruben, let's not get all sentimental now. I don't need explanations. I don't want your pretty words.' I turned to face him. 'Just tell me straight. Is it over?'

He looked me in the eye, but didn't speak.

'Well?'

'Why are you being like this, Jasmine? I don't understand.'

'I'm trying to make it easier, that's all. If you want to call it a day…'

'But I don't. You know I love… I love being with you. I thought you felt the same.'

'I do. Of course I do, but… aren't you… What was it you wanted to tell me?'

'Do you know what they call you in Spain if you're mad?'

'What?'

'Loco, psicopático, chalado, rabioso, insensato, trastornado, atrasado, chiflado, lunático...'

'What are you talking about?'

'Madness, Jasmine. Lunacy. Insanity. They take your children away from you, you know. As if any parent could harm their own newborn baby. Can you imagine?'

'You're talking about Ana?'

'She was only sixteen when we met. We were married at eighteen. She was expecting Isabella, you see. And I loved her. I did love her.'

'I know, Ruben. So, what happened?'

He turned away from me and towards the fire. 'I did everything I was expected to, Jasmine. Everything. Ana's dad gave me a job in the company and I worked harder than anyone. I didn't want to look like a freeloader.'

'I'm sure nobody thought that of you.'

'So I worked my way up faster than the others. Learnt about the importing and exporting side. Nobody else spoke decent English, so it made sense for me to help out.'

'And Ana?'

'She seemed fine. She was happy. For the first few years, at least. Always told me I was working too much though. She used to say... She used to tell me Isabella would grow up not knowing she had a daddy.' He gazed into the fireplace, silent and motionless, as tears began to roll down his cheeks.

'Ruben?'

'I was exhausted, Jasmine. I worked ten, eleven hours a day. But I was good. I brought in new contracts. Xalvador was even talking about a partnership.'

'So what went wrong?'

'It wasn't enough for her. *I* wasn't enough. I'd get in at the end of the day and she'd want to hear all about my work, and she'd tell me how she'd had friends over for lunch and how I'd never *guess* what Izzy had done that morning. She expected me to play with Isabella and give her a bath and a bedtime story. I was too tired for it all, Jasmine. And I wasn't old enough to be a husband and a father. I felt such a fraud.' He wiped the back of his hand across his face. 'So I worked longer hours. Agreed to take on the Madrid project. And Ana was so proud of me. *"What a clever daddy you have,"* she'd say to Isabella. *"Mummy will have to let you stay up later so that Daddy doesn't miss his bedtime stories!"* When Ana talked about having another baby, I thought it would be company for Isabella, and for Ana when Isabella started school. She liked having someone to fuss over.'

'So that's when you had Tomas?'

Ruben nodded, transfixed by the dancing flames.

'Is that when Ana… when she—?'

'I thought things would be easier when Tomas was born. I thought Ana would be more content, not demand so much of me. We had money – God knows I earned it; she could have had a cleaner, a nanny, anything. But she had this idea that we shouldn't *need* anyone else, that we ought to do everything ourselves or it somehow didn't count, as if we were cheating. But we couldn't do it all, Jasmine. It was too much. It was just too much.'

'And having Tomas was the last straw?'

'He wasn't an easy baby like Isabella. He would cry and cry. He'd wake up in the night and cry. Three times, four times. Some nights we barely slept. I was glad to leave the house in the mornings. That's awful, isn't it? Poor Ana.'

'Ruben, you mustn't blame yourself. You were both young. These things happen.'

'We can't run away from our responsibilities, Jasmine. You've reminded me of that.'

'Me?'

'Your amends. You're putting everything right. Some of us never get that chance.'

'But, Ruben, what happened to Ana wasn't your fault. What was it? Post-natal depression? Some sort of post-partum psychosis? It's not *that* rare.'

He turned to face me, his moist eyes narrowed. 'You don't understand, Jasmine,' he said. 'It wasn't Ana. It was me.'

He'd left for work as usual one morning and never returned. They'd found his car at the station. None of his things were missing and he'd left no note, but he *had* been growing more distant, Ana told the police, and he'd never bonded with baby Tomas like he had with Isabella. In fact last night he'd shouted so loudly at poor Tomas that he'd made both children cry.

They picked Ruben up on a beach near Málaga. Locals had informed the authorities of a strange man in a suit, sleeping rough and scavenging for food. He told police he was heading down past Gibraltar to Algeciras; he had business to attend to in Tangier, if only he could remember what it was. His name, he said, was Esteban Castillo Martínez. When asked about the woman and children in the photo they'd found in his wallet, he told them he'd never seen them before in his life. He had no idea who they could be. He'd been missing for eleven days.

By the time Ruben was well enough to go home, he had no home to go to. Ana had given up the apartment and gone to stay with her sister in Córdoba. She was afraid that Ruben might be a danger to Isabella and little Tomas, and besides, they were settled where they were now, and Tomas wouldn't even recognise his father. All in all, she said, the children were better off without him around. Ruben had no energy to defend himself. And if he was honest, he could see that his wife was probably right.

'So you never saw them again?'

'A few times. Xalvador set me up in Madrid, let me take more on when I was up to it. I went back to see the kids when I could, but Ana was right – they didn't know me.'

'But you could have gone to court, got joint custody, surely?'

Ruben shook his head. 'It doesn't work like that, Jaz. And anyway, I could barely look after myself, let alone two confused children. It wouldn't have been fair on them.'

'You stayed in touch though?'

'For a while. Xalvador showed me photos from time to time. He was a good man. Then Ana wrote to me, saying she'd met someone else. They didn't need my money any more, she said, and it might be best if I stopped writing to the children. It was unsettling for them, and they had a new daddy now.'

'Ruben, I'm so sorry. I knew you'd lost touch, but I thought that was when they were older. And I had no idea you'd been… ill like that. Why didn't you tell me?'

'When, Jasmine? The night we met at that party? *"Hi, my name's Ruben Ramírez and I used to be clinically insane."* '

'Of course not when we met. Just… later.'

'Funnily enough, there never seems to be an ideal moment for telling someone you used to be a nutter.'

'Ruben, stop talking like that.'

'Your words, Jasmine. Nutcase, fruitcake, loon – that's me!'

'I didn't mean you. You know I didn't mean you. I would never have spoken like that if I'd known. You should have told me.'

'Well, now I have.'

'So what were you doing on Saturday?'

'Saturday? Nothing.'

'You cancelled our night together. Who were you with?'

'What? No one.'

'You're sure you weren't with anyone? A woman maybe?'

'What woman? What are you on about? I needed time to think, that's all. Whether to tell you, what to tell you, how to tell you… I didn't know what you'd think of me.'

'What I think of you hasn't changed one bit, Ru. I'm just sad about what happened, and that you lost touch with your kids, and that you didn't tell me before.'

'So am I, Jaz. I'm sorry.'

I took Ruben's hands and pulled him towards me. 'You have nothing to apologise for.'

He put his arms around me, and I felt the tension in his body ease as we sat silently, holding each other tight.

'I wish my past was as simple as yours,' he said, pulling away and slumping back into the sofa. 'Stealing biscuits and dropping your sister's Kerplunk marbles down the drain – it's all so easily fixed.'

'I'm not so sure about that,' I said.

'How do you mean?'

'It's… Well, it's not *all* that simple. I don't want to think about it now though. Another day. I'm shattered, and I've got work in the morning. And you look awful.'

'Thanks,' he smiled. 'Kind of you to point that out.'

'I mean you look like you need a good sleep. You look exhausted. I'd better go home.'

'Don't go, Jasmine. I want you to stay.'

'I can't, Ru. I've got work in the morning.'

'Please?' How did he manage to look so forlorn yet so

alluring?

'OK. I'd love to stay, if that's what you want. I'll be up early though.'

'Well, that's something I never thought I'd see! Oh, come here. And thank you.'

'For what?'

'For listening to me. For being here. For not being ashamed of me.'

'Ashamed of you? Don't be stupid. Any woman would be proud to have you on her arm – intelligent, funny, solvent, handsome, charming... and did I ever mention that you have incredibly sexy eyes?'

'Once or twice.'

'And a rather seductive laugh.'

'Oh, Jasmine. I'm a lucky man. Come on. Bed.'

'OK, but I really do need to go straight to sleep.'

'No problem,' he said. 'What else did you think I had in mind?'

I watched him as he closed down the fire, turned off the lights and locked the front door. *I* was the lucky one.

In the hallway he stopped in the semi-darkness, and turned to face me. 'I really am sorry. You're right, I should have told you earlier.'

'Shush. Stop worrying about it. I'm glad you've told me now, that's all.'

He leant towards me and kissed me on the cheek. 'Thanks. And Jasmine?'

'Yes?'

'No more secrets, OK?'

I looked into his eyes, so full of gratitude and optimism and trust. 'Of course, Ruben,' I said. 'No more secrets.'

eleven

My English group's morning assembly on healthy living went without a hitch, so I treated the twelve of them to a *Scooby Doo* DVD and cinnamon flapjacks during second period. When I'd chucked the goodies into the car an hour earlier during my pit-stop at home between Ruben's and work, I was thinking they'd be more of a consolation prize than a reward, but the kids had surpassed all expectations and done themselves proud.

The rest of the school day flowed by as Fridays usually did, until Mrs Fraser's art class, where my job was to support Gemma Rees in accessing the curriculum. This mostly meant curbing her incessant nattering and preventing her from eating glitter, sequins and anything else that sparkled. After a good night's sleep and with my wits about me, these weekly craft sessions could be a lot of fun. A momentary lapse in concentration on my part today however resulted in a trip to Worcester A and E, and a three hour wait for the top consultant who'd hopefully be able to induce vomiting and retrieve the potful of silver buttons that Gemma must have swallowed when I'd turned to hand Kirsty White the Pritt Stick.

'Right then, let's have a look at you,' the bright young paediatrician piped up, just as I was resigning myself to spending the whole night in casualty. He drew a healing-blue curtain around our cubicle. 'So, young lady, what have you done with all those lovely buttons?'

Gemma grinned, took off her left shoe, and poured a trickle of shiny discs into the doctor's lap.

I spent that evening at Penny's, discussing canine hygiene and the intellectual and social superiority of classroom assistants over teachers.

Saturday was for me and Ruben: no looking forwards, no looking back. A day outside time, we'd agreed. A day to simply be.

The corridors of Valley View felt brighter and warmer that Sunday and I was eager to let Mrs Wilkinson know of my successes with the diary and television licence tasks.

'Someone's a bit perkier today,' said Mark, as he led me past the kitchen and up towards the library. 'Good weekend, I take it?'

'Very pleasant, thank you,' I replied, my mind drifting back to last night's unfinished lasagne and newly discovered delights.

'Ooh, look at you. I've made you blush! I won't ask! I won't ask!'

'I'll be fine from here, thanks,' I mumbled. 'Should know my way by now.'

'Right-e-o. Long as you're sure. I'll go and see to Mr P and his colostomy bag.'

Mrs Wilkinson was pouring tea when I entered the library. A chunky orange polo neck and A-line skirt hung from her fragile frame.

'There. Just as you like it,' she smiled, as I sat down in the armchair opposite her. 'Now, tell me all about your week.'

I gave her the highlights – one generous donation to the fantastic talking newspaper scheme and a frank and revealing conversation with my sister.

Mrs Wilkinson peered at me from over her china cup. 'Jasmine, I'm still not sure that you are approaching these things in quite the right spirit.'

'Of course I am. I want to make amends. What exactly are you getting at?'

'Calm down, dear. All I mean is that you seem to have such clear expectations every time. We can't go into these situations knowing how we want the other person to react.'

'But I don't. It's just... Take my sister and that diary – I didn't expect—'

'Don't expect anything, Jasmine. This is not a time to seek forgiveness or to apportion blame. This is your chance to be honest about what you've done, to say sorry and to move forwards in love.'

'Oh.' She was going to start talking about Jesus any minute, I could tell.

'I think it's time I introduced you to Benestrophe,' she announced.

I thought about Ruben, the way he'd touched me last night, the things he'd said.

'Jasmine?'

'Sorry. No. I mean, thanks, but I don't think it would be a good idea. Not now.'

She narrowed her eyes. 'My dear girl, this would be the perfect moment. Trust me.'

'Oh, I do. But it's not a good time. I'm just not ready. I thought I was, but I'm not.'

'You underestimate yourself. And in any case, you have already been fleetingly introduced. For Benestrophe is with us as we speak, Jasmine. Right here, right now.'

I span to face the door. Had the Greek lothario overheard my protestations? The doorway was empty. Confusion. Delusion. Poor Mrs Wilkinson.

'Are you feeling all right?' she asked.

'Me? Yes. How about you?'

'I'm fine, thank you,' she nodded.

'Good,' I replied. 'Then we're both fine. That's great.'

We looked at each other across the table for a moment before she tried again. 'Jasmine, about Benestrophe, let me explain.'

I attempted a smile. Hallucinations of foreign care workers. I wasn't trained for this. Where was Mark and his annoying wink when I needed him? Never mind. I poured us both another cup of tea and settled back into my chair to listen. One of us clearly had a weak grasp of what was going on here.

'Benestrophe is part Latin, part Greek,' she began.

Greek! Ha! I knew it!

'The word literally means *good turning*. It's the opposite of catastrophe.'

'The word?'

'Yes, Jasmine, the word. Benestrophe.' She raised an eyebrow.

'Oh. Right.'

'Benestrophe is about being here now, looking at ourselves honestly, teaching love by the way we live.'

'You mean Benestrophe's not a person?'

'A person? Jasmine, you do have some strange ideas. Here, you might like to read this.' She picked up a tiny booklet from the table and passed it to me. 'I went to a few Benestrophe Pathway meetings for a short time, but decided to stick with AA. They were a little New Age for me, but I thought that would suit you better.'

I skimmed over the pamphlet, which seemed to promise me a twelve step path to Heaven on earth. That sounded good. Actually it sounded like last night. I pushed thoughts of Ruben from my mind and tried to concentrate on the reading material. There were paragraphs about celebrating sacred relationship, loving ourselves as we are and healing our lives through forgiveness. She was right; this was pretty New Age. And as for the bit about fear blocking our experience of love, well, that was clearly rubbish.

'Thanks,' I said, 'but this doesn't really relate to me.'

'I see,' she nodded. 'And what makes you say that?'

'Listen to this for a start: "*We dissolve negativity by forgiving others' wrongdoings, sharing our innermost secrets, showing willingness to right our wrongs, and releasing all guilt and shame.*" I mean, it's a bit over the top isn't it? I'd hardly say I'm wallowing in guilt and shame and negativity.'

'Take it away and read it anyway, Jasmine. There may be something of use to you in there.'

I dropped it into my bag. I didn't want to offend her, but it was the making amends I was interested in, not all the spiritual and psychological stuff. So, *that* was Benestrophe. Good job I still had Ruben.

We talked for a while about discipline in schools and our favourite Agatha Christie novels before conversation returned to my amends. Mrs Wilkinson apparently considered this a marvellous opportunity for me to enter into an adult and truthful relationship with my parents, so picked *Mum's teapot* and *Dad's tobacco* from my first list.

'I do already have an incredibly honest, adult relationship with my family, you know,' I protested.

'Really? Well, from the way you were talking about your

sister—'

'Oh, that's different. Tasha's always tried to make me look like the naughty one. *And* she called me a brat. And a snoop. And she's *way* older than me but she was *still* trying to wind me up and—'

'Like I said,' nodded Mrs Wilkinson, 'high time for more adult relationships.'

I let out a huff. I *was* being grown-up about this. And besides, why should *I* be all mature about things if Tasha refused to do the same?

'How about I let you pick a task from your second list?' offered Mrs Wilkinson.

'Hm.' I scanned the list and pointed to an item. She scored a fat pink line through *Newspaper round* and passed the two pieces of paper back to me. The printed repetition at the bottom of the second list caught my eye: *Arnaud – I'm sorry, I'm sorry, I'm sorry*.

'Is something wrong, Jasmine?' asked Mrs Wilkinson.

'No, no. Nothing at all.' I slid the sheets into my folder and out of sight. I didn't need to think about it yet. One day at a time.

I'd been given a fortnight for this most recently set homework, as the residents of Valley View were hosting a mini film festival over the coming weekend. According to Mrs Wilkinson, Mark had organised the first one shortly after Mr Wilkinson had died, to give everyone something to focus on and look forward to. The mix of silent movies, twentieth century classics and musicals had gone down so well that the showings quickly became a regular event in the Valley View social calendar. Minibuses shipped in ageing cinema-goers from as far afield as Castlemorton and Eastnor.

I spent the Bank Holiday re-grouting the bathroom and peeling ivy off the back wall and window frames. Those were going to need sanding down and another coat of paint now. Yet another of Dan's jobs I'd had to take on.

On Tuesday evening I took out my lists and my writing paper. Mum would keep me on the phone for hours if I rang. Was I *sure* there was no going back for me and Dan? She had *so* hoped to have grandchildren one day. Relate and Viagra had worked *wonders* for her and my father...

I looked through my list to see what else might need addressing, seeing as I was about to pour my heart out to my mother. I crossed out *Bogus tummy aches*. They clearly didn't count since Mum had not once been hoodwinked by my feeble fibs and crocodile tears. Me and Tash must have had some of the best attendance records in the history of Brockhill Junior. I circled two more items and added a question mark before another. Although the *Mint ice cream > Fluffy to vet* incident did need tackling, I was uncertain as to the best course of action. I doubted whether the *Alcoholics Anonymous Big Book* or even the New Age Benestrophe Pathway booklet would contain relevant guidance. How, after all, does one make amends with a dead cat?

That left four issues for me to elaborate on in my letter. This couldn't possibly be the grand sum of misdemeanours committed against my parents, so I may as well take this opportunity to write a sort of all-encompassing confession and apology. I picked up a black biro and started to write.

Dear Mum

Just a brief note to say sorry for a few small things I did when I was little. At the time I probably didn't realise they were wrong, so I'm not sure I can actually be *held accountable. Please can you tell Dad...*

Utter drivel. I *was* accountable – that was the whole point. I scrunched the sheet of paper into a ball and threw it over my shoulder. Come on, Jasmine. Do it properly or not at all.

Dear Mum and Dad

I'm writing to apologise to you both for some of the mistakes I made when I was younger. I've reached a point in my life where it feels right to review how I've lived so far, to make up for the bad stuff I've done and see if I can learn anything from it. I doubt I will, but people keep saying I might. I'm doing this because of someone I didn't like that much at University, and also partly because of our old headmistress, the scary one from primary school. It's all to do with moving forwards, so it seemed quite relevant, what with Dan and everything. Anyway, it's a bit complicated so I'll just get on with what I have to tell you. Don't worry though, I'm fine. I'm not ill or dying or anything. Sorry to hear about Uncle Ivor by the way. He can't have been that old...

I went on to explain how I'd created the doorway in the garden fence at Briar Street, helped Dad fix it when he'd spotted the problem a couple of weeks later, then eased the nails back out over the next few evenings. On Mrs Wilkinson's instruction I omitted any mention of my sister's involvement and the fantastical land she'd promised me we would reach once I'd removed this final obstacle. Tasha owed me one.

The thing with Mum's teapot had been an accident. Or the first part had been, at least. I'd written to Stewpot from *Crackerjack* about a month before to tell him that I thought he was ace and a lot funnier than Noel Edmonds *and* Chris Tarrant, and that I really, really wanted to be on the show. If it was OK I'd like to play Double Or Drop, but I didn't mind too much what I did as long as I got a signed photograph and a *Crackerjack* pencil. Please could he let me know by saying something to me during one of the programmes because when I wrote to Sting out of The Police I never got a reply and I thought my big sister might be stealing my post.

This was the fourth Friday since I'd sent in my letter and Stewpot still hadn't mentioned me. The others had gone down to play by the brook but I'd told them I was too tired and that my knees were aching. I couldn't miss this week's show; he was *bound* to say something today.

I sat through the first part of the programme munching on my salt and vinegar French Fries, the cat curled up on my lap. Tash always laughed really loudly at The Krankies, but me and Fluffy thought they were childish. When Stewpot came back on, I jumped off the settee, turned the volume knob right up and knelt on the carpet with my face as close to the screen as possible without the static making my hair stick to it. Stewpot introduced the contestants for Double Or Drop and explained the rules for anyone who'd been born on another planet and hadn't seen the game before. Fluffy brushed up against my side but slunk out of the room when I pushed her away.

'Tell everyone the names of who's going to be on next week, Stewpot,' I whispered.

But he didn't. So I did what I did every week, and stood on one of Mum's beige cushions in the middle of the sitting room ready to answer my first question.

'What,' boomed Stewpot, 'is the capital city of England?'

Oh, I knew this, I knew this.

'Is it London?' asked contestant one.

That was *just* what I was going to say. One prize for me! I picked up Tasha's stripy pencil case and gripped it under one arm.

The next question was for a skinny blond boy in glasses who looked like the Milky Bar Kid.

'How many days are there in a leap year?'

The Milky Bar Kid bit his bottom lip.

'Easy,' I shouted at him. 'It's two hundred and sixty six, stupid!'

'I think it's three hundred and sixty six,' he said.

Dumbo.

'Well done! Pick a prize!'

The boy chose Mousetrap, which was pretty silly as it was so big that he was bound to drop it. Since I'd somehow got the answer wrong I was meant to be given a cabbage, but nobody in our house liked cabbages because of the smell, so I had three of Dad's shoes lined up on the table next to me instead. I picked up one of the brown shiny ones he usually wore to the Labour Club.

As the game went on, I gathered up more and more of the treasures I'd collected in preparation for the show. Most of them were teensy, but seeing as I was answering all the contestants' questions I thought this was only fair. When the pile ran out, I began reaching for random items off the sideboard, mostly bits of the old tea set we saved for when great aunties with moustaches came to visit at Christmas.

A dead simple question about *Doctor Who* meant I got to choose another prize, so I carefully balanced a blue and white teapot on top of the goodies I was huddling against my body. Contestant number one gave the wrong answer, stupidly confusing

Daleks with Cybermen, and then dropped his cabbage, so now it was between me, The Milky Bar Kid and the freckly girl with black plaits.

'You're doing well so far,' grinned Stewpot. 'Now, here's your next question. Think carefully. What colour is at the bottom of a set of traffic lights?'

'Red!' I yelled. 'It's red!'

Dad's grey moccasin wobbled on top of my *Bagpuss* pyjama case. I bent forwards to steady it with my chin. As the shoe stopped rocking, my Flower Fairies notelets started to slide from their box and I made a grab for them with my right hand. In an instant they were on the floor, buried in an avalanche of furry toys, size eleven footwear and Mum's best china.

I stared down at the heap. Mum was going to kill me. The spout of her best teapot had broken right off, and I'd heard her telling Mrs Clutterbuck at Whitsun that it wasn't just a tea set, it was a family hair loom. I spread the other bits and bobs back out around the room and chucked Dad's shoes behind the sofa. If Mum had heard me she'd be straight in. One of the teacups was a bit chipped but it might have been like that before and it didn't look too bad. I put it back on the sideboard on its saucer behind the others. The teapot I hid under my jumper, and sneaked out into the hallway. There should be some of that glue left that Mum had used for making our costumes for the ballet exam. With any luck it would be with her sewing kit in the cupboard under the stairs. Bingo! I crept back into the sitting room and prised the lid off the glue.

When I'd finished with the teapot, it looked as good as new. I was impressed with myself for noticing that the spout had been upside-down after my first go at fixing it. Now it was perfect. I turned the television off, watching the picture shrink to a dot in the middle of the screen. I closed the doors of the television cabinet and switched the power off at the plug in case of thunderstorms. Then I ran to get my wellies on and go and find my sister and the Hicklings down by the brook.

On my way through Stinky Alley and over Tinkers' Field I wondered whether The Milky Bar Kid had beaten Plait Girl, and whether Stewpot had invited me to the studio for next week's show. Stupid flipping teapot. Now I'd never know.

It was during Great Auntie Nell's Christmas visit that my plan, and the teapot, fell apart. It had never crossed my mind that the glue might not hold, even though mine and Tasha's white leotards shed trails of feathers and sequins each time we performed our *Swan Lake* routine.

We were in the front room, and me and Tash were wrestling over the last strawberry cream from our annual tin of Quality Streets, when all of a sudden Great Auntie Nell shrieked like a baby, and Mum used the B word, which I'm sure she'd never done before in her life. Me and my sister stopped fighting and turned to face the grown-ups. This must be serious. My hand crept out sideways for the strawberry cream which lay on the rug between us, and I slipped it into my pocket for later.

At first I thought Great Auntie Nell had wet herself. She was standing looking down at her dress, knees apart as if she was riding a horse, a huge dark patch spreading over her crimplene-covered lower half. No wonder Mum had sworn. Even the infants got told off for doing that. I dared a quick look at Mum's face, but she wasn't glowering at Great Auntie Nell. Instead her eyes darted between the body of the teapot in her own hand and its detached spout which lay at her aunt's feet in a growing pool of pale liquid. I held my breath as PG Tips dripped steadily onto the carpet from the hemline stretched between Great Auntie Nell's veiny legs.

At last Mum spoke. 'Nellie, are you all right? Do we need to get you under cold running water?'

Great Auntie Nell slowly shook her head.

'Nellie, did it scald you? I think you might be in shock.'

I remembered what Brown Owl had taught us about emergency situations. You needed someone sensible who could act maturely and take charge.

I stood up and cleared my throat. 'Mum, go and dial 999 and ask for an ambulance. Tasha, you fetch some paper towels. I'll stay with the invalid.'

'Shut up, Jasmine,' snapped Mum. 'You're really not helping.'

'Yeah,' piped up Tasha, 'and we haven't even got paper towels.'

'Any towels then, thicky. Or don't you use your initiative now you've left the Brownies?'

'Girls, please! I'm trying to think. Nell, are you OK? Do you need to go to hospital? Can you speak?'

'Of course I can ruddy well speak.'

Me and Tash giggled. Two rude words and nobody was being told off for it.

'Nell, I'm sorry, I've no idea what happened. The spout just... fell off.'

'Thank you,' said Great Auntie Nell in a voice that sounded like she didn't really mean it. 'I did notice that.'

'Nellie, we ought to get you changed and have Dr Chapman take a look at your legs.'

'Dr Chapman will not be going anywhere *near* my legs, thank you very much, and I am *not* in the habit of borrowing other people's clothes.' Now she sounded a bit angry and a bit like she was trying not to cry.

If Tash had done something like that to me I'd have hit her. What if Great Auntie Nell started a fight with Mum?

'You're sure the tea didn't scald you?' asked Mum. 'Well, at least we can be grateful for that.'

'Grateful?' started Great Auntie Nell. 'Grateful?!'

When we'd finally waved our great aunt off in the taxi, her crimplene pleats almost dried by Mrs Hickling's electric hairdryer, Mum slumped down into her chair and inspected the broken teapot yet again.

'I just can't understand it,' she sighed. 'That tea set's barely been used. Poor Nell. I feel awful.'

I smiled at my mum and patted her on the head. 'Don't blame yourself, Mum,' I said. 'I guess it's just one of those things.'

Once I'd finished the letter, I checked it through against my list to make sure nothing had been left out. Fence, teapot, toothbrush, tobacco – all there. Dad had always suspected Dougie Naylor of nabbing his Golden Virginia when he came round to fix the boiler that time. Us and the Naylors had sat at separate tables at Labour Club do's after that, and Dad and Scotty had had Dougie dropped from the Tap and Firkin skittles team. We never saw Dougie once we moved over the river, and the poor bloke must have had no idea what he was supposed to have done wrong. Now I'd set things straight I could picture Dad ringing his old drinking buddy to explain the mistake. The Naylors would book the next available flight from Birmingham to Granada, meet up with my parents in a beachside tavern and laugh off the silly misunderstanding over several jugs of sangria.

I'd skimmed over the details of why I'd needed to clean Fluffy's teeth, and what had made me choose Dad's toothbrush over anyone else's, but the sentiment was genuine and I thought that this came across well. I'd already set up an International Money Transfer, I explained, and sent what I hoped would cover the cost of a couple of meals out and something arty for the apartment. I doubted they needed a new fence panel or teapot or toothbrush, and Dad hadn't smoked since Uncle Ivor's first scare in 1993.

My repeated *sorries* and *thank yous* at the foot of the final page sounded a touch over-sentimental, but I could hardly cross them out and I certainly wasn't about to rewrite the whole thing. A postscript would have to suffice.

P. S. That last bit came out a bit soppy. I don't want you thinking I'm going soft in my old age! And seriously, Mum, don't worry, I'm really not ill or anything.

P.P.S. Let me know if you decide to come over for Christmas.

P.P.P.S. Send Auntie Lou my commiserations or whatever - I can't find her address.

Done. Phew. I crammed the sheets into an envelope and ticked off the four tasks from my list. I'd start the newspaper round mission in the week. It would take a bit of organising and there would obviously be face to face contact and a lot of explaining involved, but in a strange way I was looking forward to the challenge.

I liked this; life was at last beginning to run more smoothly. My amends were going well, the kids at school seemed to be making progress, and my relationship with Ruben was beginning to feel, well, comfy.

There were some stamps in the kitchen drawer, so I stuck on what I hoped would be enough to speed my written apology all the way to the Costa Blanca. As I popped the letter into my bag, I heard my mobile in the living room starting up a jaunty Flamenco tune – the new ringtone I'd downloaded especially for Ruben's calls. Unusual for him to phone. He normally texted. Delicious memories of Saturday night must have been playing on his mind as much as mine. Maybe he wanted to meet up sooner than the weekend. I wouldn't say no.

'Ruben, hi. A phone call. I *am* honoured.'

'Jasmine, I need to see you.'

'Mmm, just what I was thinking.'

'It's Ana. I got in touch with her like you said.'

'Oh. That was quick. That's good though.'

'Yes, well, no point hanging around.'

'So… What did she say?'

'That's why I need to see you, Jaz. She's asked me to go back to Spain.'

twelve

'Ana's asked you to go back to Spain?' I clutched the phone tightly.

'Yes.'

'And you said no, obviously?'

'I told her I'd think about it.'

I leant back against the doorframe to steady myself.

'Jasmine? Are you still there?'

'Yes. Yes, I'm still here.'

'This could be a great opportunity for me. We should at least discuss it.'

I lowered myself onto the sofa. I felt sick. 'You want to discuss it? With me?'

'Of course I do. I mean, it would affect both of us, wouldn't it?'

'Well, yes. I suppose it would.'

'So when can you come over?'

'What?'

'To talk. How about tomorrow?'

'Ruben, how can you sound so calm about all this? After Saturday night. After—'

'I know, I know. It's crazy, isn't it? I'm not really calm, Jaz. I'm not sure *how* I feel, to be honest. I'd never planned on going away, but—'

'But your wonderful ex-wife says she wants you back and

you're ready to drop everything.'

'It's not Ana who wants me back. Christ, no. It's Xalvador. He wants to pass the business on, and nobody else in the family's interested.'

'Xalvador? But why you? I mean you're not family, are you? Not any more.' So it wasn't Ana who wanted him back. Maybe this wasn't as bad as I'd thought.

'Well, we never actually divorced, you see, me and Ana, so technically I *am* family. Technically she's still my wife.'

Or maybe it was.

Xalvador had apparently been on the verge of giving up hope of tracking down his favourite half-English son-in-law when Ruben had got back in touch. It was a miracle, the old man had exclaimed, an indisputable sign of God's will for the future of the company. Sure, Xalvador loved his work, but there were other things he wanted to do before he met his maker. His empire needed a new sovereign and Ruben Antonio was the only man for the job.

'But, Ruben, I don't get it. You're settled here now. I thought you were happy.'

'I *am* happy, but—'

'And you said you hated the pressure of big business. Why throw away all you've built up here for a life of meetings and deadlines and corporate stress?'

Ruben laughed. 'All I've built up? A few hours' translation a day in a crumbling stone hovel?'

'But you *love* your work.'

'And I could take most of if with me. It's practically all done online anyway.'

'OK, so what about your cars? You couldn't leave your cars.'

'Jasmine, how often do you tell me what a waste of time and money they are? Besides, they're just something to tinker with. If I was running the business I wouldn't need anything so environmentally heinous to fill up my days, would I?'

His last words had a familiar ring to them, but I wasn't sure why. 'And the cottage?'

'Oh, I don't know. I could sell it, rent it out. I haven't thought this through yet. It's all just ideas at the moment. But I wanted to tell you straight away.'

'Thanks. I'm happy for you. Seriously. It's great. If that's what you want. It's just...'

'What?'

I didn't want to say it. No promises, we'd agreed. No commitments. If he wanted to go, I should give him my blessing, let him go.

'What is it, Jasmine? What's the matter?'

'It's nothing really,' I said, wiping my eyes. 'It's just that... I'd miss you.'

'Jaz, Jaz, I'd miss you too, you silly thing. God, I'd miss you. And after Saturday night... No, I'm not talking about going out there on my own. That's what we need to discuss. I want you to come with me.'

'I still think you're mad,' Penny said as we walked across the school car park the next afternoon. 'Eloping to Spain, it's dead romantic. Any normal woman would jump at the chance.'

'I haven't decided anything yet. There's a lot to think about.'

'Oh, come off it, Jaz. You're scared, that's all. I think it's amazing. I had no idea you and Ruben were so serious.'

Neither had I. Which was why I'd told Ruben I needed a few days to get my head round the idea, and why, having said goodbye to Penny, I was now on my way to the corner shop at the end of Briar Street instead of hurtling through Cotswold countryside to meet my lover and plan our new life together.

The newspaper round was my final task for another ten days, the one I'd chosen for its simplicity. I imagined loads of fourteen-year-olds did exactly as I'd done – took on a paper round to earn easy pocket money, realised a week later that it was pretty damn monotonous, then disposed of the papers by whatever means possible. I was sure I couldn't have been the first to carry on collecting their weekly envelope of money until customers complained and the newsagent realised he'd been taken for a ride. I'd never claimed originality in my crimes.

The old shopkeeper would be long gone, but my plan was to pay a month's bills for all the households in my old round which still had their newspapers delivered. It was a gesture; it didn't matter if none of the original householders remained. And I couldn't imagine that anybody from the corner shop was going to argue with me, unlike that Scandinavian Post Office employee and her pimply sidekick.

It was strange driving past Brockhill, and following the route which me, Tash and the Hicklings used to walk twice a day, scraping our sticks along the high factory walls as we went. A pedestrian crossing had replaced Mrs McGretton, the lollipop lady, and the Rossi Brothers' building had been converted into flats, but apart from that, not a lot had changed in the last two and a half decades. I turned down Coombe Road and passed the Oddfellows' Hall on the right and the wooden scout hut on the left. There was space to park in front of Ellie Fletcher's old house so I pulled in there and made my way up Stinky Alley towards Briar Street.

And there it was. The front lawn of number five had been

tarmacked over, and a shiny green people-carrier took centre stage. The extension that Mum and Dad had spent years saving for, then years paying off, had been replaced by an ugly white plastic conservatory, and from what I could make out by heaving myself up on the front fence, most of the fir trees from the back garden had been hacked down as well.

'Anything the matter, missus?' A round, bald head stuck itself out of an upstairs window.

I smiled up at the man. This had always been a friendly street. 'No. I'm just looking, thanks. Nothing's the matter.'

'Well it *will* be if you don't get off my bloody fence sharpish. Go on, piss off!'

I was glad our old street had been on Tasha's paper round and not mine. I clambered down and hurried along the pavement to the end of the road, brushing cobwebs and wood splinters from my jumper.

Of course, the corner shop was no longer there. The huge window which had once displayed sherbet lemons and French Fancies had been bricked up. Flowerpots and planters full of pansies and herbs now camouflaged the metal trap doors which, years ago, we'd watched being levered open every Tuesday at six for the delivery man to lower crates of Fanta and sacks of potatoes into the cellar. Fortunately I had a plan B.

Rounding the corner into Windsor Close, I was momentarily disorientated. Gone were the rows of 1950s prefabs with their identical gardens, concrete paths and sunrise design front gates. Gone were the sky blue three wheeled invalid carriages which half the householders here once used daily for the two minute drive to the shop. In their place were tidy bungalows and polished Nissan Micras. All that remained unchanged were the paving slabs, pastel coloured and ridged, which would shake our bones and our voices as we scooted or roller-skated over them.

I approached the first bungalow and rang the bell. A black-clad teenager, who apart from the mop of burgundy hair could have passed for an albino, wrenched the door open and glared out at me. A boy. Possibly.

'Hello,' I said. 'Is your mum in? Or your dad?' Maybe that was a bad question. 'Or your carer?'

The boy sniggered and turned his back on me. 'Mom,' he shouted, 'there's some woman here looking for my mental nurse.'

I strained to hear Mom's reply, but there was no need.

'Mom says if you're from social services you can get stuffed.' He began to close the door.

'I'm not,' I replied, jamming my foot between the door and its frame. 'I've come to give you something.'

The door eased open a little and the albino blew his fringe from his eyes to survey me. 'Give me something? Oh yeah? Like what?'

'My name is Ms Somers and I'm from Co-operative Publications.' I flashed my Co-op membership card at him.

'Never heard of it.'

'No, well, we're a very new company, and as such I am able to offer you a free trial of our delivery service for one whole month.'

'Free? Yeah, right. Free what, anyway?'

'We can source all national and local broadsheets, tabloids, journals, comics, magazines…'

His pink-rimmed eyes opened wide. 'Do you do *Guitar Freaks Weekly*?'

'Ah, yes. One of our more popular publications within your generation.' He'd better not be making it up.

'Awesome! Can I have that then?'

'Of course. If you could just give me your name…' I took out my pen and notepad to jot down my first order.

'Yeah, it's Oakley. Oakley Rocks.'

I looked up at the boy.

'All right, Smith. Oakley Smith.'

'And this is number two?'

'Yeah. Man, that's wicked. *Guitar Freaks* costs, like, five quid a throw. Nice one.'

Five pounds? This was not going to be a cheap assignment. 'My pleasure, Mr Smith. You can expect your first delivery within the next seven days.' I held out my right hand to shake on the deal, but the albino stared down at it as if I were proffering a rancid kipper.

'Er, yeah. Whatever. Cheers,' he said, and closed the door.

A successful transaction, but I'd been less than upfront. I really ought to be mentioning my amends. I'd try it this time at number four. I knocked loudly then stood back from the doorstep.

'Good afternoon,' I said to the stout middle-aged man with red cheeks who opened the door.

'Yes?'

'Sorry to disturb you, but I'm carrying out good turns in your area and would like to make you an offer you can't refuse.'

'I beg your pardon?'

'When I was younger, I did a few things which were wrong. I'm not ashamed of them, but I'm not exactly proud either.'

'Look, I'm not interested, OK?'

'Hear me out, please.'

The man shook his head, but seemed to want to listen.

'In my past I've made some mistakes. I'm not saying I'm a bad person, but, well, perhaps at times I was. Maybe I *have* been bad, or at least behaved badly. But then I suppose we can all behave badly sometimes. Extremely badly.' I wasn't putting this very well.

The man's face seemed to have grown redder. He looked me up and down, then both ways along the street. 'Listen, love,' he whispered, 'you're a very attractive woman, and if it was up to me I'd certainly give it a bit of thought, if you know what I mean.'

I didn't. 'It's not that I feel I need punishment exactly,' I continued, 'but I'm hoping to make up for the bad things I've done. Perhaps you can help.'

The man undid the top button of his shirt. 'And how would you... What precisely would you do to make up for being such a bad girl?'

I lowered my voice to match his. 'Well, at the moment I'm offering a free service. Whatever you want. Straight to your door. Papers, magazines...'

'You do the mags as well? Sweet Jesus, is this my birthday or something?'

It was nice that he was so excited at the prospect of a few free newspapers, but the way he was looking at me was making me feel uncomfortable. Best to hurry him up and move on.

'So what would you like?' I whispered.

He undid another button and puffed his cheeks out, releasing a long garlicky breath. 'OK, love. I'd be mad to turn down an offer like that. Come here and I'll tell you *exactly* what it is I'd like.'

He leant closer. I turned my ear towards him and stood with pen poised over my page. Before he could speak, the garden gate clanged shut and I looked round to see a haggard-looking woman walking up the path, shopping bags dangling by her sides.

The man jumped away from me and hurriedly adjusted his clothing. 'All right, sweetheart?' he called over my shoulder, a manic smile on his face.

The woman nodded.

'I was just telling this young woman here we're not interested in double glazing, isn't that right?' He was nodding at me with a fixed grin.

'Ah!' The penny dropped. We'd been talking at cross purposes. Double glazing, indeed. 'No, no, I'm not selling windows. I wanted to give you—'

'Yes, well, thank you. But as I was saying before my *wife* appeared, I'm definitely not interested. At all. Thank you.'

'Yes, but—'

'Sorry, love. Not possible. No can do.' He put an arm round his bemused wife as she attempted to sidle past us and into the house. 'We're perfectly happy with things as they are. Isn't that right, muffin?'

The woman shrugged his arm off and went inside. 'I think perfectly happy's a bit of an overstatement,' she mumbled.

'Look, I'll leave you in peace,' I said. 'Sorry to have bothered you.'

The man took a pace towards me and pulled the door to behind him. 'Friday,' he whispered.

'I'm sorry?'

'Fridays. She goes to her sister's in Brum. Out all day. Come back then and we'll, er, talk about how bad you've been and discuss your punishment.'

It was kind of him to want to get involved, but I had no need of another mentor. Besides, he was rather fickle for my liking. I told him I'd send him four weeks' issues of *Morality in Action*, and thanked him for his interest.

By the time I reached number eighteen I'd given up on any honest explanation of my motives and was simply offering free trials on behalf of my cutting edge media distribution enterprise. Being mistaken for a Jehovah's Witness or care in the community case was not doing wonders for my self-esteem. On the plus side, I'd taken orders for *The Echo*, *Fisherman's Friend* and *Watercolour World*. Two more calls then home for tea.

'I'm sure I recognise you from somewhere.' The spinster from number eighteen was scrutinising my face as I wrote down her order details. 'What did you say your name was?'

'Ms Somers, from Co-operative Publications.'

'You're not one of those Somers girls from Briar Street, are you?'

I stopped writing. Did I *know* this woman?

'Only, they used to steal our apples when we lived over by Tinkers' Field. Little blighters.'

Scrumping down by the brook. Sneaking into the orchard and filling our satchels with juicy red fruit. I'd forgotten about that. Another one for my list.

I finished writing and flipped my notepad shut. 'Sorry, madam,' I said, 'but I'm from over the river. In any case, I've married.'

'So Somers isn't your maiden name. Of course not. Silly of me.'

'Not at all, Miss Dowty. An easy mistake to make.'

'It's just that you do look so familiar.'

I avoided her gaze. 'Yes, people often say that. I must have one of those faces. Right, well, *Chrysanthemum Expert* and *Della's Delights* should be with you within the week.'

'Oh, thank you,' she said. 'I'll look forward to having some new recipes. You get tired of cooking the same meals after fifty five years. This is very kind of you.'

'All part of the service,' I smiled. 'Anyway, I'd best be on my way.'

'You're not going next door, are you?'

'I was planning to, yes. Why?'

'I'm not sure she has much call for magazines, that's all.'

I found it most off-putting, the way the woman from number twenty seemed to be focussing on a point slightly to the left of my head while I was speaking. She smiled and nodded though and showed an interest in what I was saying.

'So,' I rounded off, 'can I put you down for anything?'

'It's a wonderful offer,' she said, 'but I can't really do newspapers.'

'We have magazines as well, don't forget.'

'No good to me,' she smiled.

What was that supposed to mean? If she didn't enjoy reading, why not just say so? 'Well, I'm sorry I can't persuade you, but if you do change your mind...'

As I began to write out my contact details for her, a large golden retriever stuck its nose round the doorframe, then plonked itself down at the woman's feet.

'It's all right, Bobby. It's only a visitor. Go on in. You're not on duty now, you soft creature.' She bent to stroke the animal's head, but continued staring out beyond me into the front garden.

So *that*'s why she'd ignored my fake identity card. And that's why she didn't want my magazines. She wouldn't be able to read them.

'Madam, please accept my apologies. I'm so sorry to have bothered you. I didn't realise—'

'What? Oh, no, people often don't notice unless I'm with

Bobby. Don't worry about it. Good luck with the canvassing, though.'

'Yes, well, thank you. I'm just sorry… You know…'

'No need to apologise. Sounds like a great scheme. I dare say I'd take you up on the offer if only you'd come in and read the blasted things to me.'

Gollum! *The Talking Gazette*! Oh, I was a genius at times. He might even be able to record a magazine for the woman. I said goodbye and assured her I'd return very soon. I'd go and see old Gollum straight away. Damn, the shop would be shut by now. I'd go and see him tomorrow. Then on Friday I'd come back to call on numbers twenty two to forty. And then it would be the weekend.

Hm, the weekend. I needed to do some thinking before then. I'd see Ruben on Saturday and I'd have to tell him what I'd decided. I'd have to tell him whether I was prepared to move to Spain. I'd have to tell him whether we had a future together or not.

thirteen

I'd forgotten about the Drugs Awareness training session the deputy had signed us all up for after school. There was no way I'd make it to town before the shops shut, so I sneaked into Naomi's office again during lunch break and found Help The Aged's number in the Purple Pages. With any luck I'd be in time to order this Friday's *Talking Gazette*.

'What the ruddy hell are you talking about?' screeched Betty-the-Uncouth down the phone line and straight into my inner ear. 'Who on earth is Gollum?'

'I meant Mr Thurlow. Frederick.'

'So why d'you ask for Gollum?'

'Sorry. I've no idea. Is he about?'

'Fred!' she bellowed. 'For you. A woman.'

I had to stop thinking of him as Gollum. It was Mr Thurlow... Mr Thurlow...'

'Good afternoon. Frederick Thurlow speaking. How may I help you?'

'Mr Thurlow, hello. Yes, it's Jasmine Somers here. I'm the one—'

'Ahhh, our kind benefactress, indeed. I told you, call me Fred. Please.'

'Fred, yes, I was just calling—'

'Not wanting your money back, are you? Only I'm afraid you're a bit late.'

'No, no,' I said, 'It's nothing like that. Actually, I was hoping you could do me a favour...'

'For you, my dear lady, anything.'

I told Fred about the woman and her guide dog in Windsor Close and he said he'd be delighted to add them to the *Talking Gazette* mailing list. He'd have to speak to the rest of the team about recording a whole magazine, as it would entail a fair few hours' work, but he was confident he'd be able to persuade them. He would put forward the proposition during tomorrow's recording session and let me have their decision as soon as possible.

I was able to buy *The Echo*, *Watercolour World* and *Della's Delights* from the Happy Shopper near school on Friday. *Fisherman's Friend*, *Chrysanthemum Expert*, *Morality in Action* and *Guitar Freaks Weekly* would need to be ordered in.

'Thinking of taking up a new hobby?' smiled Mr Patel. 'Those kids not keeping you busy enough?'

'Don't worry, these aren't for me. They're for a project I'm working on.'

'No, I didn't have you down as a guitar freak.' He handed me a copy of my order form. 'Or an angling enthusiast, come to think of it.'

'Oh, don't start me on fishing.'

'I wouldn't dream of it,' he laughed. 'Right, I'll give you a ring when they're in, shall I?'

As I turned to leave, I noticed a stack of crates filled with exotic fruits and vegetables, the sort of thing we used to buy all the time in Nottingham, the sort of thing considered too outlandish for the residents of my hometown. The local Waitrose was selling okra now, but that was about the limit around here as far as ingredients for foreign cuisine went.

I picked over the contents of the top pallet. 'What's this in aid of?'

'Just an experiment, really. Most of it's what the wife cooks with anyway. Thought we'd see if there's a market for it. Take some cassava, if you want. Try it. Our nippers love it fried, with beans.'

'Could you make me up a hamper?' I asked. 'Stick a bit of everything in? I know someone who'd love to try all this.'

Back in Windsor Close, I delivered *The Echo* to number eight, shoved a celebration issue of *Watercolour World* through the letterbox of number fourteen, then rang number eighteen's bell. This I managed to do with my left shoulder; Mr Patel's sturdy box was too heavy for me to hold with one hand. I stood my ground as Miss Dowty's shadowy figure glided up the hallway towards me. Her frame had shrunk since my scrumping days, when the sight of her or her brother would send us scarpering, satchels bashing against our thighs as we raced towards the gap in the hawthorn hedge which marked the orchard's boundary and a return to safety. Through the frosted window pane I watched her take down a key from the hook on the wall.

'Who is it?' she called through the glass.

'Only me. Ms – I mean Mrs Somers from Co-operative Publications.'

'That *is* impressive service. I may well consider placing a regular order when this free offer runs out.'

Hm, that could be tricky. 'Miss Dowty, I wonder if you could open the door?'

'Just push them through,' she said, poking her fingers out of the letterbox.

'I'm afraid it's only the one today. Your *Chrysanthemum Expert* will take a little longer as it's one of our more specialist titles. But I've got you something else. And it's fairly heavy. So if you wouldn't mind...'

The key clinked in the lock and the door swung open. Miss Dowty looked over my box of obscure fruit and veg with suspicion.

'Is that meant to be for me?'

'Yes, it's a free gift that comes with this week's copy of *Della's Delights*. Should spice up your menus a bit.'

'Oh, I'm not sure about spices,' she frowned.

'Well, no, you don't have to use spices. I mean you should be able to concoct some tastier dishes than you're used to. Where shall I put it?'

'And it's free, you say?' She plucked out a star fruit and sniffed it. 'They didn't mention anything about this on the television advertisement. I know there was a complimentary egg whisk in February.'

'Ah, well, this could be a regional offer.'

'Could it?'

'Yes. In fact it is. Definitely. I remember them saying so at head office.'

'In that case you'd better bring it through to the kitchen.'

We paused by a doorway off the hall, and Miss Dowty leant into a tiny room crammed with gold Parker Knoll furniture. There in front of a gas fire sat an old man in an armchair, a crocheted blanket draped over his lap, a walking stick at his feet.

'Kenny, this is Mrs Somers who called on Wednesday. She's brought us some vegetables. Isn't that lovely?'

He turned to face us. 'Eh? Oh, yes.'

'My brother,' she whispered. 'Doesn't hear so well these days.'

The old man stared into my eyes. My heart thumped against my ribcage. I could see him now, stick in hand, hurtling behind me through the trees, yelling after me precisely what would happen when he caught up with me and my no-good friends.

'Mr Dowty. I…er… Hello.'

He didn't reply, but held my gaze. 'Where did you say she was from?'

'A newspaper shop, Kenny. I'm getting some free magazines as well.'

'Somers, did you say? She's not one of those thieving Somers girls from Briar Close, is she?'

My mouth was dry. The box was heavy. I wanted to drop it right there in the doorway and run.

'Only, I swore I'd skin those girls alive if ever I got the chance.' His eyes narrowed. 'Like rabbits.'

My breath became shallow. Blood pounded in my ears.

Beside me Miss Dowty laughed. 'Don't be silly, Kenny. Those rapscallions will be long gone. And this lady is married, aren't you, dear? Somers is her husband's name.'

I looked away from the old man and gave his sister the best smile I could muster.

'Take no notice of Kenny,' she said. 'You're an old grump, aren't you?'

Mr Dowty grimaced and shook a fist in our direction.

'There's no need to look so frightened, dear. He's only pulling your leg. He's completely harmless.'

Easy to say if you'd never been pursued across a brambly field by the maniac.

'Come on,' said Miss Dowty, leading me towards the kitchen.

I plonked the box onto the pine table and braced myself for a swift exit.

The old woman looked at me. 'It's rather strange, isn't it?' she said, shaking her head.

'How do you mean?' Had she recognised me after all?

'I mean, it's quite a coincidence. Don't you think?'

She had. She knew who I was. They both did. Why had I taken their grub-ridden apples? Why had I told her my real name? Had the Dowtys been waiting for my return all this time? The serrated blade of a black-handled knife glinted on the laminated worktop. Was this what they used for skinning rabbits? I heard the scrape of Mr Dowty's chair-legs on the sitting room floor.

'I've got to go,' I said.

'Let me get you a glass of water,' offered Miss Dowty. 'You've gone all pasty.'

They weren't going to let me out.

'It *is* a coincidence though, isn't it?' she repeated, handing me my water.

'Yes,' I said. 'A coincidence. Of course it is. What else could it be?' Somers was a common enough name, wasn't it?

'Or a stroke of luck, maybe. There's me saying I want to make more interesting dinners for me and Kenny, and then two days later you appear with this fantastic box of vegetables!'

'Vegetables?'

'Oh, and the fruit. That will be lovely too, I'm sure.'

'You're talking about the box?' I put my glass down and leant back against the worktop.

'I expect it sounds silly,' she said. 'I know it's not a big thing, but we don't often change our ways or routines. It'll be quite exciting for me and Ken. It's not *that* funny, is it, dear?'

'I'm so sorry. No. No, it's not funny at all. I'm very pleased.

Let's call it a happy coincidence then. Happy coincidences I can deal with.'

Miss Dowty nodded slowly. 'I see. You're sure you're all right, dear?'

'Absolutely fine. Never felt better. But I've outstayed my welcome, I'm sure. Lots more visits to fit in today.' I strode back down the hallway, glancing into the sitting room as I passed. The last threads of tension eased from my shoulders as I saw that Mr Dowty was still in his seat and had turned his piercing eyes back towards the fire.

Numbers twenty two to forty went more smoothly once I'd perfected my spiel. A couple of people I called on had already heard about Co-operative Publications from their neighbours, and had written out orders for me. I felt a little miserly denying the young chap from number thirty six half of his wish list, but we'd been instructed to distribute our resources as widely as possibly, I explained, and eight periodicals per household would seriously overstretch our fledgling enterprise's budget. I took down all eight titles, intending to check with Mr Patel which four were the cheapest before I shelled out for them. That would have to wait until next week now though. Tomorrow was Saturday; tomorrow I'd be seeing Ruben.

'So you seriously thought this old couple were going to skin you alive in their own kitchen?' Ruben handed me my mug of tea, and we sat down in the window seat in the living room.

'Oh no. Miss Dowty doesn't come across as the violent type. She'd probably just… I don't know… watch.'

'Jasmine, I do wonder about your sanity sometimes.'

He was hardly well placed to comment. Besides, he was twisting what I'd said to make it sound ridiculous. He hadn't been there. But I didn't want to argue. And this wasn't what I'd come to discuss.

I took a sip of tea, then set my mug down on the window ledge. 'Ruben, this Spain thing...'

'Ah, yes. That.'

'Have you thought any more about it?'

He put his mug down next to mine. 'Of course I have. I've thought about little else. I can really see it working out. Xalvador has all sorts of plans for expansion, but he trusts me to take things forward in my own way. This could be huge, Jasmine.'

'Yes.'

'No, really. He's a shrewd man, my father-in-law. Sounds like he's seen this recession coming for years and has made cut-backs and investments in all the right places. This would be such a good move for me.'

'Would it?'

'Clearly. You see, businesswise—'

'But this isn't just about business, is it?'

'Isn't it?'

'No, Ruben. It's about you and me.'

'Yes, but I want you to come. I told you that.'

'Ruben, we've barely spent a whole weekend together. And now you want me to leave what I have here and follow you to Madrid?'

'I want you to come *with* me, Jasmine, not follow me. I thought this was what you wanted.'

'To live in Madrid? I don't remember mentioning that, no. I don't even speak Spanish, for God's sake.'

'You speak French, don't you? You'd soon pick it up.'

'That's not the point. The point is I don't want to go. And I don't know why you'd think I would.'

Ruben flinched. 'Isn't that what this amends thing is all about? New beginnings, a clean slate, leaving the past behind?'

'No. Yes. But I don't want a new beginning. I like the one I've got. I don't want to leave everything behind.'

He closed his eyes for a moment. When he opened them again he spoke slowly and softly. 'But you always seem to want more. It's like I felt with Ana. It's as if this life isn't quite enough for you.'

'What do you mean, more? When have I ever said I wanted more?'

'You don't need to say it, Jasmine. OK, for a start there's your job. For whatever reason, you never finished your teaching qualification, right? Yet you make it clear you'd do a far better job than half the teachers at your school.'

'No I do not.'

'You barely mention your ex, but when you do it's to point out how dull and unattractive he was.'

'I don't think I've used the word dull. Anyway, I only mean in the last few years.'

'And then there's me. It's like you constantly want me to *say* more or *do* more or *be* more.'

'That's rubbish, Ru. You're perfect just as you are. I'd prefer it if you gave up smoking, of course, and dairy products, but I'm only thinking of your health. And I guess you could get rid of a few cars and take up a more cerebral pastime. And sometimes it seems like you're wasting your talents somehow, hiding away from the world, scraping by, translating other people's work. And then there's that thing you do when you're waiting for me to finish talking. Ruben?'

'Perfect, eh?'

'Well, maybe not. But, nobody is, are they? I'm sure even I've got the odd imperfection. The point is I still like you.'

Ruben relit his cigarette. 'Thanks.'

'Oh, you know what I mean. It works, doesn't it? We get on. It might not suit everyone, but it works for us.'

'For one night a week.'

'Meaning?'

'Jasmine, I see you one day out of seven. The other six I spend rattling round this place on my own. Most of the time I've no idea what you're up to.'

'You're making my life sound far more exciting than it is. I'm not usually up to anything. And that's what we agreed. No commitment.'

'*I know*. You don't need to keep reminding me. But what if I'd changed my mind? Then what?'

'Then I guess you'd be asking me to move to Madrid.'

We looked at each other. Maybe I did want more. Maybe one night wasn't enough. Maybe at times I *did* imagine us doing normal stuff together: Christmas shopping, visiting my sister, spending a week by the sea. But it didn't matter now. His heart was set on Madrid and it wouldn't be right for me to ask him to give up on his dream.

'Please come with me,' he said.

I shook my head. 'I can't, Ruben. There's too much for me here, and there'd be nothing for me there.'

'Except me.'

'That's not fair,' I protested.

'No, but it's the truth.'

I picked up my mug and took a gulp of tea. Stone cold. I put it back down on the ledge.

'This is all down to you,' he said. 'You're the one who made me get in touch with Ana, and you're the one who's made me realise I can do more with my life. We could make this into a great adventure, Jaz. I know we could.'

'Not in Spain, we couldn't.'

'But you'd be so much closer to your parents.'

'Is that supposed to be a plus point?'

'At least come out there and see what you think. Meet Xalvador, have a look around Madrid. It's a beautiful city. You'd love it, I'm sure. Once you're there, you might think otherwise about the move.'

A holiday together would be lovely. But that was all it would ever be.

'How about you sleep on it?' suggested Ruben. 'You don't need to give me an answer yet. You can tell me tomorrow. And you wouldn't be committing to anything. It would only be a visit. We could go at half term to test the water. Then maybe you'll change your mind.'

I looked into his gleaming eyes. My dark and mysterious lover. My beautiful and gentle friend. We had always known it couldn't last.

'I'm not coming, Ru. I'm so sorry. My answer's no.'

fourteen

'*All you need is love...*' bleated The Beatles from my car stereo as I pulled into Windsor Close after school on Wednesday. Who were *they* to tell me what I needed? It wasn't as if they'd made such a great success of their love lives. No, all *I* needed was to immerse myself in activity – my work and my amends. They'd both be easier to focus on without petty relationship-type distractions. I'd finish taking my newspaper orders this week and have Mr Patel sort out the deliveries; I was sick of these hideous bungalows and their distrustful occupants already. I switched off the engine and silenced the Fab Four. All you need is love? They should try living in the real world.

On opening the car door I was accosted by a runty version of the androgynous creature I'd seen earlier, grimacing at me from the front cover of *Guitar Freaks Weekly*.

'Hey! You got my *Guitar Freaks* yet?'

'Oakley, hello. Yes, I was about to pop it round.'

'Awesome, awesome. Let's have a look.' His burgundy tresses dangled over the bundle of papers and magazines I was leafing through.

'Maybe if you stand back... I can't actually see that well with your... Ah, here we go.' I pulled out a shiny magazine from near the bottom of the pile.

He yanked it from my hand. 'Oh my God! Johnny Skag!'

'I'm sorry?'

'Nah, no worries. Johnny Skag, see?' He blew his hair out of his eyes and gazed at the *Guitar Freaks Weekly* cover photo.

I studied the semi-bandaged musician, sprawled over a stack of speakers, fondling a lightning bolt guitar. 'Yes, he looks...' Desiccated? Decomposing? Dead? 'He looks just like you.'

'Man, thanks. That's like... wow. Johnny Skag's like, the reason I took up playing. Solo he's awesome, but with Monkskull... I just love him.'

'Forget about love,' I wanted to tell him. *'You stick with your guitar. You know where you are with a Fender.'*

'I'd better get on,' I said, nodding towards my stack of magazines.

'Who's ordered *The Joy of Compost*?' sniggered Oakley, twisting one of the three silver rings in his left eyebrow. 'Some people are right weirdos.'

It was a good job I'd been writing down all my new orders because by the time I'd hung up my keys in the kitchen and turned the kettle on I had no idea who I'd spoken to in Windsor Close, which numbers they lived at or what they'd asked for. All I could think about was Saturday night and Sunday morning, how strange everything had seemed between me and Ruben after we'd talked, how distant we'd suddenly become. It was the first time we'd ever fallen asleep not wrapped in each other's arms, the first time I'd been up early and left before he was awake. But what more was there to say? Why hang around to pick over what might have been, if only I'd been willing to go with him, if only he would stay?

The phone rang in the living room and I plodded through from the kitchen to answer.

'Hello?'

'Jasmine, it's Fred here. From the shop. I've got a bit of good news for you.'

As if that would make any difference. 'Oh, hello, Fred. Is it about the magazine?'

'Indeed it is. The group thought it was a fantastic idea, and we've recorded the whole of *Travels Through Time* already. I was wondering whether I should send it to the same address?'

'Yes please. Number twenty. That's great. Thanks.' I slumped down onto the sofa.

'Hard day with the kiddies?'

'Same as usual, pretty much.'

'Only you sound rather tired. Or glum?'

'Oh, I'm probably coming down with something. Feeling a bit, you know, under the weather.'

'Exercise. Always used to sort me out.'

'How d'you mean?'

'Well, in my younger days, if I was ever ailing or feeling sorry for myself, I'd make an effort to go out dancing. Never failed to put a smile back on my face.'

'I'm not feeling sorry for myself.'

'No, no. Not you. I meant me. Of course I don't go out dancing any more. Too old and decrepit for all that. No fandangos for Frederick Thurlow.'

No fandangos. Where had I heard that recently? Mrs Wilkinson! Mrs Wilkinson who dreamt of ballroom dresses and big band accompaniment.

'Fred, you've given me a brilliant idea. How would you like to dance again? In fact, how would you like to teach?'

Brilliant may have been an overstatement, but at least it would distract me from my own thoughts for a while. I explained my idea to Fred, who after much not-so-gentle persuasion finally agreed.

'So you want me to start the classes this weekend?' he asked.

'Well, the first session will just be for you to meet the residents and gauge their interest.'

Fred chuckled. 'Who'd have thought it, eh? An old codger like me leading a proper course in dancing. I expect I'll be a bit rusty.'

'I'm sure you'll be fine, Fred. And I know at least one lady who will absolutely love it.'

'As long as you don't expect me to go leaping about all over the place,' he warned me. 'And I shan't be performing any lifts.'

Sunday morning dragged by, and not even a spate of grizzly garrottings in Midsomer Marrow could hold my attention. When Ruben had texted on Thursday to put off our Saturday night tryst, I'd felt oddly relieved. He had so much to work through and organize, he'd explained. Well, that suited me fine, because so did I.

I picked Fred up at two o'clock from the corner of Gaol Street. He wasn't his usual eloquent self as we drove through the city's outskirts and out along the A44. I was starting to worry that I'd asked too much of him.

'First night nerves,' he assured me. 'I'm always the same. Will I remember my routines? Will I let my partner down? Will the audience relate to the performance?' His fingers were tapping on the dashboard.

'Fred, we're only looking into setting up a few classes in an old people's home. It's hardly Broadway.'

He stopped tapping and turned to face me. I didn't need to take my eyes off the road to sense his outrage.

'Broadway, RADA or Women's Institute – a true professional always gives his all in each gesture and every step. Teaching,

Jasmine, as you should know, is even more important than performing. As teachers we are the ambassadors of our art. We are sharing with the world the delight and beauty of that which we love.'

I nodded sagely. I did wish everyone would stop droning on about love.

The peeling door of Valley View swung open as we approached. Mark clapped his hands together when he saw us. I'd phoned on Friday to run my dance class idea past him and he'd mentioned swapping shifts so that he could meet Fred, but I hadn't taken him seriously.

'Come in, come in. Welcome to the mad house. I'm Mark, by the way. You must be Mr Thurlow. I've heard all about you.'

'Good afternoon. Yes, that's me. But I can't think what this young lady's been saying about me.'

Nor could I. I'd only been on the phone to Mark for about two minutes.

Mark closed the door behind us. 'Mr Thurlow, is it true that you danced at La Folie d'Or?'

Ah yes, I'd mentioned that to validate Fred's credentials, although it meant nothing to me.

'La Folie d'Or?' smiled Fred. 'Oh, that was a *long* time ago.'

Mark gasped. 'So it's true! Did you ever meet Gabriella Lacroix? Or Henri Mersault?'

'Well, Henri was on the same circuit as me for a while in his early years, and I shared a stage with Gabriella a few times before she made a name for herself. Sweet girl. Absolutely tiny.'

Mark was shaking his head, his mouth and eyes wide open. I cleared my throat loudly. He took no notice.

'You danced with Gabriella Lacroix? I can't believe that. Were they true, all those stories about her and Jürgen Littig?'

'Ha! The public didn't hear the half of it.'

Mark let out an embarrassing squealing sound. 'Oh, tell me more! Tell me more!'

I gave up on my subtle coughing attack. 'Sorry, shall I leave you to it?'

Fred looked at me as if he wasn't quite sure whether he was in trouble or not.

Mark came to his rescue. 'Yes, leave us to it. You go on up and have your chin-wag with Mrs W. Superb idea. Mr Thurlow can be my guest in the visitors' lounge and I'll bring him up when we've had a cuppa. If that's all right with you, Mr Thurlow.'

'Of course, of course. It's a pleasure to meet someone with such an interest. Do you know, the one time I bumped into Gabriella and Jürgen...'

They headed off along the corridor, leaving me to find my own way upstairs. Why hadn't *I* ever been invited to the visitors' lounge?

Mrs Wilkinson was looking particularly elegant today, her turquoise necklace and earrings exactly matching her ankle-length satin dress, her silver hair swept loosely into a bun. I couldn't help but comment.

'Glamorous?' she laughed, 'It's a while since anyone's called me that! But I thought I should make an effort for this young dance teacher of yours. Now, tell me, how have your amends been going? It's been a long time.'

She seemed more impressed with my efforts in Windsor Close this week, but questioned my reasons for withholding the true explanation for my magazine deliveries.

'It's amends by proxy,' I protested. 'Surely I don't *need* to tell the truth?'

'Amends by proxy, eh? So you *have* been reading my literature after all.' She smiled. 'And, yes, these may not be the actual people you wronged, but there is still a place for honesty. Remember that anonymity should not be used simply to safeguard our own pride or comfort. And neither should dishonesty.'

'I'd hardly call turning up on people's doorsteps remaining anonymous. And I object to being called dishonest.'

'Mrs Somers from Co-operative Publications?'

'It was only the one person who presumed I was a Mrs. Anyhow, that was self-preservation. Her brother wanted to skin me alive.'

Mrs Wilkinson raised an eyebrow. 'Let's pick you a couple of tasks for this week, shall we?' Her pink highlighter hovered over my first list as she skimmed through it.

'Actually,' I said, 'I've been thinking about this. I'd like to do the animal ones next. There's Stan the hamster. And the worms. And then there's… Then there's Fluffy.'

She scored fat lines through the three items. 'What about the fly in the Eccles cake?'

'Oh, no. That was already dead. It's more my Auntie Jean I need to apologise to for that.'

'And from the second list? We're not doing so well with that one, are we?'

I couldn't bear looking at it, that was why. My drunken rant at the bottom of the page about Arnaud and Dan – I didn't even want to think about it.

'Jasmine? The second list. Would you like me to pick something for you?'

'Yes, you choose,' I said. 'Anything you like.' But *please*, I thought, please not one of the last two.

'There. Essay-sharing. How does that sound?'

'Fantastic. Well, not fantastic. Essay-sharing sounds bad, clearly, not fantastic at all, but it should be fine, I mean.'

Mrs Wilkinson put my papers away. 'And do you want to discuss your approach? Or any of the animals?'

Poor little Fluffy with her bad breath and stubby tail. 'No. I know what I'm doing with these.'

'Just remember what I said about honesty, Jasmine. I can't emphasize its importance enough. Now, where *has* this dancer of yours got to?'

While we waited, Mrs Wilkinson enthused over the movies she'd watched during last weekend's Valley View Film Fest. I'd never heard of any of them apart from *Brief Encounter*, which I'd only watched to the end to find out which of the main characters threw themselves under the train. At last there was a knock on the library doors.

'That'll be them,' I said, getting up to let them in.

'And you're quite sure he's not some whippersnapper who'll have us all break-dancing and moon-walking?' Mrs Wilkinson asked.

'I'm quite sure.' I pulled the doors open and Mark bustled in.

'Your visitor has arrived,' he announced. Then turning slightly he whispered to Fred over his shoulder, 'Don't worry, she'll love you.'

This was *my* introduction. I took a step forward and positioned myself between Mark and Mrs Wilkinson. 'Fred, I'd like to introduce you to—'

'Margaret Cooke!'

'No, Fred, this is Mrs Wilkinson.'

His cheeks had grown pink and he looked even more awkward than he had on the journey here. 'Margaret Cooke! I'd recognise that smile anywhere. And your poise. But, I must apologise. How rude of me. You wouldn't remember. My name's—'

'Freddie Thurlow! It is, isn't it? My goodness. Freddie Thurlow. Dapper as ever, Freddie. How *are* you? Do come and sit down.'

I turned to Mark in hope of an explanation. He shrugged and skulked out of the room.

'I didn't realise you two knew each other,' I said. Both were leaning back in their armchairs surveying the other.

'But Jasmine, this is Margaret Cooke. I think I may have mentioned her. We moved in the same circles many years ago.' He nodded at me as if I really ought to know what he was talking about. 'Village dances and the like.'

'Oh, so you two are old friends?'

'Unfortunately not,' said Mrs Wilkinson. 'Young Freddie was far too aloof to bother with my sort. And what a dancer!'

'Aloof?' said Fred. 'Is that how you saw me?'

'I always wished he'd ask me for a dance,' confided Mrs Wilkinson, as if Fred couldn't hear, 'but I'm afraid the steps have never come naturally to me. My two left feet probably scared him off!'

'Two left feet? Margaret, you were as graceful as a ballerina.'

'Freddie, you're making me blush. What a shame you didn't ever ask me for that dance. I kept hoping, you know.'

'I never had the chance. You had so many suitors. And then Harry Wilkinson came along.'

'Ah, yes. Harry. Not one of nature's great movers. But an incredible mind, he had. And such a generous man.'

Fred shuffled his feet and looked down at the floor. 'Yes, I'm sure. Good, good.'

I was so slow at times. Mrs Wilkinson was the girl who'd broken his heart. Mrs Wilkinson was the reason he'd moved away when he was young, the reason he'd never married, the reason he'd lived to dance. Poor Fred.

'Look,' I said, 'these dance lessons… I'm wondering whether they might be a little on the energetic side for all the… more mature residents here. Perhaps a new card game would be more appropriate. How about canasta?'

'Nonsense!' cried Mrs Wilkinson. 'I've waited half a century for a dance with Freddie Thurlow. Canasta indeed. I may be getting on a bit but I'm not as decrepit as you might think.'

I opened my mouth to defend myself.

'Oh Margaret,' gushed Fred, who seemed to have regained his composure, 'nobody is calling you decrepit. Look at you, as radiant and lovely as the day I first set eyes on you.'

'Freddie, shush!'

'And I must say, this dress brings out the blue of your eyes so beautifully.'

'We're going to have to watch this one, Jasmine. A smooth talker if ever there was one. I always did have a soft spot for these handsome, roguish types.'

'Right,' I said, 'I think I'm going to pop downstairs and find Mark for a minute. I've just remembered something really urgent I need to discuss with him.' I wasn't sure that either of them had heard me. I headed towards the doors.

'So, tell me, Freddie,' said Mrs Wilkinson, 'where did you disappear off to all of a sudden? We came back from our honeymoon and you'd vanished. I thought I saw you across the churchyard at our wedding, you know. Ridiculous, isn't it? Wishful thinking I suppose…'

I pulled the library doors closed behind me. It was lucky I had nothing to get home for. Fred and Mrs Wilkinson had a lifetime of catching up to do and were likely to be some time.

fifteen

The RSPCA were booked up until after Christmas, but the woman from the third animal shelter I tried said she'd be happy to come in to assembly one day this week to talk about her work. My explanation – that I'd not been the world's best animal carer as a child and wanted the children to be more aware of animal welfare issues than I had been – was frank, if not full. Tuesday suited us both, and fitted around my cloakroom monitoring duties and her mucking out rota. The members of my French Club were grateful for another week to rehearse their assembly on French pop music.

'Good morning, children,' began the jolly, weather-beaten animal rescuer, following my brief introduction.

'Good mor-ning, Mrs Pratley. Good mor-ning everybody,' chorused the children.

Mrs Pratley shot a look in my direction. I nodded for her to continue.

'Right, well, I was asked to come in today to talk to you about the importance of correct animal care. Hands up if you've heard of Pratley's Animal Shelter. Quite a few of you. Good. Well, that's where I work, and I'll tell you all about what I do in a moment. But first I'd like to thank Ms Somers for inviting me here. Now, Ms Somers wants me to teach you how important it is to be kind to animals, because it sounds to me like Ms Somers wasn't always very kind to animals when she was a little girl. Isn't that right,

Ms Somers?'

Two hundred and thirty four pairs of incredulous eyes fixed on me as my face burned and my palms grew moist. Nicholas Ashcroft shook his head at me and tutted.

'Now put your hands up if you have any pets at home,' said Mrs Pratley.

The children turned back to face the front, hands shooting up, my inhumanity forgotten.

I'd have to use the remainder of her talk to prepare my defence, in case she planned to return to me at a later point in the proceedings. Chopping worms in half would be easy to explain. Me and Gabriel Dukes had simply been experimenting to see whether they really did survive and become two worms instead of one. His sister had tried it and said they multiplied forever, like Mickey Mouse's broomstick in *The Sorcerer's Apprentice*.

'Guilty,' I was ready to plead. *'But who hasn't chopped a few worms in half in their time?'*

I did feel bad about Stan the hamster though. I'd saved up for months to buy Stan from the pet shop in Elgar Street. It wasn't just the hamster you had to think about; there was the cage, the bedding, the exercise wheel, the water bottle, the ceramic food bowl, all sorts. I'd promised Mum I'd feed him and give him fresh water every day, as well as cleaning his cage out once a week.

Stan was my best friend. I told him all my secrets, and got him out for a cuddle whenever I felt sad. Stan was always there for me. He always listened and he never laughed at me or told my secrets to anyone else. When Tasha told me the truth about Father Christmas, Stan was the only one who understood. He was the only one who didn't tell me how ridiculous it was for a girl of my age to be that upset about something so silly.

Then in January, Elizabeth Hetherington started at my school. On her first day, she chose to sit on my table at lunchtime, and from then on we were best friends. I stopped telling Stan all my secrets, and most days I was too busy for cuddles. Elizabeth said pets were unhygienic, and she called Stan a rodent. I started moving his cage to the box room when she was visiting, and then it seemed easier to simply leave him there. Sometimes I forgot to feed Stan, but I always made up for it the next day and gave him extra. If I was in a hurry I'd cover Stan's toilet corner with newspaper and sawdust to keep him going until I had the chance to give him a proper clean-out. Elizabeth was right: human friends came first, and after all, Stan was really no different from a rat.

It was a Friday in mid-February when Stan disappeared. I'd been looking forward to going round to Elizabeth's all week. Her gran had given her Buckaroo as an early birthday present and she'd invited me round to play it with her and to have tea. Fish fingers, chips and spaghetti hoops, she'd said. But that lunchtime we'd fallen out over a game of marbles – she'd called me a cheat when she wasn't even watching properly – so she'd invited Karen Phillips round instead. When I got home after school that day I ran straight up to the box room for a snuggle, but Stan was gone. His cage had gone, with his little wheel and play-tube, and the only sign that he'd been there was a faint oblong-shaped sawdust outline on the carpet, the imprint of where his cage had been.

I raced down to the kitchen. 'Mum, Mum, someone's stolen Stan!'

My mum put the vegetable knife down, wiped her hands on her apron and slowly turned to face me.

'Mum? What's the matter?'

Dad always shouted when he was cross, but Mum just did it quietly. 'Jasmine, you swore you'd look after that creature. How *could* you?'

What on earth was she on about? It wasn't me who'd stolen him. 'But, Mum—'

'Have you *any* idea what state that thing was in?'

What was she talking about?

'Don't try acting all innocent. You know very well what I mean. That cage can't have been cleaned out for weeks.'

It might have been a bit dirty, but that hardly mattered now it had been stolen.

'That water bottle was green, Jasmine. Green! And God knows when the poor thing was last fed.'

That wasn't fair. I'd missed a few days lately, but I'd put loads of food in Stan's bowl yesterday before school. Or was it the day before?

'Well? What have you got to say for yourself?'

I sniffed. 'Mum, Stan's gone.'

'I know he's gone, you silly girl. He's been gone since Tuesday.'

I stared at my mum. I'd only just fed him a couple of days ago, hadn't I? But why would she lie about it? And who would take him? 'Where did he go?'

'Back where he came from,' said Mum.

'The desert?'

'The pet shop. They didn't want him, said he was too emaciated to sell on, but the equipment was worth a bit so the man said he'd feed him up himself and keep him on the counter for customers to look at.'

'You gave Stan away?' How could Mum be cross with me when she'd done something so spiteful?

'Don't you dare whine at me, Jasmine. That animal was practically dead.'

Hot tears rolled down my cheeks and into the corners of my mouth. I'd done my best. I loved Stan. But I'd been busy. And now I'd never see him again. I slumped down onto the kitchen floor and covered my face with my arms. 'I want to see Stan,' I wailed. 'I wanted a cuddle!'

'Pssst! Ms Somers!'

I glanced down to see Nicholas Ashcroft pulling at my trouser leg. As I looked around the school hall I realised that once again two hundred and thirty four heads had swivelled in my direction. Our very own St Francis of Assisi in the vaguely feminine guise of a pock-marked farmer's wife was frowning at me expectantly.

'Sorry,' I said, 'I was lost in thought for a minute there. Thank you. Your talk has certainly given us lots to think about, hasn't it children?'

'Quite,' said Mrs Pratley. 'But what do you think of the sponsorship idea?'

She wanted to be my sponsor as well? Was she on The Programme too? Not another recovering alcoholic, surely? But then that would at least explain her complexion.

'Sponsorship?' I said, 'I'm not sure—'

'Yes, we were talking about the whole school sponsoring one of our rescue animals. You could come and visit it at the centre and you'd receive photos and regular updates on your animal's progress and development until we find him or her a permanent home. Most people find sponsorship very rewarding. And it's not as costly as you might expect.'

'We'd love to. Yes. Thank you. We'd like a hamster.'

Nicholas Ashcroft sniggered.

'Most schools like to take on a larger animal,' said St Pratley. 'A goat for example, or one of our dogs.'

'Yes, a goat,' I nodded. 'Wonderful. And a hamster.'

'Right, well, we can go over details in a moment. But if there are no more questions I think I'm about done.'

'Mrs Pratley, can I ask you something?'

We'd completed the sponsorship paperwork and she was about to head back to her ark.

'Of course, ask away,' she replied, 'but it's all fairly self-explanatory.'

'It's not about the goat. It's just something someone wanted me to check with you. Somebody else. Not me.'

'Go on.'

'A pupil. It was a pupil. She wanted me to talk to you for her. She was a bit scared to do it herself. You know what kids are like.'

'Yes?'

'Well, she was wondering whether a cat could be poisoned by mint ice cream.'

'Mint ice cream? That's a rather strange question.'

'Yes. Ha ha. That's precisely what I said. But what do you think?'

'I've never known of a cat being harmed by eating ice cream, although we do recommend recognised brands of cat food rather than scraps from our own diets.'

'Yes, yes, but is it possible? Could a cat die from eating too much mint ice cream?'

'I really don't imagine so, but I'm no vet, Ms Somers. I could send you an information sheet on cat care to pass on to her if that would help.'

'Pass on to who?'

She paused for a second. 'The girl with the cat.'

'Oh, yes, her.' I noticed my nails digging into my palms and made an effort to unclench my fists.

'Sorry if that's not much help.'

'What if the ice cream was homemade?'

Mrs Pratley laughed. 'I'm afraid that wouldn't make much difference.'

'Yes, but if it was made with toothpaste, vanilla ice cream mixed with mint toothpaste, lots of it, what about that? Could *that* kill a cat?'

Mrs Pratley zipped up her bag and hoisted it onto her shoulder. 'Ms Somers, all I can say is that if this child thinks mint toothpaste is a suitable diet for a domestic animal, I would recommend that she be prevented from owning a pet for the foreseeable future.'

'Longer than that,' I could have added. *'And she should go vegetarian too. Prevent any more unnecessary deaths. Then turn vegan when she's old enough. As soon as she leaves home and can cook for herself.'*

Maybe I'd started making my amends a long time ago.

Tash had come home early with a migraine and gone straight to bed, Phil told me when I rang that evening, so I tried her mobile first thing the next morning. She was about to go into a meeting with some government advisor – something to do with literary bursaries and university funding. What I wanted to discuss was important though.

'Tash, I need to know what the vet said about Fluffy. Mum wouldn't tell me.'

'Bloody hell, Jasmine. You said it was urgent. The future of my department's at stake here.'

'Was it the ice cream? Is that what did it?'

'What ice cream? Jasmine, we're talking twenty whatever

years ago.'

'Fluffy ate some ice cream the day before she died. I cleaned her teeth afterwards, but… Is that what killed her? Was she poisoned?'

'Of course she wasn't poisoned. She was run over.'

'Run over? But Mum said Fluffy was feeling poorly and had to go to the vet.'

'Yeah, because she knew you'd bawl your eyes out otherwise.'

'Fluffy was run over?'

'Yep. Mr Hickling reversed straight over her in his Morris Minor. Flat as a pancake, Dad said. A pancake with jammy stuff oozing out the edges.'

'Tasha, stop it!'

'Look, sis, I've got to go. This really doesn't look too professional.'

'But why didn't anyone tell me?'

'Oh God. *I* don't know. Fluffy feeling poorly and falling into a long, peaceful sleep probably sounded less distressing for our sensitive little Jazjaz. Ask Mum. It was her idea.'

'So I didn't kill her?'

'Not unless you were in the car with Mr Hickling. You weren't, were you?'

'Of course I wasn't. Don't be stupid.'

'That's it. I'm going. Lovely speaking to you again, sis. It's been fascinating.'

Great. So now I was going to have to ring her back later to apologise. Some of these tasks seemed to be self-perpetuating. I was off the hook as far as cat-killing was concerned though. Mr Hickling. I'd never trusted him, with his straggly moustache and gold tooth. I used to watch him from my window, crank starting that rusty old car in the winter. Thank goodness I hadn't been watching when he squashed Fluffy. This was great though. I wasn't to blame! I hadn't killed the cat! I swung my front door open and inhaled the cleansing morning air. What a beautiful day. What a wonderful world.

The postman waved an envelope at me as he came up the path. 'Morning. That was good timing! Have you been waiting for me?'

'Nope. I was just appreciating... you know, nature, life. You're early today.'

'Nature? Bit rubbish, if you ask me. Anyway, what are you looking so pleased about?'

'I just found out my cat was run over,' I beamed.

'Your cat?'

'Fluffy. A neighbour drove right over her. Splatt!'

'But she's OK?'

'Christ, no. Dead as a doornail. Or a dodo. Both, actually.' I closed my eyes against the morning sun and took in a long, deep breath. I was innocent! My, that felt good.

'Are you all right?'

'Absolutely. Never felt better. And a letter for me too? Perfect.'

'Yes. Handwritten. Airmail. From Spain by the looks of it. A proper letter. Not that I've had much of a butcher's.'

'Fantastic,' I said, taking the letter. A thank you note from my mum, no doubt. 'Have a marvellous day!'

'Huh,' grunted the postman. 'That's highly unlikely.'

I checked my watch – I'd better get a move on or I'd be late for work. I slipped Mum's letter into my bag and went through to the kitchen to grab my keys.

I had put that evening aside for my essay-sharing amends. It would only involve a few phone calls and some brief apologies. I mean, overall I'd managed pretty skilfully to combine typically irresponsible undergraduate behaviour with attaining half-decent grades. When Melanie Dickson had asked me one Thursday night at Rock City if I too was celebrating handing in our mid-year assignments for Feminism in the Humanities, due in the following afternoon, I was gutted. How dumb could I be? Dr Peetz would kill me! Still, it shouldn't take more than half a day to write three thousand words comparing the work of Marilyn French with that of Erica Jong. I was sure I could knock something out in time. What was the point of subsidiary subjects in any case? I was a philosopher, not a feminist. I bought myself another pint of snakebite and decided to think about it tomorrow.

I'd only gone up to the feminism corridor to grovel for a week's extension on compassionate grounds, but when I saw all those completed assignments in Dr Peetz's pigeonhole I couldn't resist a quick read-through. My fellow students had based most of their exposition on what we'd all discussed in class. There were references to many of the texts from our reading list, which I too could easily have quoted from if I'd had the time to study them. So now I had a choice. Basically, I could spend days and days in the library, slogging my guts out to produce the exact same piece of work I could cobble together in a few hours right now. All I had to do was to lift the most pertinent paragraphs from a few essays and blend them together in my own unique way. I plucked out four files at random and scuttled off to find an empty study.

It was more difficult than I'd imagined tracking down females, as they so often changed their surnames. Melanie Dickson was now Melanie Chan and was living in an artists' community in New York. Sonal Pandya had become Sonal Nguyen and had adopted two Vietnamese orphans with her concert pianist husband Giáp. Debs Malone had married and divorced three times and was now circumnavigating the globe in search of husband number four. She'd have to make do with the explanation and apology I'd left with her son.

Melanie was extremely generous with her forgiveness. Yes, she'd been shocked when Dr Peetz had accused her of plagiarising my superb essay, but had also been flattered to have her work compared with mine. My writing was always so thorough yet concise. I was quick to grasp a concept and masterful at propounding an argument. This is how Dr Peetz had immediately concluded that my fellow students had copied *my* work, and not the other way round.

Sonal was not so understanding. She'd suspected foul play on my part all along and was convinced that Dr Peetz had marked her down for the rest of her university career for daring to question her judgement.

'I'm sure that's not true,' I told Sonal. 'Dr Peetz would have marked you on merit alone.'

'So you're saying my essays were just rubbish?'

I couldn't win. 'Not at all. And anyway, a 2.2 is still a good degree.'

'I got a third,' she replied. 'And what was yours? Oh yes, of course, a 2.1.'

'Well yes, but I mean a third's nothing to be ashamed of.' I'd have been mortified.

'I've a good mind to get in touch with the vice-chancellor and have your degree revoked,' she threatened.

'Look, how about I contact Dr Peetz to put the record straight?'

'Forget it,' she spat. 'Let's just let sleeping dogs lie, shall we?'

'If that's what you want,' I agreed, although it didn't much sound like she wanted to let them lie at all.

I reminded myself of the teachings of the Benestrophe Pathway literature: I was responsible only for making my apology in a fitting way, not for the reaction of the person I had wronged. In other words, if Sonal didn't like what I had to say, that was tough. I decided not to mention that to her though.

'Well, Sonal, I can tell that this is still an emotive issue for you, but I hope one day you'll find it in your heart to forgive me.' Insincere, but she was bugging me.

'Some things are not so simple to forgive, Jasmine.'

For goodness sake, it was one damn essay. 'No. You must feel very hurt. Believe me, I'm finding it hard to forgive myself. I am truly remorseful.'

'Yes, yes, OK. Is that it?'

'It is. Thank you so much for listening. You've been very understanding.'

'Yes, well…'

'Ooh, hang on, Sonal. Can you remember who else's work I looked at? There was you, Debs and Melanie, and I'm sure there was someone else. Must've been someone I didn't really know. I seem to have completely blanked them out.'

'Sounds about right. It was Sophie, Sophie Styles. What was it you and Dan used to call her? Soppy Soph? So tactful.'

Sophie Styles? Oh my God, it was. And she'd been devastated at being called a plagiariser. No wonder I'd blocked it out. OK, so now it was *my* turn to ring Sophie and apologise to *her*. Strange, the way things can turn around. Did I really have to phone her? Look at the ridiculous mission I'd ended up embarking on the last time we'd spoken. Still, the damage was done now. And this amends thing wasn't so bad. Besides, she'd hardly be putting any more outrageous ideas into my head. *I* was the one phoning *her* after all. What was I worrying about? It wasn't as if she'd be able to suggest anything else that would turn my life upside-down, was it?

sixteen

Sophie wasn't answering her phone. Probably in one of her AA meetings, or off making her own amends. I pushed my mobile back into the side pocket of my bag and fished out a now crumpled envelope. Mum's letter – I'd forgotten about that. I stuck a fingernail under the flap of the envelope and peeled it open.

Dear Jasmine,

How lovely to get a letter from you. It reminded me of when you were in student digs and had no phone.

You're right about your Uncle Ivor – he was four years younger than your father. Very sad, but it didn't come as much of a surprise, I'm afraid.

Talking of surprises, we've been having terrible problems with our sewers. There's a lovely couple from Huddersfield in the apartment above us. He's a retired builder so he's had a good poke about, but says the system just wasn't built to service all these new developments. The bureaucracy here's unbelievable and the officials hardly speak any English, which really doesn't help matters.

Anyway, regarding your letter – I shouldn't worry about your Auntie Nell and that old teapot. The only injury was to her pride, and on the plus side, her Christmas visits were always fleeting after that. Thank you for telling me about breaking the fence. I'd always presumed that it *was another of your father's botched DIY attempts. He <u>will</u> be pleased. As for Dougie Naylor and the tobacco, I suppose it's best that your father knows the truth, although I can't see him going out of his way to rekindle the friendship. After all, Jasmine, this did all happen a very long time ago. What did you want with Golden Virginia anyway? I do hope you're not a secret smoker. We've decided to spend the money you sent us on a new gas barbecue for the patio. It will be lovely sitting out under the stars with some nice sausages sizzling and a decent bit of bacon. Not that this would appeal to you, of course.*

We won't be back for Christmas, no, but you're always welcome to come and stay if you're worried about spending the festive season on your own. I'd always hoped that you and Dan would come and see the place some time, but I suppose it's too late for all that now. It really is <u>such</u> a shame about you two. He was <u>so</u> right for you, and the <u>perfect</u> son-in-law. I presume you've heard his news...

Of course I hadn't heard his news. Why should I be interested in his latest promotion or golfing trophy? It was none of my business any more, and that was exactly how I liked it. Mothers – they couldn't resist interfering.

Right, I'd give Sophie one more try, then I'd go up to bed. Two more days till half term. I was so looking forward to a proper rest.

Sophie picked up straight away. 'Hi, Jasmine. Sorry, I saw I had a missed call from you. I meant to phone back. I was doing my yoga. Did you get the card?'

'Yes, and the money, thanks. I bought a lovely scarf, hat and gloves.'

'Oh, good. It's very satisfying when one of my missions turns out well.'

'Missions?'

'My amends. That's what I call them. Makes it sound more exciting. Anyway, how are you?'

I told her I was fine. I told her how she'd inspired me to make my own amends. Then I told her about the essay of hers I'd copied.

'Oh my God, Jasmine. You mean you cheated? That's, I don't know, intellectual theft or something.'

'I know. I'm sorry, Soph. I guess you're not the only one with a dodgy past.'

'Sonal warned me not to trust you. I told her she was being paranoid. I said Dr Peetz must have made a mistake. I can't believe I stuck up for you!'

'Thanks, Sophie. That was good of you.'

'It was only because you seemed so honest.'

'I was. I am. Generally. I just got my priorities wrong that time, I suppose.'

She paused. 'Yes, well, we've all done that.'

'Look, if there's anything I can do…'

'Oh, forget it! I guess it was a big deal at the time but… Well, I've been learning to let that kind of stuff go. No point holding on to negative emotions.'

'No,' I agreed.

'But thanks for telling me. I appreciate it. You're lucky though.'

'Lucky?'

'Yeah. It must be easy doing just those two steps without the whole addiction thing to battle with as well. I envy you.'

'You *envy* me?'

'You know what I mean,' Sophie sighed. 'No dreadful skeletons in your closet. No demons to exorcise. Just simple little apologies.'

'They're not all simple.'

'No, sorry, that came out wrong. All I mean is that I'm happy for you if all you have to feel bad about is stuff like looking at other people's essays. It's on a different scale from the confessions I've heard at my meetings. Addicts can stoop pretty low. I should know. Sorry. Too much information probably.'

'Not at all,' I said. 'I'm interested. Really.'

'Well, I can't go into detail – confidentiality and all that – but what I *will* say is that some people I know have committed some terrible wrongs and then they really get stuck trying to sort them out. You can start to sail through the small stuff. It can even be fun in a weird kind of way. Feels like you're getting somewhere, making progress, then boomph.'

'Boomph?'

'Yeah, it's like you hit a brick wall. Most people have a couple of biggies they really don't want to tackle. Don't even want to think about them sometimes. I've known people drop out of The Programme because they're too scared to face one of the issues from their own past. Such a shame.'

'Yes.'

'And it's a terrible waste, Jaz, because they've done so much work already but don't have the courage to take on what really matters. You can't move on until you're at peace with your own past, you see. It's like you have to forgive the old you to be able to know and accept the you that you are now. Does that make sense?'

'It does.'

'Anyway, my point is that you aren't in that position. You're not going to have some massive unresolved issue or shocking revelation to offload onto anyone. You're lucky.'

I lay in bed that night, replaying our conversation. I couldn't put this off any longer. Dan and Arnaud. Arnaud and Dan. I had demons and skeletons all right. Demons and skeletons which crowded my dreams and taunted me in my sleep.

Ruben cleared our bowls away and began to roll himself a cigarette. 'You're quite sure you won't come with me? Not even for a look? It's not too late to change your mind.'

'It is, Ruben. You're going in two days.'

'Yes, while you're still off work. I'm sure we could find you a flight.'

I shook my head. What would be the point? We sat in silence.

Ruben lit his cigarette. 'So, your amends. What's that evil headmistress got lined up for you next?'

'I'm not seeing her until tomorrow. But I've made up my own mind this week, more or less.'

'Sounds rather vague. What is it this time then? More broken china and filched fruit?'

'This isn't a joke, Ruben.'

He reached out and stroked my arm. 'I know, Jaz. I'm only teasing.'

I stood up and walked over to the window. The sunlight was fading and a swirling drizzle filled the air. Maybe I should go home.

'Come and sit down, Jasmine. Tell me what you're planning. I'd like to know.'

I could have told him about France, about everything I'd done, the lies I'd had to tell, but why bother now? In a few weeks he'd be starting out again in Madrid. Spain was where his past was, and his future too. My future was here, alone. I should never have imagined anything different.

Ruben sidled up behind me and slid his arms around my waist.

He rested his chin on my shoulder. 'So, you're not going to tell me?'

I stared out across the garden to the field beyond. 'Of course. It's just something with someone I knew while I was studying in Perpignan.'

'Well, that's specific.'

'Sorry, it's not really a big deal, that's all.'

'So what are you going to do? Phone them? Send a letter?'

'I haven't decided yet. I guess so.'

'Is this someone you started your teacher training with?'

'What? Oh, no, it wasn't anyone from my course. He was a local. We made friends when I was out there.'

'Oh, it's a he, is it? Friends, eh? Sounds like I might have a bit of competition.'

I turned round and hugged Ruben. He was trying his best. And we might as well enjoy what time we had left. 'No competition, don't worry.'

'Glad to hear it.' He yawned loudly. 'Are you tired, Jasmine? Only I was thinking of getting an early night.'

'Oh, were you? No, I'm not tired at all.'

He smiled and kissed me. 'Good. Neither am I. Come on then. An early night it is.'

The next afternoon at Valley View, Mark ushered me along the corridors towards the library. 'They're up there waiting for you,' he said.

'They?'

'Yes. Fred and Mrs W.'

'Fred Thurlow? What's *he* doing here?'

'Courting, I'd say. He's been here every day this week. Most evenings as well.'

'Really? But, that's—'

'I know, it's sooo sweet, isn't it?'

'Hm, yes, I suppose so.' They were so *old* though.

'Blimey,' huffed Mark, 'these stairs'll be the death of me, I swear.'

'Oh, I'll be fine from here,' I said. 'Don't worry about me.'

'I wasn't. I promised Fred I'd pick him up when you arrived. He's brought in some old newspaper cuttings to show me. We thought you'd appreciate a few minutes on your own with Mrs W.'

'How considerate.'

'Here we are.' Mark tapped on the library doors. 'Hello? Anybody in? Are you decent?' He turned and winked at me.

I pretended not to notice. 'I think they said to go in.'

Mrs Wilkinson was sitting in an armchair, silken hair framing her beaming face, a bottle green trouser suit enveloping her frail body.

Fred stood up, still chortling at some private joke. He took Mrs Wilkinson's hands in his and kissed them. 'I shall see you very soon, my dear. You must tell me all about Trebetherick.' He turned towards me and Mark. 'So, you'll be wanting to see my photographs then? And you, young lady, don't you go keeping my Margaret nattering for too long, will you?'

So now I was on a time limit. Great. The doors swung shut behind me as the men headed off downstairs.

Mrs Wilkinson gestured towards Fred's empty chair. 'Sit, Jasmine, sit. You heard the man. Time is of the essence.'

I sat down. Where should I start? Should I tell her about the goat and the hamster, the bisected worms and the flattened cat? Was it worth mentioning my plagiarism or was it better to spend our few minutes talking about the next tasks and the most sensible course of action?

'He is wonderful, don't you think?' asked Mrs Wilkinson.

'Sorry? Who is?'

'Freddie. What a fascinating man. I noticed him straight away, you know. He always stood out from the crowd. A girl would never approach a young man in those days though, not a nice girl anyway.'

'I see. Yes, he's very pleasant.'

'Oh, he is, Jasmine. A deep thinker and incredibly intuitive. I'm sure he knows what I'm about to say before I do sometimes.' She was gazing into space beyond my armchair.

'Lovely. Listen, I think I know what I'm going to look at next.'

Mrs Wilkinson shifted her attention back to me. 'Look at?'

'My amends. I was talking to an old friend, well, not exactly a friend... But anyhow, she made me realise that there's something I've been avoiding. I know you've picked up on it before and—'

'Jasmine, whatever it is, I'm sure you'll manage admirably. You're a very capable girl.' Her eyes flitted away from me for a second as she checked her watch.

'Yes, I know. It's just, I'm not sure how to approach this next one. I mean, everyone keeps on about honesty—'

'Its importance can't be overestimated, Jasmine. We all need to face our own truths. If only Freddie had been true to himself all those years ago... Well, who knows? Honesty and bravery – our happiness depends on them, I'm certain.'

'That's what I've been realising,' I said. 'I have to tell the truth.' I meant it; I would tell Arnaud the whole and absolute truth. And then I would tell Dan. I just needed to know what she thought was the best way: letter, email, phone call? She knew the rules better than I did. I wasn't asking for help, but with all her experience, a little advice would surely be useful. 'Mrs Wilkinson?'

She'd started humming a little tune. It was shaky, but sounded like Frank Sinatra's *You Make Me Feel So Young*.

'Mrs Wilkinson – my amends?'

'Sorry. Yes. Good,' she nodded. 'You're doing well. It sounds like you don't need my input then if you've already decided what to do next.'

'Well, I haven't exactly—'

There was a knock at the door.

'Aha! Right on time,' said Mrs Wilkinson. He's showing us a rhumba this afternoon, you know.'

'Super. Can I just ask—'

'I'm afraid I can't keep Freddie waiting,' she laughed. 'Says he's missed out on quite enough without me keeping him hanging around any longer.' She pushed herself up out of her chair.

'I was only going to ask—'

'Stop worrying, child. I've told you, I have every faith in you.'

She hobbled over to the doors. I couldn't imagine her dancing.

As she reached the doorway she turned back to say goodbye. 'Whatever you do, you can tell me all about it next weekend,' she smiled. 'And just remember – honesty and bravery, Jasmine. Honesty and bravery.'

Honesty I was ready for. I could put it in a letter, write it all down. It would be like telling a story. Was it really my own story? It was so far away, so long ago. I could distance myself from it like that. It would be easy. But where was the bravery in that? Writing my truth in the sanctuary of my own home. Sending a letter to intrude into the life of a man I no longer knew. And how long would I be waiting for a response before realising that I might never get one, that this might never be finished? No, if I was going to do this, I would do it properly. I would face my demons squarely, confess my sins and accept the consequences. I would go to France and find Arnaud. I would tell him I was sorry and tell him everything I'd done.

seventeen

I opened my window as the taxi pulled out from Perpignan airport to begin the four kilometre journey into town. The air felt warm against my face, despite the haze which veiled the morning sun in the sky. I'd been lucky to find a last minute flight from Birmingham, even if it *had* meant having to wake up so early.

The last time I'd made this trip it had taken us twenty four hours, taking turns at driving while the others rested, all of us too excited to sleep as we headed through the brand new channel tunnel and southwards across the whole of France. The five of us had agreed to keep contact to a minimum outside classes at the university and our work experience placements. We'd come here to improve our French, so mixing with other English-speakers would have defeated the object of our stay.

I watched the shops and houses stream past as we drove through unfamiliar streets. Would I recognise anything I'd known back then or would everything have changed? We waited at a busy junction for the lights to change, then turned left into Avenue de la Liberté.

'Arrêtez!' I shouted at the driver. 'Arrêtez, s'il vous plaît!' That was the canal we used to walk along, I was sure.

The driver pulled over. 'Madame?'

'Je veux, euh... I want to get out. Merci.'

He surveyed me in his mirror. 'Madame, ees a long way to 'otel. Ees near citadel, non?'

'Yes, oui. Don't worry, I can walk. If you could get me my case.'

'Please, more slowly, Madame.'

'My case. Um, ma valise, s'il vous plaît.'

The driver shrugged and turned off the engine. I pulled some notes from my purse. They hadn't had Euros the last time I was here. I thanked the driver as he extended the handle of my new pink suitcase and handed it to me. I'd packed the minimum for my two night stay, so the walk along the canal wouldn't be too strenuous. I set off across the grassy bank away from the traffic and towards the shimmering water.

I loved the smell of this place. I didn't know what it was exactly – the cypresses and eucalyptus, the faint aroma of croissants and coffee, a hint of sea spray or mountain zephyr mingling with the city breeze. I closed my eyes and inhaled, filling my lungs with the air I hadn't breathed for fourteen years. The air of Perpignan, the scent of France.

I lifted my case to lug it down the shallow steps which led to the canal-side path.

'Madame!' a voice called behind me.

I turned to see the taxi driver waving both arms above his head. He stopped when he realised he'd caught my attention, and gestured in the opposite direction to the one I was heading in.

'Madame,' he repeated, 'the centre of the town, the 'otel, ees that way!'

After half an hour I found a bench and sat down to look at my map and eat my apple. Each place name on the map brought back different memories of my time here with Arnaud and the hours we'd spent meandering through Perpignan's narrow streets, hand in hand. How struck I'd been by the magnificence of the

Cathédrale St-Jean, constructed with a million river pebbles and topped with red slate. How stunning I'd found the red brick Castillet and Le Palais des Rois de Majorque which crowned the hill dominating the southern part of the old town. Arnaud delighted and inspired me with his enthusiasm and his love of history. As we explored shops and cafés in the maze of lanes in the Arab and Romany quarters of town he would recount stories of Majorcan Kings and Cathar crusades. How could I help falling in love with such a beautiful and fascinating place?

I folded up my map and pushed it into my pocket. If I dropped my bags at the hotel I could spend the day revisiting old haunts, strolling along tree-lined boulevards between elegant pink and turquoise houses, taking in the fine buildings with their gargoyles and balustrades. Maybe tomorrow I'd head out through Elne towards Argelès-sur-Mer. Or perhaps if this evening went well, Arnaud would take me out to our favourite spot at Canet-Plage.

I could picture him now, the way he captivated me when we first met. I'd just finished university for the day and had come to eat my lunch by the fountain in the park. I'd noticed him looking at me, of course. As I stood up to leave, he ran over to me and spoke.

'Excuse me, I couldn't let you go. You're English?'

A strange introduction, but something about him enthralled me.

'I'm English, yes. How can you tell?'

He pointed at the book in my hand – Sartre's *Being and Nothingness*. 'You should be reading this in French.'

I laughed. 'He's opaque enough even in my own language.'

'I'm sorry?'

'It doesn't matter. Look, I really should go.'

He took no notice. 'So, you are a philosopher? I knew I would like you.'

I stepped back to look at him properly. He was tall and slender, the blackness of his long pony tail accentuated by his white linen tunic. I imagined him as heir to an ancient Moorish throne.

'I do like the existentialists,' I said, 'but I'm more of a language student than a philosopher these days.'

'No, you are a philosopher. It is in your eyes. You are a deep thinker. I see into your soul.'

My cheeks grew hot, but I couldn't look away. I hadn't met this man before, I couldn't have, but somehow I felt I knew him. Maybe he *could* see into my soul. I shut my eyes and shook my head. I was being stupid – too much sun and too little contact with home. I didn't want to appear rude, but I really had to get away. I opened my eyes. 'Well, it was nice to meet you.'

He nodded. 'You believe in reincarnation?'

'Not really, no.'

'I think that sometimes, when two people meet in this world, they have already been together in another life. They know each other already.'

I stared at him for a moment. 'I'm... I'm going.' I turned to leave but instantly regretted my decision.

'Perfect,' he replied, keeping up with me. 'Then I shall go with you. Beginning with the finest of bookshops, I shall show you every corner of this town. Welcome to the magical capital city of French Catalonia.'

When I finally dumped my case in the tiny room at the Hôtel de la Loge, I could see why the taxi driver had questioned my decision to walk. I was tempted to lie down for a while, but the solid bed with its unyielding bolster reaffirmed my resolve to see as much of the town as possible before my rendezvous tonight. Would Arnaud even turn up? Prudence rather than cowardice had led me to ring after closing time to leave a message at his bookshop. If we'd spoken on the phone, he was bound to demand an explanation. I wanted to have this conversation face to face, not at a distance of seven hundred miles with an ocean between us. If he didn't appear, I still had tomorrow to find him, so unless he was away for the week… No, he'd come, I knew it.

I left my key at reception and headed for the museum in the Place de Verdun. If I could find a decent food shop I'd buy something to eat in the park afterwards. Just some fruit maybe, and a fresh baguette.

I thought of those lazy mornings with Arnaud, the hours spent in his tiny room overlooking the square. While I showered, Arnaud would fetch breakfast from the bakery opposite – warm ficelles straight from the oven, topped with avocado and black olives or a simple tomato and pepper sauce. In the evenings, while I studied, he reinvented Moroccan and Catalan specialities to include all our favourite ingredients and cater for my awkward diet. Roasted vegetable and couscous tagine, spiced aubergine moussaka with dates and almonds, sautéed polenta with butter beans and spinach… He *had* looked after me well.

I stopped when I reached another crossroads. Was it straight on again here or right? I looked around for signposts, and seeing none, settled for a right turn. I rounded the corner and there it was – the Cinéma Étoile. Arnaud had taken me there a week after we'd met; Gazon Maudit was showing and he'd been desperate to introduce me to the exceptional Victoria Abril. Afterwards, he'd taken my hand as we spilled out of the cinema into the cool March night. When we reached the bench at the end of the street I stopped and faced him.

'You do know we're just friends, don't you, Arnaud?'

His smile was luminous, his dark eyes shone. He took my other hand in his. 'Of course we're friends, Jasmine. What else?'

I gazed up at him – his haughty posture, his fine cheekbones, his soft lips.

He gently let go of my hands and smoothed the hair back from my face. 'Did I tell you,' he said, as he began to kiss me, 'that you are very beautiful?'

I found the museum, but didn't stay for long. Everything I looked at, everywhere I went, Arnaud's ghost was with me, guiding me, teaching me, laughing with me. As I walked through the park he teetered around the stone rim of the fountain, then picked me a single yellow rose. As I sat drinking coffee outside Le Chat Noir his shadow watched the passers-by with me, speculating as to their prospects in health and happiness and love.

It was a relief to get back to the hotel. I could be on my own there and prepare myself for the evening ahead. Oh, Arnaud, I hadn't meant to leave like that. At least now I could explain. I never meant to hurt you. Never. But what else could I do?

At six o'clock I left the hotel and set out for the restaurant. Judging by their website, Le Dauphin looked like my best bet for a decent meal. It seemed that even France catered pretty well for vegetarians now, so I was hopeful for something more imaginative than pommes frites and bread.

The walk didn't take long and I arrived at Le Dauphin with quarter of an hour to spare. I gave my name to the woman at the reception desk and settled on one of the sofas in the window. The street outside was filled with people making their way home from work or coming back out for an evening with friends or lovers. I watched them hurrying along on their own or sauntering across the cobbles in groups and in pairs, arm in arm or hand in hand.

That had been us once. What would he look like now? Would his hair still be long? Would his features have softened with time or grown more refined? Would people still watch him as he passed, wondering who he could be to walk with such self-assurance and grace? He'd always refused to speak French with me. His was far too diluted with Catalan, he'd said, and he'd only teach me bad habits. So unless I wanted to learn Arabic we'd have to stick to English. I was glad he'd opened his bookshop. Apart from making him easy to trace, it meant he'd followed his dream. I hoped it had made him happy. I hoped it had been everything he'd wished for.

To my left, somebody coughed. 'Excuse me,' said a low voice.

I turned to see a balding man with a slight stoop and tiny glasses balanced on his long thin nose. He appeared overdressed for a waiter, but suitably morose.

I smiled. 'I'm fine, thanks. I'm just waiting for a friend.' I checked my watch. Twenty five past. He shouldn't be long.

The man didn't move. Behind the glasses, his narrow eyes looked hollow and black. There were traces of wrinkles on his face, but no laughter lines. The hair he had left was streaked with greys and whites like a badger's. Perhaps it made him look older than he was.

'You don't recognise me.'

I glanced out of the window. He'd be here any minute. 'I'm sorry. I think you've got the wrong—'

'I recognised you straight away, Jasmine.'

I looked up at him again. He took off his glasses and slid them into his top pocket. The high cheekbones, the long limbs – those were the same, but everything else...

'You've scarcely changed, Jasmine. You look beautiful.'

I stood up and kissed him on both cheeks. 'And you, Arnaud...'

'Don't tell me I've not changed,' he said, with melancholy in his voice. 'I know how much I have.'

My heart was pounding and my legs shook. Could this really be him? 'Shall we see if our table's ready?'

'Let's just sit a while,' he replied, and we sat down on the sofa.

He stared out through the glass, and I searched his profile for something familiar – some vitality, some spark that could link this stranger with the Arnaud I had known. I followed his gaze to the pavement opposite, where a young couple had stopped to embrace.

'Why did you leave?' he asked.

I'd prepared myself for this. So why was I so scared? 'I'm sorry, Arnaud. I didn't mean to hurt you. I had no choice.'

'We always have a choice, Jasmine. And you did hurt me. I loved you. You knew I loved you.'

I was glad he wasn't looking at me. 'Arnaud, we were only together a short while, and we were—'

'Four months, Jasmine. It was four months. That's sufficient to know when something is right.' He turned to face me, his chin high, waiting for my response.

I saw it now, his old passion, his old poise. I'd loved him too. 'But we were both—'

'Don't tell me that we were too young. Don't you dare tell me this. I was twenty two, Jasmine. I knew what I wanted. I *had* what I wanted.'

'But you didn't, Arnaud. Not really.'

'I tried to find you after you left. I wrote to the university.'

'I know.'

'I kept hoping that you would return. That you would miss me as I missed you and come back. Were you afraid, Jasmine? Were you frightened of the intensity between us? Is that why you left?'

'No. No, it's not.'

'Because *I* was afraid. But I have never been more alive. Not before and not since.'

'Arnaud, I—'

'Just tell me this one thing. What we had… Have you *ever* felt the same way with anyone else? Tell me honestly.'

I thought of Dan. Then I thought of Ruben. Maybe in the beginning… Maybe it could have been… But it was too late now. I shook my head. 'No, Arnaud. It's never been the same.'

'So why did you go? It makes no sense to me. Why did you disappear?'

I took a deep breath. This was what I'd come to tell him. 'I'm sorry, Arnaud. I'm so sorry. I was pregnant.'

He leant forwards, head in hands, elbows propped on bony knees. His palms pushed against his temples as if trying to contain his thoughts.

'Arnaud?'

His voice was barely audible. 'There was a baby? There was… there was a child?'

I swallowed. 'No. There was no child.'

He raised his head and turned towards me, his forehead lined. 'I don't understand.'

I took another deep breath. I'd never told anyone before. Not ever. 'I was pregnant, Arnaud, but there was no child. I didn't have our baby. I couldn't.'

His dark eyes fixed on mine. Was he hoping to look into my

soul again, to find a place where what I'd told him wasn't true?

'No, Jasmine! No, that can't be!'

'I'm sorry, Arnaud.'

'But how did it…? When could it—?'

'That night in Collioure. It must have been.'

He shut his eyes, bowed his head and let out a long sigh.

Collioure. How I'd loved that place with its seafront palms and mountainous backdrop. Leaving Arnaud's scooter in a cobbled street near the beach, we would wander through galleries and bays, revelling in the sun-drenched iridescence that had so captivated Matisse and Derain. The blueness of Heaven and the sea seemed to hang in the air itself. Pastel-hued houses echoed a time when sailors would paint their boats then use what was left to decorate their homes.

'If God had really created the world,' I used to tell Arnaud, 'he would have made it all like Collioure.'

I looked up to see a waiter standing beside Arnaud.

'Is everything OK, Monsieur, Madame? Your table is ready.'

Arnaud opened his watery eyes but didn't speak.

'We're fine,' I replied. 'If you could just give us a few minutes?'

The waiter nodded and slipped away. Arnaud was looking into the distance, shaking his head.

'Arnaud, are you… Are you all right?'

'That night at Collioure…' he began.

'Yes?'

'I took you to the fortress and we ate our picnic in the vineyard on the hill.'

'Yes, I remember.'

'We bought wine and carried it down to the beach below the church.'

'Yes.'

'I told you the whole history of Notre Dame des Anges, its bell tower, its prisoners, the lighthouse. You remember the little stone carvings inside? Of anchovies. You laughed at that.'

'Arnaud, why—?'

'And the sun went down and I said I should take you home. But you didn't want to go home. You told me you would stay there with me forever if you could.'

'Arnaud, please…'

'And now you say we made a child that night? You could have stayed forever, Jasmine. I would have been so happy. I would have done anything. It could have been perfect.'

'No, Arnaud. It couldn't have been perfect. It wasn't real, don't you see? It was a dream. We were in our beautiful little bubble for a while but it had to end. I had to go. I *had* to.' I was shaking again now. My nails were digging into my palms.

'But *why*, Jasmine? I know you hadn't planned to stay, but plans can change. This is life. You say you *couldn't* stay, you *couldn't* keep our baby. But *why*?'

'Because… I'm sorry, Arnaud. Because I was engaged.'

He screwed his eyes shut and covered his face with his hands. Slowly he began to rock back and forth. The waiter approached but I gestured for him to leave us alone.

'Arnaud,' I whispered, 'people are staring.'

He stopped rocking and opened his eyes. Without looking at me he stood up, turned his back on me and walked away. I watched as the door slammed shut behind him and he ran out into the bustling street.

'Would Madame care to be shown to her table now?' The waiter stood calmly at my shoulder, a menu in his hand.

'No,' I snapped, heading for the door. 'Madame couldn't give a toss about her table.'

Arnaud had reached the other side of the square by the time I caught up with him. He'd stopped to catch his breath and was leaning against the wall of the old library. I wanted to explain, to make it better.

'Arnaud, I didn't mean for it all to happen. I tried to tell you we could only be friends.'

'You didn't try very hard, Jasmine.'

I knew he was right. 'I didn't mean to fall in love.'

He laughed. 'So you admit you loved me.'

'You know I did. But it wouldn't have worked. I had my life in England. I had a home; I had my family; I had plans.'

'Oh and I got in the way. Like our baby. It must have been easy for you to leave then, and easy to get rid of it.'

I remembered sobbing as my coach left Perpignan. I thought of the cold grey corridors of the clinic, the blank eyes of the girls and women there, each of us alone, each facing the horror of having a part of ourselves destroyed forever.

'It wasn't easy, Arnaud. It wasn't easy at all.'

He looked at me as I wiped a tear from my chin. His face softened. 'Oh, my poor Jasmine.'

Perhaps we still had a connection. Maybe if we could sit and talk properly he'd be able to understand. But then his expression changed. What I'd taken to be a smile became a sneer.

'Poor little Jasmine,' he spat. 'She kills my baby and is surprised when it hurts.'

'It wasn't like that.'

'So why come and tell me now? And this husband of yours, does he know you have come?'

'We're divorced.'

'Of course! It makes sense! So you come here to ask me back?'

'Don't be ridiculous.'

He winced. 'Ridiculous is it?' He ran a hand over his thinning hair. 'Yes, perhaps you are right. It would be ridiculous.'

'Arnaud, I didn't mean it like that. Look, I came here to say I'm sorry, that's all.' How could I mention my amends? How could I tell him that this was part of something I'd started as a challenge, a fun way to make myself feel better about my past?

'So what do you want from me?'

I shrugged. 'Nothing. I don't want anything.'

'You would like my forgiveness.'

I looked into his eyes. This man had taught me so much about humanity, about living, about love.

'Yes,' I said. 'You're right. I'll always regret what I did. But if you could forgive me—'

'Well, I can't. You broke my heart when you ran away and now you come back and tell me you killed my child and you break my heart again. Some things can never be forgiven, Jasmine. Never.'

'Arnaud, please—'

'Stop. I don't want to hear any more. When I first spoke with you, Jasmine, I thought I could see into your very soul. I thought you were a good person. I thought I knew you. But I was wrong. I see now that I *never* knew you. You did not deserve my love. But our baby deserved love. And look what you did to it! Jasmine, I hope you find peace, but if it is forgiveness you search for, you will not find it here.'

'*You did know me!*' I wanted to shout. '*I sometimes thought you knew me better than I knew myself. And I am a good person, but there was no other way out. I longed to stay, to keep our baby and do all those things we talked about. But I had another life too. I'd made promises. People were counting on me. Don't you see?'* I wanted him to hold me. I wanted him to tell me he forgave me and that everything would be all right.

Instead we stood in silence, what bound us forever together tearing us both apart.

He shook his head. 'I pity you,' he said, 'and I wish we had never met.'

He turned away, and I watched as he trudged across the square, hands in pockets, hunched over as if against the cold. He paused by the fountain on the corner, and for a moment I thought he might turn back. Had he realised he'd been too harsh? Had he remembered all there'd been between us and found that he *could* forgive me after all? The bells of the church clock began to chime. I checked my watch. Seven o'clock. We'd barely been together for half an hour. I looked back to the corner where he stood. A taxi stopped and Arnaud climbed in. He pulled the door shut behind him, and in a second he was gone.

eighteen

I didn't make the return journeys to Argelès or Canet Plage, and as my plane slid into the clouds and France disappeared below me, I knew I never would. Perhaps I'd been expecting too much of Arnaud. Maybe if I just gave him some time… No, there was nothing I could do. All I could hope for was that Dan would show more acceptance, more understanding. We'd been together for so many years and been through so much. We knew each other in a different way. We'd been partners, best friends. Yes, Dan would understand. And even though Arnaud never could, if Dan would only forgive me… But I didn't want to think about that now. I wanted to sleep. I wanted to get home and I wanted to talk to Mrs Wilkinson and ask her how it could all have gone so wrong.

As I lay in my own bed that night I thought about Arnaud – the Arnaud I'd once known so well and the stranger I'd just left. Did he have someone to go back to, someone to comfort him? I'd never asked. I thought of Ruben. He'd be in Madrid now, making connections, making plans. He was getting ready for a new beginning, a fresh start. I didn't blame him. I thought about Dan and how he'd taken care of me after my sudden return from France all those years ago. Exhaustion, I'd told him. Being on my own in a foreign country, the language barrier, the prospect of a whole year of teacher training ahead, I explained, it had all got on top of me.

An image of Dan's face drifted into my mind. For hours he'd sat at the end of my bed as I hid from the world, bringing me books to read and application forms for easy jobs in local schools.

'I don't want to get up, Dan,' I'd tell him. 'I don't want to go anywhere and I don't want to do anything.'

He would smile and stroke my hair. 'You're just tired, Jasmine. It'll pass. I want you better for our wedding day, you know. We'll make a great team, you and me.'

As sleep approached, three sinister figures seemed to float by my bedside. They scowled as they looked on, shaking their heads.

'She murdered my baby.'

'She didn't deserve another one.'

'She deserves to be alone.'

The shadows merged and leant over me where I lay. A suffocating weight pushed down on my chest, and before blackness came I heard their three voices speak as one; I heard what they all wanted me to know.

'We wish we'd never met you.'

I spent Saturday cleaning and tidying. The freezer needed defrosting, the kitchen cupboards were due for a clear out and I'd been neglecting the garden for long enough. My clematis and a few of the borders weren't in too bad a state, but why did everything have to grow so damn fast? Why couldn't things ever stay as they were? Filthy and too worn out for thought, I fell into bed that night and slept a dreamless sleep.

At three o'clock on Sunday I knocked on the library doors of Valley View. Fred had already scurried off to the visitors' lounge with Mark to give me and his beloved some privacy. So my trip to France had been a disaster. At least Mrs Wilkinson would appreciate the courage I'd shown. It made all the difference, knowing that somebody was on my side.

'You did *what*?' Mrs Wilkinson bellowed, her pink dress shaking with a rage that surprised me.

'Honesty and bravery, you said. I *had* to tell him. He needed to know the truth.'

'No, Jasmine. *You* needed him to know the truth. There's a difference.'

'But The Programme—'

'The Programme asks that you make amends wherever possible, except when to do so would harm yourself or others. *Or others*, Jasmine. What were you thinking?'

I bit my lip. 'I thought he might forgive me.'

She paused for a moment, then spoke more calmly. 'I presumed you had a better grasp on this process than is the case. Evidently I should have given you more guidance.'

'It's not your fault,' I said.

'I *know* it's not my fault,' she barked.

I didn't know what to say.

'I'm sorry, Jasmine, I'm not feeling my best today.'

'Shall I come back another time?' I suggested. I'd so wanted to come here but now I'd be quite happy to leave.

'No. I'll be fine. This is important. What you must realise, Jasmine, is that this isn't all about you. Other people have feelings too.'

Did she think I didn't know that? Couldn't she see how hard it had been for me to leave Arnaud in so much pain? I said nothing.

'We can't separate our past from our present or our future. It's no good attempting to put right something from our past if it causes more suffering now. We have to look at life as a whole, you see. Not just our own lives but other people's. Sometimes, if we're fortunate, making amends will bring about healing and love. But sometimes the truth will only bring misery and suffering.'

'And what about honesty? I thought that was what was most important?'

'Nothing is more important than compassion, Jasmine. Compassion and love. Not even the truth.'

'But he *might* have forgiven me. It *might* have worked out.'

'Worked out for whom, Jasmine? Did you really go to France thinking you were doing the best thing for *him*? Or were you thinking of yourself?'

That was unfair. 'It was his baby. He had a right to know.'

'At the time, yes. But you chose to keep that from him. How could you ever have thought that telling him after all this time would help him?'

I didn't know. I just remembered how she'd spoken about honesty and bravery. And I remembered what Sophie had said about people being too scared to face their demons. I hadn't wanted to give up on this. I didn't want it to be one more thing I'd never managed to complete. I wished it had gone differently in France, but there was nothing I could do about it now. I had to look forwards. Perhaps I shouldn't have told Arnaud everything, but with Dan it would be different. I *had* to tell him. He'd never suspected a thing, but it had coloured our whole lives together. If only I could explain it all properly, he'd see why it had always felt like there was something missing. He'd understand why I'd refused the tests and why I'd never bothered to reapply for teacher training.

'Jasmine! You mustn't tell him! Have you not heard a word of what I've been saying?' Mrs Wilkinson looked outraged.

I didn't need this. I wasn't ten years old any more. 'I have. Of course I have. But you don't know Dan like I do. I know how he'll react.'

'Like you did with Arnaud?'

She wasn't going to get it. There was no point in arguing. 'Dan was my husband and he ought to know the truth. I'll even tell him with compassion if you like.'

She ignored the tone of my last remark. 'Jasmine, I know you well enough to realise when to leave you to make your own decision. All I can hope for is that when the time comes you will do what you know to be right. And please keep in mind what I've said. Whatever choices we make in this life, whichever path we take, we must do so with compassion and love. Always.'

The week at work dragged by. I'd mentally prepared myself for my confession to Dan but wanted to wait until the weekend in case of any unpleasant emotional aftermath. On Tuesday, Toby Stone reminded me about the French Club's postponed assembly. We limped through our presentation on pop music from the nineteen seventies to the present day. French culture was the last thing I wanted to think about right now.

On Saturday morning I stuffed Dan's mildew-covered hold-all into the boot of my car. If he hadn't missed these last few odds and ends by now, I doubted he ever would, but it had given me a plausible excuse to arrange a visit. It had been months since I'd last seen Dan. He'd popped in on his way past some time in the New Year to pick up his post. Penny bumped into him now and then in Sainsbury's and always said he looked happy and well. Penny was usually a most reliable informant, but that didn't sound at all like Dan to me.

It wasn't far to his flat. We did well at never seeing each other, considering. I pulled up outside the building and switched off the engine. How much should I tell him about France? Should I pretend that what had happened with Arnaud had been an accident, a one off? Or should I tell him everything? That despite what I felt and despite what my heart was yearning for, I came back to him, I came back and married him because I'd promised that I would. I opened the car door. I knew what I had to say. I'd come to tell the whole truth and nothing less would do.

I climbed the stairs to the second floor and rang the bell.

'Won't be a sec,' called Dan from somewhere inside. 'Sorry,' he said, as he opened the door. 'Just sorting out the spare room.' He peered at the ground by my feet as if he was expecting to see something.

'Dan, what are you doing?'

'I thought you were bringing my tools.'

'Ah, yes. They're in the car. But I wanted to speak to you anyway. Can I come in?'

'Yeah, of course. Sorry.'

I followed him into the hallway.

'It's a complete tip, I'm afraid. We're in the middle of decorating.'

'Oh yes, and how is, um…'

'Ravindra. She's very well. She's only popped to the retail park to buy some more paint. Shall I put the kettle on?'

'No, no. I won't stay long. It's just—'

'Come and sit down at least.' Dan led me into an almost bare room. 'Hang on, let me move those for you.' He pushed a pile of dustsheets off a wicker chair for me and perched himself on a wooden footstool.

I looked around the room and back out along the hall. 'You've got your work cut out for you here.'

'I know. It's almost as bad as *our* house was when *we* moved in. Remember that wallpaper in the bathroom?'

'Oh, don't!' I said. 'That was hideous. What about the wiring though? You were lucky you weren't electrocuted.'

'*I* was lucky? You were the one who was meant to turn the supply off.'

He was laughing at the memory. Penny was right – he did seem happier now. I laughed with him. There was no point making an issue out of it now but the electricity thing had definitely been *his* fault.

'So,' he said, still smiling, 'what was it you wanted to talk about? If it's about my stuff in the attic, I can fetch it whenever suits you. I didn't want to... you know... intrude.'

'No, it's nothing like that. It was about you and me, and about moving forwards.'

'Great. Yes, we've been talking about that too. Listen, I'm going to stick the kettle on. I'm parched. I'll be back up my stepladder as soon as you've gone.'

He darted off into the kitchen and I heard the clattering of crockery and the banging of cupboard doors.

'Got some digestives here. Ah, but they've got milk powder in. Fancy a banana?'

'No thanks.'

'I think we've got some Earl Grey. Oh no, no soya milk. Chamomile?'

'Yes, OK. Whatever.' I didn't want a drink. I wanted to get this over with. I sat and waited in the empty room while Dan made our tea. The walls and ceiling needed a lick of paint but apart from that it didn't look too bad.

Our house really had been a dump when we'd bought it, but we'd both seen its potential. And it was so exciting to be able to call something our own after renting that dismal flat. Dan had been happy for me to take things easy work-wise, especially while there was so much to be done on the house.

'Don't you get doing too much though,' he'd tell me. 'We can't have you making yourself ill again.'

He was right. We *had* made a good team.

'Milk's gone off anyway,' said Dan, passing me a mug. 'I've got flipping chamomile as well.'

'Thanks,' I said, and took a sip.

Dan scraped his stool across the floor and sat nearer to my chair. 'Bet I can guess why you've come,' he said.

I shook my head. Poor Dan. He wouldn't have a clue.

'It's about the baby, isn't it?'

Blood pounded in my ears. My arms grew numb and I felt sick.

'Christ, Jasmine. What the... Here, give me your drink.'

I felt the mug being taken from my hand. Then as my head dropped back against the cushion of my chair, I felt my feet being gently lifted and laid down again on something hard. I sat with my eyes closed, the chair swaying beneath me. How could he have known? Had somebody seen me at the clinic? I'd thought we'd simply grown bored of each other but maybe he'd hated me all along for what I'd done.

Gradually the giddiness subsided and I opened my eyes.

'Bloody hell, Jasmine. I thought you'd fainted. Are you all right?'

'I think so.'

Dan was standing next to me, the footstool he'd been sitting on now propping up my feet, a blanket draped over my legs. His face was white. 'God, you gave me a fright.'

'Sorry,' I said. 'It's just... You mentioned the baby. It was a bit of a shock.'

'Jesus, Jaz, I'm sorry. I thought you knew. I thought your mum would have told you.'

I stared at him. 'Told me what?'

'About Ravindra being pregnant. My mum phoned yours a few weeks ago.'

I remembered Mum's letter: *I presume you've heard Dan's news...* She'd been supposed to tell me.

'We weren't sure how to break it to you. I was worried you'd be... you know...'

I couldn't speak.

'God, Jaz. Sorry. I should have told you earlier. But I wasn't sure how you'd react. Because the whole baby thing was always so... sensitive.'

'You're having a baby?'

'I know. Weird, isn't it? I mean I told Ravindra I probably couldn't. I was convinced it was me. But there you go.'

'Well... Congratulations.'

'Thanks. Means we're in a mad rush to get this place finished though. Are you sure you're OK?'

'Yes. I'm fine. It's just... A baby. Wow.'

'I know.'

I lowered my feet to the floor so that Dan could have his stool back.

He passed me my tea and sat down. 'I thought that's why you'd come round, because of the baby.'

'How do you mean?'

'I thought you might be worried about my share in the house.

Like I was suddenly going to want all the money you owe me.'

'Oh, right.'

'But I don't, it's not a problem. We had the cash from Rav's apartment so there's no hurry.'

'Thanks.'

'Actually, Jaz. There's something we wanted to ask you. It was Rav's idea. You know I said we'd been talking? About moving forwards?'

I nodded.

'Well, I realise it's rather early, but she suggested that we ask you to be godmother.'

This *had* to be a joke. 'Dan, I'm an atheist. And so are you. And isn't Ravindra a Buddhist or something?'

He frowned. 'She was brought up as a Hare Krishna.'

'Surely they have their own kind of ceremony? With incense and chanting and stuff?'

'Probably, but she doesn't call herself a Hare Krishna any more.'

'Then what's with all this church business?'

'Well, I'm not fussed either way, but Ravindra's agnostic and she's determined to get the baby christened. Just in case.'

'Dan, I've never heard anything so barmy.'

'What? You mean the christening or you being godmother?'

'Either. Both. Why me?'

'Ravindra thought it would be, you know, symbolic. Putting the past behind us. But acknowledging what has been. I don't know.'

'But why choose an atheist?'

'Well, like I said, she's hardly religious. It's more about moral guidance, I think. I guess she's been impressed when I've told her about your ethics and whatever.'

'My ethics?'

'Oh, you know, how you'll go out of your way to do the right thing. Make life bloody awkward for yourself so that you can stay on the moral high ground. I mean that in a nice way.'

'Of course.'

'Anyway, maybe you could think about it. The godparent thing. We'd have a few. It's not like we'd leave our daughter's moral integrity completely in your hands.'

'You're having a girl?'

'Bugger. That was meant to be a secret. Don't let Ravindra know I let it slip, will you?'

I didn't imagine I'd see her. 'No,' I said. 'Your secret's safe with me.'

'Thanks. So, can I tell Rav you'll think about it? She'd be so chuffed. We both would.'

It was a ludicrous idea, but what the hell. 'Go on then,' I said. 'Why not?'

'Great. What was it *you* wanted to talk about then?'

It would hurt him less now. He had his baby and he had his new life. What I'd done would still be hard for him to face, but he'd get over it, and he did deserve to know the truth.

'Dan, I'm glad you've told me about Ravindra and the baby—'

'It's a weight off my mind, Jaz. I was so worried about you.'

'I'm pleased you're moving on—'

'I know, and I'm serious about the christening. I know things all went a bit strange between us for a while, but it's really nice to see you again. And to talk normally without, you know, arguing. Like friends.'

The best of friends. What had happened? We grew apart. We got bored. Maybe it was nothing to do with the baby. Maybe it was nothing to do with France. But I still had to tell him. Because he was happy now. Everything was fine for him, so surely he'd forgive me and…

And then I realised why I was there. It wasn't for his sake at all, it was for mine. Mrs Wilkinson was right: what good would it do Dan now to know the truth?

'Jaz? Sorry, I'll shut up. I was getting all sentimental there for a minute. I'm convinced this baby's done something to my hormones.'

'I'm not sure it works like that,' I smiled.

'You still haven't told me what you were going to say.'

'Oh, it was nothing really. A few things I've been thinking about lately. But they needn't affect you. I'm sure I can deal with them on my own.' I handed Dan the blanket from my lap and stood up to leave.

'Independent as ever, eh? A fine trait, Jasmine. As long as it's not overdone.'

'And what's that supposed to mean?'

The smile left Dan's face. 'Nothing. Listen, let's not fall out now. Ignore me, OK?'

Dan as peacemaker? He really *had* changed. Could we be friends? There was so much about him that annoyed me. It would take some doing. And as for me being a godmother… Actually, I kind of liked the idea. Which moral philosopher's work would be best to give as a christening present? Mill perhaps, or Singer. Godmother… Friends… Yes, I could do that. Maybe.

nineteen

I was up early on Sunday. I couldn't wait to tell Mrs Wilkinson what I'd done. Or rather what I hadn't. It was as if everything she'd been telling me about making amends, everything I'd read and all that Sophie had told me, had been seeping into the outer layers of my consciousness. And yesterday, at Dan's, it had finally sunk in. I understood with heart and mind how this thing worked. Yes, honesty was crucial, but *I* was the one who needed to face the truth. And if forgiveness came from others, well, that was grand, but if I hoped to come to terms with my own past, the only person's forgiveness that would help me was my own.

At noon I took a plate of sandwiches out into the garden and sat under the apple tree. Cowslips and cornflowers clustered around my untamed lawn edges, nasturtiums spilled from the disused vegetable patch, and foxgloves and aquilegia towered above overgrown flowerbeds. I should start coming out here after school. I used to love my gardening hour, my quiet time before Dan got in from work. It wouldn't take much to get this garden back into shape. I thought of Ruben's garden with its dappled shade by the stream. I remembered our languid Easter morning outside, the nights he'd taken me down to the woods to listen for foxes and owls. He'd be back by now, back to make arrangements, to finish what needed finishing before he left for good.

I carried my plate back into the kitchen. It was fine that Ruben was going. That was just the way life worked. Things changed, people moved on. Surely I could do the same? There was plenty left on my lists to concentrate on, but I'd slow down now, take it easier. This wasn't some assignment I could dash off and scrape through. I wanted to do it properly. What was that word I'd scoffed at in the Benestrophe Pathway bumf? Mindfulness. I wanted to do it mindfully.

Mrs Wilkinson would be so proud. Jasmine Somers – star pupil. Had I been rude to her last week? Maybe a little. But she'd still trusted in me again. Had she known I'd make the right decision when it came to telling Dan? How pleased with me she would be.

I left the house shortly after two. I'd pick up some flowers for Mrs Wilkinson on the way, a sort of thank you for everything she'd done so far. The landline rang as soon as I'd pulled the door to. Probably Penny about tomorrow's maths session. I'd ring her when I got home.

I bought cream coloured roses at the garage. Not my flower of choice, but I knew Mrs Wilkinson would like them. Wouldn't it be funny if she was wearing cream today? She was like that woman in the poem who wanted to wear purple when she grew old. Except that the woman in the poem planned to wear a red hat too. Mrs Wilkinson would *never* do that.

As I pulled out from the forecourt into the stream of traffic, my mobile rang. Penny, no doubt. Oh well, I could hardly answer it now. I switched the stereo on. Louis Armstrong sang in gravelly depths about fields of green and skies of blue. He was right: it *was* a wonderful world. My phone rang again. I fished it out of my bag and switched it off.

Swinging into the driveway of Valley View, I passed an ambulance on its way out. Another broken ankle or fractured hip. As long as it wasn't Berny. Mrs Wilkinson wouldn't be impressed at losing her most formidable poker opponent on a Sunday afternoon. I parked my car and walked around to the back door. When nobody answered after a minute or two I decided to try the other entrance to the side of the fire-escape. I gave one last knock and turned away.

'Mrs Somers?' called a voice behind me.

'Mark, hi. I was about to give up on you.' I walked back to the doorway.

His eyes were bloodshot, his face pale.

'Are you all right?' I asked.

'You'd better come in.'

I followed him inside and along the corridor. We didn't turn off towards the staircase and the library, but carried on past sitting rooms and offices until we reached a door with a sign which read *Visitors' Lounge*.

Mark pushed open the door. 'Come and sit down,' he said.

We faced each other across a cheap pine table. I laid my roses down carefully between us.

'Mark, what's going on?'

'I'm sorry, Mrs Somers,' he said. 'I've been trying to phone you. It's Mrs W. I'm afraid she died in the night.'

I shook my head. 'I'm seeing her at three o'clock.'

'I'm sorry, love.'

'I've brought her some flowers.'

Mark nodded. 'Roses. Her favourites.'

'I don't know what to do. What shall I do with her flowers?'

'Don't worry about that now. I'm sure—'

There was a knock at the door and Mark got up to answer it. I heard a whispered exchange as my eyes tried to focus on the table.

Mark put a cup and saucer down in front of me. 'There you go,' he said. 'Sweet tea.'

I took a sip. 'It's cold in here,' I said, noticing my hands shaking.

'No, you're in shock. I'm sorry, I was hoping to catch you before you set out. I thought there might be someone there to look after you.'

'No. There's no one.'

We sat for a while. I didn't understand. She was supposed to be in the library. I was meant to be seeing her at three. 'What happened?' I asked.

'We're not exactly sure. It can be so quick sometimes, once it's taken hold. I think it became too much for her body to fight in the end.'

'What did?'

'The cancer. She was very brave.'

'Mrs Wilkinson had cancer?'

Mark's eyebrows knitted together. 'Are you telling me you didn't know?'

'Yes. No. I didn't.'

'So what on earth… What did you two talk about for so long every week?'

I looked down into my trembling lap. 'Me.'

According to Mark, she'd been diagnosed a few months ago, but it was already too advanced for them to operate. Chemotherapy might have slowed things down, but she rejected any treatment or intervention. Didn't want to be poked and prodded about by a bunch of young medics, she'd said. And besides, if her time was almost up, she was damn well going to make the most of it. From now on, she'd declared, she would do exactly as she pleased.

'But what about all the hours she spent with me?'

'Oh, she looked forward to your visits. Always insisted on looking her best, whatever kind of week she'd been having. I expect she liked having something else to think about.'

I should have been with her right now, yet here was Mark, talking about her in the past tense. He must be used to this. But it was wrong. It was all wrong. There were things I had to tell her, things I hadn't said. She couldn't be dead. She just couldn't be.

Mark reached over and rested a hand on my shoulder. 'It's all right, Mrs Somers. Don't mind me. You have a good cry.'

I don't know how long we'd been sitting together when there was another knock at the door. A white-haired old man came in and for a moment I couldn't think what he'd be doing there. Then I remembered.

'Fred, it's awful. Have you heard?'

He nodded. 'I was with her, Jasmine. It was very peaceful.' He smiled as his eyes rested on the bouquet I'd brought. 'Lovely,' he said.

What was there to smile about? How *could* he? 'I don't know how you can both be so... calm!'

Fred pulled up another chair and sat down between Mark and me. 'We knew it was coming, Jasmine. And the end wasn't so bad.'

'But she's gone. You'll never see her again. It's... it's too cruel.'

'None of us is immortal, Jasmine. One day our time will come too.'

'But don't you care?'

'Mrs Somers,' began Mark, rising to his feet.

Fred put up a hand to stop him. 'It's all right,' he said.

Mark sat back down.

Fred let out a long sigh, then turned to face me. 'These last few weeks I've had with Margaret – they've meant so much to me.'

I shook my head. What difference did *that* make?

'I gave up hope of seeing her again years ago. Decades. Each day I've had with her has been so precious. Of course I care, Jasmine. I care very much. But I feel blessed as well.'

'I'm sorry,' I said. 'I shouldn't have said that. It's just…' I pulled my hanky back out of my pocket.

Fred smiled. 'I know. We'll all miss her.'

I *would* miss her. And I hadn't told her about Dan and the baby and about me being godmother and about how I understood what making amends really meant now and how I was going to do my best to forgive myself and…

'Mrs Somers?'

I looked up. Mark was standing by the door, holding it open. 'I'm afraid I have to get back to work. You take your time. Stay here as long as you like. Are you sure there's nobody I can call for you?'

'No,' I sniffed. 'There's nobody.' I looked at Fred, who was cradling the roses, tracing their outline with one finger.

'She was a fine woman,' he said.

'Fred, was she… The last time we spoke… Do you think she was disappointed with me?'

He shook his head. 'Never. She thought an awful lot of you. You should have heard the way she talked about you. Sang your praises, she did. Strong-headed but soft-hearted, she called you. I think you reminded her very much of herself when she was young.'

'But I didn't tell her everything I wanted to.'

'That's the mistake I once made. I shan't do it again. It's never too late to learn.'

'I don't mean that. There's stuff that happened yesterday and... It doesn't matter.'

'You can tell me if you like. I'm a good listener too, remember?'

What a gracious man. Ready to help me even now. But he wouldn't understand what I was saying like Mrs Wilkinson would have. If only I could tell her that I *had* made the right decision. I hadn't told Dan anything. I'd done what she'd hoped for: when the time came I'd done what I knew was right.

'Fred, you're very kind. But it was her I wanted to tell. There's nobody else I could explain it to properly. It wouldn't be the same.'

'I know what you mean,' he said. 'She was a special lady, my Margaret.'

I stood up. I didn't want to be here any more, at Valley View, Mrs Wilkinson's home, with her no longer there. 'I've got to go,' I said. 'Will you be all right? Do you need a lift anywhere?'

'No. Thank you. I'll be fine. I'd like to stay here awhile. Talk to the others, go and sit outside, on the lawn. Here, your roses.'

'They're not mine, they're... You keep them, Fred. You look after them for her.'

I left him with his flowers and his thoughts, and drove slowly down the avenue of limes and out through the wrought iron gates for the last time. I should have asked where they'd taken her. I should have asked about the funeral. But there would be time for all that. I pressed the accelerator to the floor, opened my windows and let the air stream through. Right now, all I needed was to drive and drive. The only person I wanted to talk to was Mrs Wilkinson and she was the one who'd gone. There was nobody else in the world. No one.

I slammed my breaks on. A white transit van swerved out behind me and hurtled past, horn blaring. There *was* someone. Ruben. I needed to see Ruben. I turned the car around, dried my eyes, and headed for the main road. I didn't want to be like Fred. If Ruben was leaving, then there were things I ought to say. There were things I had to tell him, before we said goodbye.

twenty

It wasn't until I reached his village that I realised Ruben might not even be there. He'd been due back that morning, but there might have been delays, he could have decided to stay on in Madrid, he might have come home and gone out again. We'd never met up without arranging the whole thing in advance, not once.

I was halfway along Ruben's lane when his silver Jaguar flashed past in the opposite direction. Damn. What had possessed me to drive all this way without phoning ahead? I slowed down to a crawl. Now what? I couldn't go back to Valley View, and I certainly didn't want to go home. Maybe I could go over to Penny's for a while. I didn't mind what state she saw me in. I pulled into Ruben's drive and called Penny's mobile: no response. Then I tried the landline.

'Hi. You've reached Penny's answer phone. That probably means I'm at work or out with the dog. Leave me a message and I'll get back to you when I've cleaned the mud off.'

I dropped my phone onto the passenger seat. Where *was* everyone when I needed them? Of course – it was Sunday. Penny would be on her hot date at the garden centre with the new woman from her dog obedience class. Should I try Tash? No, she'd be watching the boys play rugby, or cooking Sunday dinner and attempting to save her marriage. Perhaps I'd have to go home after all.

I jumped as my car door swung open.

'Hey, Jasmine! A surprise visit – I like it!'

'Ruben. How did you… I just saw you heading for the village.'

'What? Oh, the Jag. Sold it. Liquidating my assets. Well, some of them.'

Of course. He could hardly take them with him. I got out of the car. 'Hello,' I said.

'Hello, you.' He hugged me tightly. 'Mmm, it's been a long time.'

'Two weeks.'

'I was going to call you later. Shouldn't you be at your old people's home gassing with Mrs Wilkinson? Jasmine?'

I locked my arms around his waist, leant my head against his shoulder, and cried and cried and cried.

I hadn't planned to tell him about Arnaud and the baby and Dan. But once I'd started, the words kept coming, tumbling and spilling out, and there was nothing I could do to stop them. He heard it all – how I'd stupidly let myself fall in love with Arnaud when my heart wasn't free to give, how the bleakness of the clinic had shadowed me through my marriage, how I'd never be able to let Mrs Wilkinson know I'd at least made one right choice.

At some point Ruben must have led me inside, but still he held me, rocking me gently, stroking my hair. For a moment I closed my eyes, and when I opened them the light seemed dimmer, the room cold.

'Ruben? What's happened?'

A shape moved beside me and I felt Ruben's warmth again. 'You fell asleep, Jaz. I thought I should let you rest.'

'What time is it? I need to get home. I've got work tomorrow.'

'You're staying here, Jasmine. I'll ring work for you and tell them you're in no fit state to go in.'

'But I—'

'Sorry, Jaz, but for once you're going to have to do as you're told.'

In the morning I awoke to the smell of fresh coffee and fried breakfast. I pulled the duvet up over my head until Ruben came in, humming the tune he'd just been listening to on the radio.

'Morning, Jasmine! How are you feeling today?'

My head was aching and my eyes were sore.

'I know you're awake,' he said. 'Look what I found – fake bacon from that health food shop in Cheltenham.'

I sat up.

Ruben handed me the tray. 'You're so easily manipulated, once you know how. The trick is to let you think you're in control.'

I smiled. 'If there wasn't a tray of food on my lap, I'd kick you off the bed.'

'I know. That's precisely why I gave it to you before I spoke. You see? I know exactly what I'm doing.' He sat down next to me.

I took a sip of coffee. 'You not eating?'

'I already did. About two hours ago. I've got a lot of sorting out to do.'

Of course. For Spain. 'Yes, you must have.'

'Xalvador gave me a letter from Izzy while I was over there.'

'Your daughter? Wow.'

'With a photo of her boys. Antonio and Orlando. Antonio looks just like my little Tomas.'

He reached down beside the bed for another pillow. 'Here,' he said, 'lean forward and I'll put this behind your back.'

'Ruben, I'm fine. Stop fussing.'

'Seriously, Jaz, how *are* you?'

'I'm OK, I think. Tired though. Drained. I'm sorry about last night.'

'Don't be silly. You have absolutely nothing to apologise for. Your past is an important part of you. I'm glad you opened up.'

'I shouldn't have. I'm not sure it was fair.' Maybe if he'd been staying… 'Really, Jaz, I'm flattered that you came all that way to tell me, that I'm the one you wanted to see.'

I rolled the fake bacon up and pushed it around the plate. 'Actually, that's not what I came to talk to you about.'

'You mean…' Ruben sat back and surveyed me. He swallowed. 'You mean there's more?'

I laughed. 'No, no. Don't panic. That's about as shocking as it gets.'

His shoulders dropped a little. 'So?'

I chewed on the bacon. It wasn't bad. 'Look, this probably isn't fair either, but I don't want to do what Fred did.'

'Fred?'

'I don't want to go through life feeling like there's stuff I should have said.'

'Go on.'

I took a deep breath. 'OK. I should have said this earlier but… I'm not great at, you know, talking emotions.'

Ruben waited.

'I told you I'd miss you if you went to Spain, and I really did. It was weird knowing you were so far away. Horrid.'

He took my hand.

'And I know it's too late now and it's all been agreed, but, well, I never really told you how much I, you know… care.'

'I know, Jasmine. I know exactly what you mean. That's why

I asked you to come with me.'

'But I can't. I don't want to leave what I have here. That hasn't changed. And I know it makes no difference now, I know it's far too late. I wouldn't want to stop you anyway, it's what you want to do, but...'

'What?'

I couldn't read his expression. I had no idea what he thought. 'It's been lovely, what we've had, Ru. Really lovely. And if I was going to be completely straight with you and upfront and... well... selfish, I'd tell you... I'd tell you that I didn't want you to go.' I put down my knife and fork. 'I don't want you to go to Spain, Ruben. I want you to stay here, with me.'

He nodded towards my breakfast. 'Are you going to eat that?'

'What? I don't know. I'm not that hungry, to be honest. Did you hear what I said?'

He lifted the tray from my lap and pushed it onto the bedside table. Then he slid under the duvet and snuggled up beside me. 'Of course I heard you.'

'Oh. Well, you don't have to say anything. I just wanted you to know.'

'I don't have to say anything?'

'No, Ruben.'

'So you don't want me to tell you about the deal I've been negotiating with Xalvador for the past fortnight?'

'I guess. If you like.'

'It's pure business, Jasmine. Won't interest you, I'm sure, but he's agreed to stay on very part time to help run the Madrid branch as a kind of satellite. I've gone through everything, looked at it all in detail, and so much more could be done virtually. The Spanish teams can mostly work from home. We'll save a fortune on office space, and the HQ can be elsewhere. That's where I come in.'

'So you'd be, what, in Barcelona?'

Ruben smiled. 'No, Jaz, I'd be right here.'

'What? But I thought... But you're selling the cars...'

'Well, there will have to be a few changes. I figured I could convert the garage into an office. It'll involve quite a bit of travel, this job, but that's not exactly a hardship.'

'I thought your mind was made up. You said it would be an adventure.'

'And it would have been. But do you know what? When I was out there I wanted you to see everything I was seeing. I wanted to show you the Puerta del Sol and the Torre de Lujanes; I wanted to take you to a show at the Teatro Real. On my own it felt like a bit of a waste.'

'Really?'

'And then I thought, that's sort of what you and me are doing anyway.'

'What is?'

'Wasting time.'

'Oh. Are we?'

'Yes. I don't mean together. I mean not together.'

'You've lost me.'

'Sorry, Jaz. I guess I'm not great at this either.' He pulled me closer. 'What I mean is, I've been quite content bumbling along, treading water, waiting to see you at weekends.'

'But?'

'But now I want something more.'

'Like what?'

'Christ, I'm not talking marriage or anything. That would be preposterous.'

'Yep. Plus you're already married.'

'Oh, yes,' he nodded. 'I forgot that.'

'So? What did you have in mind?'

'Well, I was thinking you could come over here more often. In the week maybe. And I want to come to yours sometimes too. If that's OK with you.'

'Of course it is.'

'And if I can wangle my business trips to be in the school holidays, I'd love you to come with me. It'll be Spain mostly, but there'd be the odd trip to Mexico and the US.'

'I'm sure I could handle that.'

'And I know we said no commitment, but I think I'd relax a lot more if I knew we weren't going to, you know, spend time with anyone else.'

I laughed.

'I'm sorry,' said Ruben. 'It's unreasonable of me to shift the goalposts now.'

'Don't be stupid,' I said. 'I haven't even thought of being with anyone else since I met you.' I hoped Benestrophe didn't count.

'Really? So you wouldn't mind? I've been so worried about not giving you your space. I know how independent you are.'

'Overly so, apparently.'

'What?'

'Nothing. Yes, Ruben. Yes to everything. Yes to all of it. Yes.'

He frowned. 'So, is that a yes or a no then?'

'Oh, shut up before I change my mind.'

He ran his fingers through my hair, and kissed me.

I pulled away. 'If you stay at my house, are you going to expect me to get up first and cook breakfast?'

Ruben looked serious. 'I realise I said there'd have to be some changes, Jaz, but you getting up before I do? I think you're taking things a bit too far.'

I kicked him in the shin and he screwed his eyes shut.

'And don't expect me to fall for that one again. Anyway, shouldn't you be getting on with stuff? I thought you had things to organise.'

He wriggled further down under the covers and pulled me after him. 'I have,' he said. 'Loads. But I was planning on staying in bed for a while first. If you have no objections.' He squeezed his one arm underneath me, and with the other hand began to gently stroke my back. Softly he kissed my shoulders, my face, my neck...

'Objections?' I sighed. 'I'll let you know if I think of any.'

I checked my reflection in the mirror again.

'Honestly,' said Ruben, 'Stop worrying. You look great.'

'Great? What does great mean? Do you think it's too flamboyant?'

'It's fine. Now put your jacket on and let's go. We're meant to be there in half an hour.'

I followed him downstairs and out of the door. 'Hang on,' I said, 'I forgot the flowers.'

On the kitchen table lay a small bouquet of cream roses. I scooped them up and headed out to the car.

'Morning!' exclaimed a cheery voice from along the pavement.

I turned to see the postman and his paunch jogging towards me.

'Or should I say *good* morning? For this morning is indeed good.'

I smiled. 'Glad to hear it. Look, sorry, I've got to dash. Is there anything for me?'

'Hang on... Just this. So, are you off somewhere special with this new beau of yours?' He gestured towards my car where Ruben was waiting.

'St Stephen's, actually.'

The postman gasped. 'I should have known it! The posh dress, the pretty flowers. Well, good for you. You have a wonderful day.'

I nodded and walked past him.

'You'll never guess what I got on Saturday,' he called after me.

I paused on the kerbside. 'You're right, I can't guess. What did you get?'

'A Fathers' Day card from my Catherine. She's a good'un, that one.'

Damn. I'd missed it again.

'A week early, mind, but it's the thought that counts, eh?'

Fantastic. I'd send Dad a card as soon as we were back from the reception. I said goodbye, opened the car door and climbed in beside Ruben. 'Take me to the church,' I said. 'And put your foot down.'

Fred was waiting in the porch when we arrived. 'Jasmine dear, you look stunning. And the flowers – how lovely.'

There was a pause in the organ music coming from within.

'I'm sorry we're late. The traffic on the new bridge was terrible.'

'Don't you worry,' he said. 'We could hardly start without you, could we? Now, go on inside.'

We hurried in as the organist struck up a new refrain. The whole place was crammed with people, young and old, all dressed in vibrant colours, all here in celebration and in love. Flowers were everywhere, their sweet fragrance hanging in the still church air. Stained glass filtered the midsummer sunlight, creating rainbows on marble pillars and carved oak beams.

Ruben squeezed my hand. 'Are you OK?' he whispered.

I nodded. I'd have to be.

Every head turned as the arched wooden doors swung open, and in she came, her fine mahogany coffin held high on the shoulders of her four pallbearers. Fred walked beside her, his own beautiful bouquet in his arms. He smiled at me as he passed. No moping, she'd insisted. No moping and not one single thread of black.

'Thanks for coming with me,' I said to Ruben as we pulled away from the church hall.

'You don't have to thank me, Jaz. Besides, I quite enjoyed myself dancing with some of those old biddies.'

'I noticed. And it was nice to see Fred again.'

'How's he doing?'

'Not bad. He seems OK. He's talking about turning one of the sitting rooms at Valley View into a mini dance studio. The Margaret Wilkinson Memorial Dance Hall. I think that's a great idea.'

'And how are you, Jaz? Really?'

'I'm not sure. All right. Kind of. Oh!'

'What?'

'I didn't tell you, that card I got earlier was from my nephews. They said they'd love to come and stay next weekend. You don't have to get involved though if you don't want to.'

'I've told you, I'd like to help out. And I'm dying to meet this bossy big sister of yours.'

'Did I call her bossy? Tasha's not that bad really.'

'Nothing like you then?'

I turned the radio on. It would do Tash and Phil good to have a break together.

Ruben leant over and switched the music off. 'Stop ignoring me.'

'Then stop trying to tease me.'

'I'm not trying,' he said. 'It comes quite naturally.'

I watched out of the window as we left town and headed for the A44.

'This may be an incredibly tasteless thing to say about someone at a funeral, but you did look rather gorgeous.'

'Thank you. But yes it is.'

'What?'

'Tasteless.'

'Sorry. Radiant. Radiant was the word that sprung to mind.'

'While you were sashaying with Doris and Ethel and Nancy?'

'Jealousy's such an ugly trait, Jasmine. No, seriously. You looked weirdly content.'

'Dancing in the perfection of each moment.'

'Eh?'

'Something Mrs Wilkinson told me I should do. And I'm going to try. I've been thinking about going back to college.'

'What – to do teacher training?'

'No. Something different. French. Or Spanish. Architecture maybe. Or art.'

'No specific plan then.'

'Nope. Apart from doing something I really love.'

'You're a strange woman, Jasmine, but I quite like you, you know.'

'Well, that's a good job because I quite like you too.'

'I was planning on staying at yours again, by the way. Is that OK?'

'That would be magnificent,' I said. 'Life is far too short to go squandering. We never know when our time will be up.'

'You mean we could die any minute. I realise we've just come from a funeral, but that *is* rather maudlin.'

'Not at all. I mean it in a good way.'

Ruben smiled, but shook his head. 'Sometimes, Jasmine, I have no idea what you're on about.'

I looked out across golden fields beneath cloud-scattered skies. I opened my window and filled my lungs with the sweetness of life. 'What I mean, Ruben, is that every second we have on this earth is precious. From now on I'm going to make the most of absolutely everything. From now on I will not waste a single moment of my time.'